PRAISE FOR *SHADOWSHAPER*

"Magnificent. . . . A world that readers cannot help wanting to live in." — Holly Black, *New York Times Book Review*

"Older's book is a first-rate example of how representation, diversity, and themes of social justice and identity can be skillfully woven into a narrative — not so that they disappear, but so that the story pivots on them in a way that is authentic, exciting, and ultimately satisfying."
— Cory Doctorow, *Boing Boing*

"The strength of Older's tale is in his meticulous attention to the details of the life of a brown-skinned, natural-haired Puerto Rican teenage girl. Older's storytelling is rich. . . this is a world that will stay with readers long after the last page."
— *Los Angeles Times*

★ "Warm, strong, vernacular, dynamic — a must."
— *Kirkus Reviews*, starred review

★ "Excellent diverse genre fiction in an appealing package."
— *School Library Journal*, starred review

★ "What makes Older's story exceptional is the way Sierra belongs in her world, grounded in family, friends, and an awareness of both history and change."
— *Publishers Weekly*, starred review

★ "Smart writing with a powerful message that never overwhelms the terrific storytelling."
— *Booklist*, starred review

"Older not only gives readers a diverse cast, but he stays true to their background, language and community, lending an authenticity to his work. . . . If you're a YA urban fantasy reader looking for something creative and different, try *Shadowshaper* on for size."
— *Romantic Times Book Reviews*

SHADOWSHAPER

SHADOWSHAPER
CYPHER
BOOK 1

DANIEL JOSÉ OLDER

SCHOLASTIC INC.

For Darrell, Patrice, Emani, and Jair

Copyright © 2015 by Daniel José Older
Map copyright © 2017 by Tim Paul

Arthur A. Levine Books hardcover edition designed by Christopher Stengel, published by Arthur A. Levine Books, an imprint of Scholastic Inc., July 2015.

All rights reserved. Published by Scholastic Inc., *Publishers since 1920.* SCHOLASTIC, the LANTERN LOGO, and associated logos are trademarks and/or registered trademarks of Scholastic Inc.

ISBN 978-1-338-03247-5

10 9 8 7 6 5 4 3   17 18 19 20

Printed in the U.S.A. 40
First printing 2016

Book design by Christopher Stengel

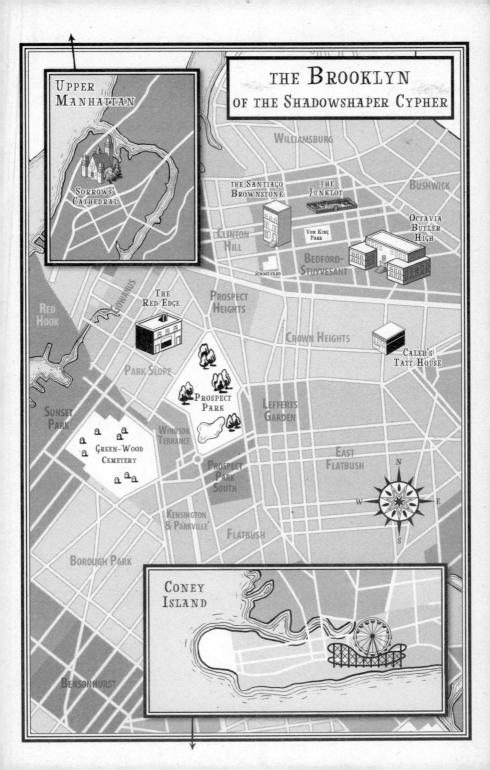

ONE

"Sierra? What are you staring at?"

"Nothing, Manny."

Blatant lie. Sierra glanced down from the scaffolding to where Manny the Domino King stood with his arms crossed over his chest. "You sure?" he said.

"Yeah." Sierra looked back at the mural. She hadn't been making it up: a single tear glistened at the corner of Papa Acevedo's painted eyes. The tear wasn't moving — of course it wasn't moving: It was paint! But still: It hadn't been there yesterday or the day before.

And the portrait was fading; it seemed to disappear more and more every hour. This afternoon when she arrived at the Junklot to work on her own mural, it took Sierra a few seconds to find the old man's face peering out from the brick. But fading murals and crying murals were totally different flavors of weird.

She turned back to her own painting, on a much newer concrete façade adjacent to the old brick building from which Papa Acevedo's face stared out. "Hey, Manny," Sierra said. "You sure the people who own this building won't be mad about my mural?"

"We're sure they *will* be," Manny chuckled. "That's why we asked you to do it. We hate the Tower. We spit on the Tower. Your paint is our nasty loogie, hocked upon the stupidity that is the Tower." He grinned up at Sierra and then turned back to an old typewriter he'd been tinkering with.

"Great," Sierra said. The Tower had shown up just over a year ago, totally unannounced: a five-story concrete monstrosity on a block otherwise full of brownstones. The developers built the outer structure quickly and then left it, abandoned and unfinished, its unpaned windows staring emptily out into the Brooklyn skies. The Tower's northern wall sat right on the edge of the Junklot, where mountains of trashed cars waited like crumpled-up scraps of paper. Manny and the other old guys who played dominos in the lot had immediately declared war on it.

Sierra dabbed dark green paint along the neck of the dragon she was working on. It reared all the way up to the fifth floor of the Tower, and even though most of its body was just an outline, Sierra could tell it was gonna be fierce. She shaded rows of scales and spines, and smiled at how the creature seemed to come to life a fraction more with each new detail.

When Manny first asked her to paint something on the Tower, she'd refused. She'd never painted a mural before, just filled notebook after notebook with wild creatures and winged, battle-ready versions of her friends and neighbors. And a whole wall? If she messed up, all of Brooklyn would see it. But Manny was persistent, said she could paint anything she wanted, said he'd set up a scaffolding. He added that if her old Grandpa Lázaro was still talking in full sentences instead of laid up from that stroke he'd had, he would've wanted her to do it too.

That last one sealed it. Sierra couldn't say no to even the idea of Grandpa Lázaro. And so here she was, on the second day of summer break, adding a few more scales along a pair of dragon wings and worrying about crying murals.

Her phone buzzed with a text from her best friend, Bennie:

*party at sully's tonight. First of the summmmmmer!!!!
Imma meet you at your house be ready in an hour.*

The first party of the summer was always amazing. Sierra smiled, pocketed her phone, and started packing up her supplies. It was nine p.m. The dragon could wait.

She looked back at the mural of Papa Acevedo, barely visible now against the crumbling brick wall. It wasn't just that there was a new tear on his face; his whole expression had changed. The man — the painting, rather — looked downright afraid. Papa Acevedo had been one of Grandpa Lázaro and Manny's domino buddies. He'd always had a kind smile or a joke for Sierra, and whoever had painted his memorial portrait had captured that warmth perfectly. But now, his face seemed twisted with shock somehow, eyebrows raised, the edges of his mouth turned down beneath that unruly mustache.

The glistening painted tear trembled and slid out of the old man's eye and down his face.

Sierra gasped. "What the —!"

The scaffolding shivered. She looked down. Manny had one hand on a support beam, the other cupped around the phone earpiece he always had in. His head was bowed, shaking from side to side.

"When?" Manny said. "How long ago?"

Sierra looked one last time at Papa Acevedo and climbed down the scaffolding.

"You are sure?" Manny looked up at her and then back down. "You're sure it was him?"

"You okay?" Sierra whispered.

"I'll be right there. Ya. Ya vengo, ahora mismo. Dentro de . . . quince minutos. Okay." Manny poked the button on his earpiece and stared at the ground for a few seconds.

"What happened?" Sierra asked.

"Reporter stuff," Manny said. He closed his eyes. Besides being the self-appointed Domino King of Brooklyn, he published, wrote, and delivered the *Bed-Stuy Searchlight*, churning out the three pages of local gossip and event updates from a little basement printing press over on Ralph Avenue. The *Searchlight* had been coming every day for as long as Sierra could remember.

"Somebody you know?"

Manny nodded. "Knew. Ol' Vernon, we called him. He's gone."

"Dead?"

He nodded, shook his head, nodded again.

"Manny? What does that mean?"

"I have to go, Sierra. You finish this painting, you hear me?"

"What? Tonight? Manny, I . . ."

"No! Ha." He looked at her, finally smiled. "Of course not. Just, soon."

"Okay, Manny."

In a flurry of jangling keys and heavy breathing, Manny shut down the industrial lights and let them out of the iron fence around the Junklot. "Have a good time tonight, Sierra. Don't worry about me. But be careful!"

Sierra's phone buzzed as she watched Manny rush off into the Brooklyn night. It was Bennie again.

You comin right?

Sierra texted a quick *yeh* and pocketed her phone. An early summer breeze wafted through her hair as she fast-walked past brownstones and corner stores, rounded the corner onto Lafayette, and headed home. She had to get ready for the party and check on Grandpa Lázaro, but all she could think about was Papa Acevedo's teardrop.

TWO

Grandpa Lázaro sat up in bed when Sierra walked into his apartment on the top floor of their brownstone. He regarded her with a concerned shake of his head, the jowly folds under his chin waving back and forth, his clawlike hands clutching the sheets. The old man had barely said anything since his stroke, but occasionally he'd blurt out random boleros from back in the day. Today he seemed different, though: his gaze was sharper and his lopsided mouth curved into a frown. "Lo siento lo siento lo siento," he muttered.

"What, Abuelo?" Sierra said. "What are you sorry for?"

Lázaro looked away, scowling. Ceiling-high windows around her grandfather's bed made the room feel like the crow's nest on some urban pirate ship. Outside, streetlights blinked to life along the streets of Bed-Stuy as the swirling orange clouds gave way to dark blue. All over Brooklyn, folks were heading out to their stoops and strolling the avenues to take in another warm New York night.

Sierra's phone buzzed again. Bennie was probably trying to rush her along so they could get to the party at Sully's.

Sierra double-checked that Lázaro's meds were all in order, his glass of water filled, his slippers by the bed.

"Lo siento lo siento lo siento," Grandpa Lázaro muttered again.

Another buzz. Sierra growled and looked at her phone.

You comin??

Ya mama down here talking my ear off Sierra cmon girl

if you dont come ya ass downstairs in the next 2 minutes im OUT i sweartagawddd sierra

She rolled her eyes and pocketed the phone. "You good, Abuelo?"

The old man looked up suddenly. His dark brown eyes locked with Sierra's. "Ven acá, m'ija. I have to speak with you."

Sierra stepped back in shock. His eyes were clear and serious. Lázaro's stroke had left him with full movement of his body — he could take care of himself for the most part — but this was the first time he'd made any sense in a year.

Grandpa Lázaro lifted a skin-and-bones arm and waved Sierra closer. "Ven acá, Sierra. Quickly. We don't have much time."

She crossed the room. His warm brown hand wrapped around her wrist. Sierra almost yelped. "Listen to me, m'ija.

They are coming. For us." Tears appeared in Lázaro's foggy eyes. "For the shadowshapers."

"The who? Abuelo, what are you talking about?"

"I'm so sorry, Sierra. I tried . . . to do right. ¿Entiendes?"

"No, Abuelo, I don't understand. What's going on?"

"¡Oye!" María, Sierra's mom, called from downstairs. "Sierra, you coming? Bennie's here and she says you're late!"

"Finish the mural, Sierra. Finish the mural quickly. The paintings are fading . . ." His voice trailed off and those old eyes blinked a few times. "Soon we'll all be lost."

"Abuelo! What do you mean? The mural in the Junklot?" Manny had just said the same thing to her. But it wasn't anywhere near done. "That's gonna take me all summer. I can't finish anytime so —"

Lázaro's eyes sprung open again. "¡No! ¡No puede! You must finish it, Sierra. Finish it now! As soon as possible! They are . . ." He squeezed her wrist tighter. She felt his hot breath on the side of her face. "They are coming for us. Coming for the shadowshapers." He released her and slumped back against his pillows.

"Who's coming, Abuelo? What are the shadowshapers?"

"Sierra?" María called again from the first floor. "You hear me? Bennie says . . ."

"I'm coming, Mami!" Sierra yelled.

Lázaro shook his head. "The boy Robbie will help you. Ask him for help, Sierra. You need help. I can't . . . It's too

8

late." He nodded his head, eyes closing again. "No puedo, m'ija. No puedo."

"Robbie from school?" Sierra said. "Abuelo, how do you even know him?" Robbie was a tall Haitian kid with long locks who had shown up midyear with a goofy grin and wild drawings covering every surface of his clothes, his backpack, his desk. If Sierra had been the kind of girl who gave a damn about boys and their cuteness, Robbie the Walking Mural would find himself somewhere on her top-ten list.

"He will help you," Lázaro whispered, his head drooping. "You need help, Sierra. They are coming for us all. We don't have long. I'm . . . I'm sorry."

"Sierra!" María called.

Lázaro closed his eyes and let out a loud snore. Sierra backed toward the door. Her phone buzzed again. She turned around and ran down the stairs.

"And so I looked at the headmaster," María Carmen Corona Santiago said to Bennie as Sierra walked into the kitchen, "and I said, 'Yes, my students will be reading that book today.'" She slapped the kitchen table. "And they did!"

"Wow," Bennie said. María turned to face Sierra, and Bennie made a "help me" face.

"So you finally decided to show up!" María said. "I was just telling Bennie about the time they tried to ban those books."

Sierra bent down and kissed her mom on the cheek. María was still in her crisp blue pantsuit. Her graying black hair was pulled back into a sharp bun and her makeup was immaculate, even at the end of a long day. "I'm sure she was thrilled to hear that story again," Sierra said.

María swatted her away. "Who taught you to be so sarcastic?"

"I can't imagine."

"And why aren't you changed yet? I thought you said you were ready."

Sierra looked down. She was still wearing the same T-shirt with torn-off sleeves, pleated skirt, and combat boots she'd been painting in, and her fro stretched magnificently around her in a fabulous, unbothered halo. She'd stopped by her room just long enough to throw some extra bangles around her wrists and beaded necklaces over her head, and that was that. "I mean . . ."

Bennie stood. "I think you look great, Sierra!"

That was definitely not true: Bennie and Sierra had almost opposite styles, and they never got tired of letting each other know their opinions. Tonight, Bennie had on creased gray slacks and a button-down maroon top that matched her tortoiseshell glasses. "Well, it's been lovely, Mrs. Santiago. C'mon, Sierra," she said, smiling a little too hard. She took Sierra's arm and led her toward the door. "We're gonna be late."

"Bennaldra! Since when you have taken Sierra's side on a fashion issue?" María demanded. "You know what? Never mind. Have fun, girls. Be safe, okay?"

Sierra stopped at the doorway. "Hey, Mami, have you checked on Abuelo in the past day or two?"

"What's that, m'ija?"

"He seemed upset just now. He was . . . talking. Whole sentences that made sense. Have you ever heard of the shadowshapers?"

Something happened in María's face — the slightest clenching of her cheek muscles, maybe, or perhaps her eyes narrowing the tiniest bit. Whatever it was, Sierra had seen it happen again and again throughout her life: Ask the wrong question, mention some untouchable topic, just catch her mother at the wrong moment, and it was like some invisible barrier sprang into place.

"I don't know what that is, Sierra." María smiled, just a little, but her voice was ice. She turned quickly back to the dishes.

"That's weird," Sierra said, "cuz you look an awful lot like you know what I'm talking about."

"Sierra. I said I don't know. I'll check on your grand-father later."

It would've been so much better if she'd just yell and scream like a normal mom. Instead, she didn't even raise her voice. Sierra knew that was that — the conversation was over, the battle lost.

"Fine." Sierra turned. "C'mon, Bennie."

"Sierra, come back," María called, but her voice sounded empty.

THREE

"What was that all about?" Bennie asked. They were fast-walking down Lafayette toward downtown Brooklyn. Some little kids zipped past on scooters. A group of middle-aged women sat in lawn chairs outside a brownstone, sipping beers and laughing.

Sierra shrugged. "Nothin'."

"Right, cuz that wasn't awkward at all."

"C'mon, B! I thought you didn't wanna be late."

The Bradwicks' elaborate Park Slope brownstone was bursting with teenagers when Sierra and Bennie got there. Just about every ninth, tenth, and eleventh grader from Octavia Butler High was running around the backyard or exploring the winding passageways of the house. The sound system alternately blared hip-hop and grungy emo rock as various DJs took turns pushing one another out of the way. Some kids stood in a little circle out back, beatboxing and freestyling, inventing brand-new ways of putting one another down and sending up wild cheers when a dig found its mark.

Sierra's eyes jumped from face to face, but Robbie's drawing-covered clothes and slender locks were nowhere to be seen. She watched Big Jerome pick up Little Jerome by the scruff of the neck like he was a puppy and toss him into the pool, upsetting the Marco Polo players. Over at the free-style circle, her friend Izzy delivered a crushing sixteen-bar denouncement of another kid's mama. Tee cheered her girl-friend from the crowd. Bennie joined the circle, laughing along with each line. Izzy wrapped up with a triumphant and brutal verse rhyming *spastic*, *sarcastic*, and *less than fantastic*, and the crowd erupted in thunderous applause. The other kid, an extra-short and elegantly dressed tenth grader named Pitkin, recognized defeat and stepped back into the crowd with a gentlemanly bow.

"Sierra! Bennie!" Tee shouted, running over. "Y'all seen my baby shred that tiny dapper kid?"

"Hey!" Pitkin yelled.

Tee cringed and then rolled her eyes beneath her per-fectly coifed pompadour. "'S'all love, bro!"

"I did what I do." Izzy grinned and walked over, making a little curtsy. She had been entertaining everyone with her perverse rhymes since the fourth grade. "King Impervious on the mic!" she yelled. "Waddup, Brooklyn!"

"Who's King Impervious?" Bennie asked.

"That's my MC name, you ain't know?"

"How she gonna know, Iz?" Tee chided. "You came up with that this morning!"

"But I'm already a global phenomenon!"

Everyone groaned. Izzy was a wisp of a girl, both skinny and short, but she sported a meticulously groomed mane of black hair that added a couple of inches in all directions. She sighed and rested her head on the shoulder of Tee's designer polo shirt.

"Hey, c'mon now," Tee yelled, stepping away. "This polo brand-new. Lean on Sierra, her T-shirt been around since the seventies."

Izzy made a pouty face.

"I'm all set," Sierra said. "Y'all seen Robbie?"

"You mean Weirdo McPainting Dude?" Tee said.

"You mean the Cartoon-Covered Haitian Sensation?" Izzy suggested.

"You mean the Human Walking Stick?" Bennie offered.

Sierra shook her head. "I hate you one and all. And Bennie, he's not even *that* tall and skinny."

Izzy scoffed. "He's eight feet tall and two inches wide, Sierra."

"When he walks down my block," Tee said, "all the telephone poles be like 'Ay bruh, what it do?'"

Izzy spat her drink back into the red plastic cup and dapped her girlfriend. "Good one, babe."

Behind them, someone screamed. Sierra whirled around, but it was just Big Jerome, finally succumbing to the team of ninth graders that Little Jerome had rallied. Big Jerome hollered and tumbled headfirst into the pool, taking at least three younger kids with him. The whole party burst into jeers and laughter.

When Sierra turned back to her friends, both Bennie's eyebrows were arched. "You shook up, girl. Talk to me."

Sierra rolled her eyes. "Why don't you go help your boy?"

"Don't even start," Bennie said. Big Jerome had harbored a gigantoid crush on her for as long as anyone could remember.

"Y'all seen Robbie or not?"

Bennie snickered. "Why you wanna know?"

"I gotta ask him some stuff."

"Sierra!" Izzy yelled. "Why didn't you tell us you had a crush! We woulda gone easier on the guy."

"What? No!" Sierra rolled her eyes again. "First of all: No, you wouldn'ta. And secondly, a girl can't ask a guy stuff without everyone launching interrogations? I'm not tryna . . . no!"

"It's cuz you both draw?" Tee suggested. "Because a lotta people draw. If you go to art school, you will find a whole teeming buttload of drawing dudes."

"Please," Izzy said. "Never say 'teeming buttload' ever again."

"You guys are literally useless," Sierra said.

"He's right over there," Tee said, "by the mango tree or whatever that is, in that little dark garden area. Being creepy like always. Hey, where you going?"

Sierra made her way up a narrow path surrounded by an herb garden and some scrawny trees. The light was dim deeper into the shrubbery, and Robbie's slender form blended so well with the curling vines and branches it took Sierra a few seconds of squinting to find him. Robbie sat with his back against a tree and a sketchbook propped on his bent knees.

Sierra's policy on cute boys, and really, boys in general, was this: *ignore, ignore, ignore.* They usually ruined all their cute as soon as they opened their mouths and said something stupid, and she had more fun hanging out with Bennie and the crew anyway. Robbie had always seemed a little different, though. He was mostly quiet and didn't have that insistent hunger for attention about him. In school, he just sat there sketching and smiling like he was in on some joke no one else got. Which would normally be annoying, but Sierra found it endearing.

All that only made her more dedicated to sticking to the triple-*I* policy. Inevitably, Robbie would open his mouth and end up an idiot like the rest of them. Why bother? But here she was standing at the edge of this weird garden in Park Slope, a house full of partying teenagers behind her, and a bizarre mandate from her normally incoherent abuelo to recruit Robbie to finish a mural. She sighed.

"You just gonna stand there sighing," Robbie said, "or you gonna come say hi?"

Sierra cringed. "I . . . Hi!"

"Hi! I'm Robbie." His hand poked out of the bush.

She laughed and shook it. "I know who you are, man.

We were in Aldridge's American History AP class together, aka naptime."

"I knew that!" Robbie said. "And I knew who you are, Sierra Santiago. I just don't really expect people to, you know . . . notice me? I don't really say much."

"You really don't." Sierra parted some branches and entered the shadowy grove. "But you draw and I draw . . . er, paint, mostly, so I noticed you." She found a spot beside him.

Robbie gasped through a mischievous smile. "How ever did you know I like to draw?"

"Sir," Sierra said.

"But seriously, I didn't know you did too. What you paint?"

"Actually, that's what I'm here to talk to you about." But how to explain? She peered at Robbie's picture. "What you makin' there?"

"Just sketchin'." He held up his drawing pad. Thick graffiti letters sprang from a swirly garden not unlike the one that surrounded them. The letters *B U Z Z* wound and looped with exaggerated grace; here they were brick, there balloony with globs of shine. "You like it?"

"I do."

Robbie smiled and went back to his drawing.

"Listen, Robbie." Words failed Sierra. Drawing was so much easier. She waved her hands a few times in the air. "I'm working on this mural."

Robbie looked up briefly and nodded, still drawing. "That's cool. I do murals too."

A shout rang out from the party. Both Jeromes were in the pool now, each with a tenth-grade girl on his shoulders. Everyone was yelling. Some stupidity was surely about to commence.

"The thing is, my grandpa actually told me I gotta finish this mural like . . . quickly. Right? Which is weird, cuz he —"

"Who's your grandpa?" He shaded a thick loop of the letter Z with slanting lines.

"His name's Lázaro. Lázaro Corona."

Robbie looked directly at Sierra. She caught her breath. He had big brown eyes, kind eyes, but something else danced behind them now. Was it fear?

"You're Lázaro Corona's granddaughter?" he said.

Sierra scrunched up her face. "Yes. That mean something to you?"

Robbie just nodded. His eyes didn't leave hers.

She decided to ignore his stare. "Well, he's been pretty much out of it since last year when he had this stroke, but tonight he told me to . . . He told me to find you, and to get you to help me finish the Junklot mural, and to do it fast. He said the murals were fading and that someone was coming for us, and something about shadowshapers . . ."

And the painting was crying, Robbie. It was fading and crying. The words lingered at the edge of her tongue, made her mouth feel heavy. No. He'd think she was crazy. Or maybe they'd just sit there for ages and stare at each other and not say anything.

And as she looked again into his brown eyes, in a weird, quiet way, that was what Sierra wanted.

Finally, Robbie looked back at his sketch, his brows creased in concentration. "Lázaro told you about the shadowshapers, huh?"

"He just mentioned them," Sierra said. "Didn't explain. You know about 'em?"

"A thing or two."

"Well, that's gratingly vague. You gonna help me with this mural or not?"

"If Grandpa Lázaro said I gotta, then I guess I gotta." He looked up and smiled.

"Oh, great, don't do it for me or nothin'. I see how it is." She took his notepad from him and scribbled her number on the cardboard backing. "There. You got the digits and you didn't even ask for 'em."

Robbie laughed. "Look, the shadowshapers . . . It's a lot to explain. I'm not really sure where to start . . ."

A hubbub was rising from the party, some yelling and cursing — a fight perhaps. Robbie was staring through the tangle of vines around them. He stood up suddenly.

"What's wrong?" Sierra said.

"It's begun."

Sierra got up too. "What has, man? Talk to me."

"We have to go," Robbie said. "Right now."

FOUR

The commotion from the pool area got louder. Through the forsythia and pumpkin vine, Sierra saw a middle-aged man stomping through the party with an even gait. He wore an old winter jacket and stained khakis that didn't quite fit. His skin was pale, like hospital fluorescents, and dull, cataracted eyes glared out from his grayish weathered face. Kids stood back, giving the stranger a wide berth.

Robbie shoved the notebook into his shoulder bag. "We gotta go," he said again.

"What's going on?" Sierra's hand wrapped around his arm. "Who is that?"

"I don't have time to explain," he said, backstepping deeper into the bushes. He took Sierra's hand and pulled her toward the garden wall. "Hop over this wall and run. You hear me? Go!"

"But what about you?"

"I'm going to lead him off somewhere else. He'll chase me. You get out of here."

"Chase you? Robbie, no —"

But he'd already disappeared into the underbrush. Sierra took a quick look around. The party was trying to get itself started again. Apparently, the stranger had wandered off; she could hear kids carrying on about messing that dude up, wherever he was.

A movement caught Sierra's eye in the bushes where they had just been sitting. As she turned her head, the man stepped out with a muffled grunt. His unblinking eyes stared down at her.

Sierra's yell got stuck somewhere in her throat. She took two steps backward.

"Where's Lucera?" His hoarse whisper sounded somehow dissonant.

"What?" Sierra was whispering too, and she had no idea why. A stank, heavy air invaded her nostrils. It was the same smell they couldn't get out of their basement after a rat died inside one of the walls.

"Where . . . is . . . Lucera?" he growled again.

She took another step back. "I don't know what you're talking about."

The thing — it didn't seem like a man at all anymore — tensed as if it was about to pounce. One thick, bluish hand grabbed Sierra's left wrist. It was cold, like a slab of raw meat. "Tell me." It pulled her arm toward its face, eyes twitching.

Sierra yanked her hand free. "Get away from me! You talkin' to the wrong girl!" She walked backward, keeping her eyes on the thing.

"Sierra . . ."

It knew her name. She glanced up. It was smiling.

Sierra turned around and ran. She reached the wall and scrambled up over it, scratching her fingers badly on the sharp stones but not caring. The only thing she could think about was the thing rushing up behind her, the cool grasp of its hand. She landed on the pavement of a quiet side street, the vibrations of her fall shooting up her legs and back. She broke into a run, glancing back just quickly enough to see the thing lurch off the wall and stumble to the ground. She turned a corner and headed uphill toward Prospect Park.

"Sierra," it brayed. It stood at the far end of the block, panting.

"Stay away," she yelled. She dipped around another corner, then another. She heard heavy footsteps clomping the pavement on a nearby street. She ran harder. Where was Robbie? How could he just vanish like that when she needed help?

She stopped to catch her breath on the wide avenue where the spiraling mansions of Park Slope met the edge of Prospect Park. The streets around her were empty — no creepy dead-looking guy.

She sighed. Even on a creepy night like this, the park's darkness seemed welcoming somehow, its shushing leaves beckoning her from across the street. When Sierra was little, Grandpa Lázaro and Mama Carmen used to take her there for picnics. Each tree and stone brought with it a story, and little Sierra could dance for hours, imagining the adventures those silent field dwellers may have seen. When she became a teenager, the quiet and beauty of the park was her solace when the rest of the world just seemed too overwhelming to handle.

But tonight there wasn't time for solace or peaceful moments in nature. Someone — something — was after her. It knew her name. It had found her once and probably could again. She had to get home. She took off at a jog toward the bright lights of Grand Army Plaza.

Back in Bed-Stuy, police lights pulsated up and down Putnam Avenue. Ambulances were parked at urgent angles alongside the rows of SUVs and hoopties. Folks from the neighborhood crowded around, gazing down the cordoned-off block to see who had been shot this time.

"You know what happened?" Sierra asked an elderly lady with a handcart full of freshly laundered sheets.

The old woman shook her head. "Another young something-something gone to dust, I'm sure." She shrugged and walked on, her pushcart squeaking crankily with each turn of its wheels. The cops keeping people away looked bored. *Just another shooting, ho hum.* Sierra scowled at one of them and he scowled back.

"Ay!" someone yelled. Sierra spun around, her whole body tensed to strike, but the corpse-like man was still nowhere to be seen. Some old guy banged on the bulletproof-glass window of Carlos's Corner Store. "Ay, C!" the guy yelled. "Gimme a loosie, man! C'mon, wake up!"

Further down Gates Ave, a couple of guys were throwing dice in front of the Coltrane Projects. "Why you frownin', girl?" one of them called out as Sierra walked past. "Smile for us!"

Sierra knew the guy. It was Little Ricky; they'd played together when they were small. He'd been one of those boys that all the girls were crazy about, with big dreamy eyes and a gentle way about him. A few years ago, Sierra would have been giddy with excitement to have his attention. Now he was just another stoopgoon harassing every passing skirt.

"I ain't in the mood, jackass," Sierra muttered, hugging herself. She was still shaky from the horrible night and she knew any sign of weakness would encourage them.

The guys let out a chorus of *ohs* and pounded one another. "I'm just saying, Sarcastula," Ricky called after her. "C'mon back when you in the mood . . ."

Sierra kept walking. At her block, she paused to make sure the creepy guy was gone for real. The trees shushed their quiet night song and Rodrigo, her neighbor's cat, strolled by. Otherwise, the block was deserted. She made her way inside, crept up the stairs, and collapsed into her bed, trying not to think of the hideous voice whispering her name.

FIVE

"Aw, damn, y'all you seen this?" Across the kitchen table, Sierra's godfather, Neville Spencer, held up a page of the *Bed-Stuy Searchlight*. The wide grin he usually wore was gone.

Sierra squinted. It was ten in the morning. She'd only gotten about three hours of sleep, and woken up to some weird texts from Robbie saying he was okay and he'd explain later, and another from Bennie, demanding to know where she'd run off to. "I can't see anything, man," Sierra said. "I ain't put my contacts in yet."

"What happened?" Dominic Santiago, Sierra's dad, appeared in the doorway, wearing his pajamas. He was short and stocky with black hair exactly everywhere on his body except his face and the very top of his head. "Lemme see. What mess Manny shedding light on this time?"

Neville passed the paper to Dominic. "Bottom of page two. You didn't work last night, D?"

"Nah, the hospital just hired a bunch of new security guys and I took a much-needed personal day, thank you very much." He looked at the paper. "Oh, man, that's a shame."

"You guys! What's a shame?" Sierra forked a load of French toast into her mouth.

Neville shook his head. "Nobody safe anymore."

"Whatsit say?" she asked. "Pass it over."

Dominic handed her the *Searchlight*.

"Ol' Vernon missing," Dominic said.

Sierra almost spat out her French toast. There, squished in between a wedding announcement and an article about yet another double murder at the Coltrane Projects, was a black-and-white picture of the thing that had attacked her last night. Ol' Vernon had a big smile, and his eyes were wide open like he expected something great to happen at any moment. He looked a world away from the whispering fiend from the party.

Vernon Chandler, 62, has been reported as missing from his Marcy Avenue apartment. Vernon was last seen two days ago; family members stated he had been acting unusually quiet the past week. Vernon has no history of mental illness and no criminal history. No note was found at his domicile. A spokesman for the NYPD's 38th precinct said that if anyone has any information about Vernon's whereabouts, they should contact the police or medical services. Otherwise, the spokesman said, "He was probably just out for a stroll."

"Wasn't he a buddy of Lázaro's from back in the sh —" Neville said.

"Yeah." Dominic sat at the table and poured himself a

cup of coffee from the carafe. "But you know . . ." He nodded toward the kitchen, where María was preparing another
batch of French toast. "She don't like to talk about all that."

"Dang, still?" Neville whispered.

Dominic shrugged. "I mean . . . It just upsets her."

"Why . . . what don't we talk about, Dad?" Sierra said.
"What'd he have to do with Grandpa Lázaro?"

"It's nothing, baby. Old family history. Drama."

"You want French toast, mi amor?" María called from
the kitchen. "I don't have to be at the graduation till noon."

Dominic cleared his wife's paperwork off the table.
"Sure, babe."

"Seconds, Neville?"

"Only if it's you that's cookin' 'em," Neville hollered a
little louder than necessary. "Sierra, baby, why is your hand
shaking?"

Sierra put the newspaper down. "I dunno. Probably just
too much coffee, I guess." She stood up. "I gotta . . . Imma
go upstairs, 'kay? Still worn out from the party last night."

"You going to start job hunting, m'ija?" María called
over the din of clanking pots and sizzling butter.

"Of course, Mami."

"That's my girl."

On the second floor, Sierra poked her head into her brothers' room. Her two older brothers could not have been more
different. Gael's walls were completely blank, while glossy

photos of fancy guitars and half-naked zombie girls stared out from Juan's side. Gael could talk through the night about all kinds of random ridiculous facts, while Juan spent his days crafting a careful casualness and practicing guitar at all hours. Then Gael became a marine, which surprised no one, and Juan's salsa-thrasher band Culebra got a record deal, which shocked everyone, and both disappeared suddenly and completely from Sierra's daily life. Now Gael was a three-page letter every month about waiting for something to happen in Tora Bora, and Juan was a rare and awkward phone call from Philly or Baltimore or wherever his latest gig was.

Sierra continued past her own room to the third floor. The murky smell of incense and ramen noodles at the landing meant Timothy Boyd was home and trying to cook. He'd been renting the Santiagos' extra apartment while he finished up his final visual arts degree at Pratt, and he pretty much stayed out of sight.

Sierra went up another flight and knocked lightly on the wooden door. She always performed this useless *tap-tap*, even though Grandpa Lázaro never opened it or even responded. When she walked in, the gorgeous morning sky over New York unfolded before her.

"Lo siento lo siento," Lázaro muttered. He was sitting up in his chair, eyes watery. His fingers were clenched tightly around a scrap of lined paper.

"You back to that?" Sierra crossed the room. "What are you sorry about? What is it?" She tried to see what he had clutched in his hand, but Lázaro pulled the paper tighter to himself and turned away.

"You okay, Abuelo?" Sierra plopped into the bedside easy chair. "Cuz I'm not. I found Robbie like you said but . . . I don't know what to tell you. I'm in over my head already. I don't understand any of this. This guy Ol' Vernon you usedta know? He showed up last night and chased me and . . ."

Lázaro lifted one trembling hand, his index finger extended.

"What?" Sierra turned and followed an invisible line from his finger to the far wall, where Lázaro's gallery of family photographs stared back at her.

"Lo siento lo siento lo siento."

She stood up and walked across the room. She had never paid the old pictures much mind. There was Tío Angelo, who'd fought with the Macheteros rebels outside of San Juan. There was Uncle Neville hanging with Sierra's mom and dad back in the eighties, all three of them looking wildly happy outside some nightclub that had long since burned down. There Sierra's mom and Tía Rosa stood next to each other outside a skating rink on Empire Boulevard, all dolled up and smiling. Sierra's grandmother, Mama Carmen, glared out of another photo; she had that look that used to light up her eyes right before someone got beat. Mama Carmen had died a few months before Lázaro's stroke. Sierra missed her grandmother's hugs more than anything — it was like a secret world of warmth and love every time they'd embrace.

But what was Lázaro trying to show her?

In the middle was a large group photo. Grandpa Lázaro beamed from the center of it, wearing the same creased khakis and guayabera that he'd always worn when he was with it. He was grinning that sweet abuelo grin of his, staring down the camera with an almost fevered excitement. Next to him, a young white man with a pouf of dirty-blond hair stood with one arm wrapped around Lázaro's shoulder. His eyebrows were arched up, his mouth creased into a surprised half smile, as if he'd been caught off guard by the photographer. Someone had written beside him *Dr. Jonathan Wick* in elegant, old-fashioned script. On Wick's other side, a group of about a dozen men stared intently at the camera without smiling. Each had their name written near their head. Sierra knew most of them from around the neighborhood, but a few were strangers to her. There was Delmond Alcatraz and Sunny Balboa from the barber shop, and there was Manny, looking uncharacteristically solemn, and Papa Acevedo . . . She squinted at the picture. The man next to Papa Acevedo had a black fingerprint smudged over his face. Beside him was his name: *Vernon Chandler.*

"What the . . ." Sierra said out loud. Her voice sounded

strange in the quiet room. She looked back at her abuelo. Grandpa Lázaro had slumped over the side of the easy chair, a strand of drool stretching from his mouth to his stained white T-shirt. He let out a high-pitched wheeze, laughed a little, and then snored again.

Sierra crept toward him, her heart thundering in her ears. Lázaro's right hand clenched the armrest. She crouched beside him and peered at the edges of his fingertips. There was no ink stain on any of them, from what she could tell. Lázaro snored again and startled himself awake. He looked warily around the room.

Sierra took a deep breath and studied her old grandfather, the blue veins along his crinkled arms, the deep-brown eyes. "Abuelo, your ol' buddy Vernon went missing," she said, "and now there's a smudge over his face in the picture." The old man shook his head slowly back and forth; the news hadn't registered. "And last night he showed up at the party acting like a creepy freak and looking for someone named . . . what'd he say? Lucera."

Lázaro sat up and sputtered, "Lucera . . . back?"

"I don't know. Who is she, Abuelo? Who's Lucera?"

He snapped his head toward Sierra, his eyes once again sharp. "Sierra, if Lucera is back, she can . . . she will help you, m'ija. I never should've . . . I'm sorry. I'm so sorry." He shook his head, eyes glazing over again.

"Abuelo, I don't know where she is. Where's Lucera, Abuelo?"

Lázaro shook his head and placed the crinkled scrap of paper in Sierra's hand. "I'm sorry," he moaned.

Sierra uncrinkled it. In the same elegant script as the names on the photograph, someone had written:

donde mujeres solitarias van a bailar

"Where lonely women go to dance," Sierra translated. "This where Lucera is?"

Lázaro nodded, his eyes faraway again.

"What does it mean, Abuelo?"

"Lo siento lo siento lo siento," he whispered.

Sierra stood and gave her grandfather a kiss on his forehead. "That's all you got for me, huh?" She pulled out her phone and dialed up Bennie as she headed downstairs.

"What it do?" Bennie said. "Did you have fun with your secret lover man last night?"

Sierra rolled her eyes. "No, B, I had fun running away from that freaky guy that showed up at the party." She packed her bag and slung it over her shoulder.

"What? That guy chased you? What the hell happened?"

"I don't even know what to tell you." She waved at her dad and Uncle Neville and walked out the front door. "But I need a favor."

"Are you okay?"

"I'm alright." Outside, it was a perfect summer day. Sierra's next door neighbors, the Middletons, had set up a kiddie pool, and a bunch of the little ones were screaming and splashing around in it. Mrs. Middleton waved at Sierra from her stoop. Sierra smiled and waved back. "It's just a lot going on," she said to Bennie. "Listen, can you check up on someone named Jonathan Wick?"

"*Wick* like candle?"

"Right."

"What you wanna know?"

"I'm not sure. He's in a picture with my granddad and some cats from around the way, but like . . . he's just a random young white dude. Just seems kinda odd."

"You seem kinda odd," Bennie said. "But that's nothing new. I'll see what I can find."

Sierra turned a corner and stopped in her tracks. The portrait of Bennie's brother Vincent, which was painted along the side of a laundromat, had faded just like Papa Acevedo's, but there was something else about it . . .

"Sierra?"

"Yeah, I'm here. Thanks, B. I'll hit you later." Sierra hung up and pocketed her phone.

Vincent had been killed by the cops three years back. His towering image stood tall against the cement wall, arms crossed over his chest, his name written in bubbly letters across the front of his favorite hoodie. The artist had painted him smiling that terrific Vincent cheeseball grin he'd flash after making a really stupid joke. Now, his eyebrows arched and his jaw jutted out with a sharp frown as he glared into the distance.

Sierra looked around. It wasn't just Papa Acevedo's mural. *What is going on?*

SIX

"¿Qué pasó?" Manny the Domino King peered at Sierra across the game table in the Junklot. Rutilio and Mr. Jean-Louise sat on either side of him, each decked out as always in their best guayaberas and Stetson hats. Two empty chairs sat at the corners of the table — one for Lázaro and one for Papa Acevedo, both longtime domino warriors, now departed.

"I was gonna ask you the same thing," Sierra said.

"Trouble at school, Sierra?" asked Mr. Jean-Louise. "Public school is a cesspool of poisonous bile."

Manny threw his hands up. "¡Cállate, viejo! The child needs her education. Don't ruin it for her just because you dropped out of kindergarten."

"When I am finished this move, Manny," Mr. Jean-Louise declared, "you will be in that nursing home on Classon Ave, rotting like a forgotten cabbage."

"If you take any longer," Rutilio chortled, "Sierra here will be in the nursing home by the time you're done. Anyway, your entire family tree is a sad weed that I pull from my garden and spit on before I feed it to the rats."

"School's out for the summer," Sierra said. "And y'all ridiculous. Hey, I was wondering what happened to that guy Ol' Vernon because —"

"Nothing." Manny shifted his considerable weight on the little wooden chair and fussed with his skinny goatee. The other old gentlemen exchanged frowns. It was the only time Sierra had ever seen them look seriously at each other. "No pasa nada."

"What do you mean *nothing*? You said he was missing in the *Searchlight* this morning."

"Yep, he's missing," Manny said.

Mr. Jean-Louise smacked a domino on the board. Rutilio cursed under his breath.

"That's it?" Sierra crossed her arms over her chest.

Manny kept his eyes on the board. Dominos clacked against each other.

"Alright," Sierra said. "I'm gonna go paint. Manny, let me know when you feel more talkative."

"Make sure you cover that nasty tower with every wild monster you can imagine, Sierra," Mr. Jean-Louise said.

"Top to bottom," Rutilio added.

"I'll drink to that," Manny said. They each produced a brown paper bag with a bottle inside. One by one the three friends poured a little splash of rum out for Papa Acevedo and then swigged. "Ah! It's the wall I think that bothers me the most," Manny continued. "We used to be able to see all the way down the block, past Carlos's Corner Store to the church, and then down beyond that the hospital. ¿Ahora? Carajo. The blankness of void vacant estupid."

"If you don't make a move soon," Rutilio said, "I will make sure that that's what they write on your gravestone."

"It's not even my go, coño, it's Lenel's."

"Here lies Manuelito," Mr. Jean-Louise said. "The blankness of void vacant estupid." He shrugged. "He was somewhat liked." He and Rutilio crossed themselves. Manny grumbled and shuffled his pieces.

"Good-bye, weirdos," Sierra said.

Papa Acevedo's face could barely be seen now. Sierra looked up at it as she walked to the foot of the Tower. If no one would answer her questions, she would do what she'd always done when people she cared about stonewalled her: She'd lose herself in art.

She'd already finished most of the dragon's mouth — its lips snarled back to reveal huge razor teeth around an explosion of hellfire. Today it was time to get the eyes on point. Sierra put her headphones on and let the crashing salsa-metal fusion of her brother Juan's band, Culebra, wash over her as she climbed the scaffolding.

"*Cuando la luna llena,*" a voice crooned, "*mata al anciano sol.*" It was all she could hear before Juan's thrash of electric guitar exploded across the song, blotting out the rest of the lyrics. The creeptastic night before still lingered in her mind, but the music kept the chills at bay.

Sierra set up her paints and dabbed a few slender blobs of white on the dragon's pupil. When she was done with the eye, she'd start filling in some of the scales along the neck. It was more monotonous work than the face details, but it had to get done. Cymbals crashed; Juan's wailing guitar and the swirl of keyboards all screeched to a halt. *"Mira que los enemigos se caen,"* came an urgent whisper, *"La voz del espíritu llama / Y la energía surge como . . ."* and then bam! Culebra burst back in as one: guitars, bass, drums, and keys a single, relentless electric roar.

Sweat poured down her back, and she was glad she'd worn a T-shirt with the sleeves torn off and shoulders open. She'd tucked her fro under a red bandana and removed all the jangly bracelets and necklaces she usually wore.

Sierra dipped her brush in the white paint again just as the scaffolding shivered. She took off her headphones. Someone was coming up. "Hello?" she called.

"Hey!" Robbie's face appeared a floor below her.

"Robbie!"

He climbed onto the platform next to Sierra and paused to catch his breath. "I was worried about you last night. You just . . . you disappeared!"

Sierra put her hands on her hips. "Actually, *you* disappeared, sir. What I did was called running for my life."

"I looked for you!" Robbie raised his shoulders all the way up to his ears. "I swear! I just . . ."

"Uh-huh." Sierra raised an eyebrow at him and realized

she was enjoying Robbie's discomfort. "Here." She handed him a paint roller. "You can make it up to me by laying down some primer and then painting something cool over there to go along with this dragon."

"Anything I want?"

"Go to town."

"Nice!" Robbie crouched over the tray, popped open a can of white primer, and gooped some in. "I mean, the thing is . . . I was really scared too, especially when you disappeared, and . . ."

"Ran for my life."

"Right, when you ran for your life and I wasn't sure what to do." He covered the roller and started spreading paint evenly across the wall.

"Dang, you really know what you're doing, huh, Robbie?"

He shrugged. "You know I've done some murals here and there. Anyway, when you . . ."

"Any I've seen?"

Robbie stopped painting and looked at her. "Actually . . ." He nodded toward Papa Acevedo's frightened face.

"You did that? I had no idea!"

"Yeah, he . . . yeah." He shook his head and turned back to the wall.

"What's wrong, Robbie?"

"Nothin'."

Sierra clenched her teeth. No one ever wanted to talk about what was bothering them. She swallowed a sigh of frustration — who was she to Robbie anyway? He didn't owe her any explanations. She turned back to the dragon eye.

"I mean," Robbie said. He was facing the wall, his eyes closed. "I don't know how to talk about it."

"Does it have something to do with the murals fading?"

He nodded sadly. "You noticed, huh?"

"I saw it and . . . yesterday, there was a . . ." Sierra took a deep breath, felt Robbie's eyes on her. "There was a tear. It came out of Papa Acevedo's eye and slid down his face."

Ever so slightly, Robbie smiled, but he looked like he was about to burst into tears. "You saw it."

Sierra nodded. He didn't call her crazy. He knew. It felt good. For a few seconds, their eyes held each other's.

"So you wanna tell me what the shadowshapers are?" Sierra said.

Robbie looked away.

One of Juan's heavy metal songs started blasting from Sierra's pocket. She made a face at Robbie. "To be continued." She stepped away and tapped her phone. "Yeah, wassup, B?"

Bennie sounded excited. "That cat you asked me to check up on? Doctor Wick?"

"Yeah." Sierra walked quickly to the other side of the scaffolding, cradling the phone with her shoulder.

"¡Oye!" Manny yelled from the ground, where he was laying down some more primer. "Esafety first, nena! And we're about to break for lunch, so let me know what you want me to order from Chano's."

"Okay, Manny!" Sierra waved at him. "What about him, B?"

"He's a Columbia professor. Or was."

"How'd you find out?"

"This amazing thing they have now. It's a web and it's mad wide. Like, worldwide."

"Wow." Sierra rolled her eyes. "I coulda Googled his ass myself. I wanted you to, you know, go deeper! Get all Bennie-nerdtronic and get me his ATM pin and favorite colors or something."

"Whatever, girl, listen: I need you to suppress the urge to make a corny pun about what I'm about to say."

"I'll do my best."

"He has a Wikipedia page."

Sierra bit her lower lip. "You're no fun at all."

"Believe me, whatever you were gonna say, I already thought of it. Anyway, there's not much on there except that he's a big anthropology whiz, expert in something called *urban spirituality systems*, went to Harvard, worked at Columbia, and then fell off the side of the earth. Dude's old-fashioned for his generation. It's not like he was out there liking people's angry gerbil videos or nothing. So that's as far as it goes, at least on the Internet streets anyway. There is, however, one place where there's quite an extensive collection of Wick memorabilia. Or Wickabilia, as we say in the field . . ."

"Bennie."

"I made *you* promise no corny puns. I made no such promise."

"That wasn't even a . . . You know what, just go on."

"He has a paper trail. I know, seems so archaic, right? It's at the Columbia anthropology archive."

"Sweet!"

"Good luck getting in, though. Not like you can just dougie on through the front gates."

"Ha. I got people that are experts at these things. Thanks for the help, B."

An anthropology expert. Maybe Wick had been studying Grandpa Lázaro's shadowshaper thing, whatever it was. If she could find him, maybe he could help her figure out what was going on. Maybe he'd know how to find Lucera.

Robbie had started painting another intricate Robbie-design, some kind of skeleton woman unraveling across the Tower wall. It was perfectly creepy. Sierra sized him up. "I'm not through interrogating you, bro."

Robbie kept his eyes on the painting. "I know, sis."

"I'll be back later." She shook her head, scrolled quickly through her contacts, and made a call.

"What it do, Sierra baby?" Uncle Neville sounded chipper as ever.

"How you feel about doing your goddaughter a solid on this lovely Saturday morning and taking a quick ride uptown?"

SEVEN

"So when popo came around the block, we just laid low," Uncle Neville said, smiling at his own memories with those big, nicotine-stained teeth. "You know, acted like we was all some dumb stoop Negroes with nothing better to do."

"And what happened?"

"Well, Hog knew better than to make a move. He was scared of us but he was just as scared of the cops. But when they rolled past, he tried to break out. T-Bone tripped him and we let him have it."

All the windows were rolled down in Neville's dark blue 1969 Cadillac Seville, and the wind whipped across Sierra's face as they zipped north along the FDR. Manhattan was a towering mass of skyscrapers on their left. To the right, the East River sparkled orange in the midday sun.

"You killed him?"

Neville exploded with laughter. "Naw, girl! What kinda gangster you think your ol' godfather be?" Sierra wasn't sure how to answer that, but fortunately he just kept talking. "We'da never done that to the brother. Then we'da been just like the police, and that'd defeat the whole point. We just turned him upside down a few times, you know, and sent him on his way, never to be seen from again. Think he landed in Tennessee or somethin'."

"He hurt Sheila pretty bad?"

"Spent three weeks in the hospital. And she never spoke to a single one of *us* again."

"Dang . . ."

When Neville smiled, his narrow cheeks seemed to fold into themselves to make room for that great wide mouth. He always got happy talking about the good ol' days, even though most of his stories ended with people getting messed up. Sierra and Bennie had stayed up entire nights trying to work out what exactly it was Neville did for a living. Asking directly seemed like a breach of some unspoken protocol. Anyway, it was more fun to guess.

"What is it we doin' up at Columbia again?" Neville asked. He gripped the leather steering wheel with one hand and fished around inside his jacket for another cigarette with the other.

"It's hard to explain," Sierra said. "But basically, I need to do some research on something. Kind of about my family — my grandpa Lázaro, actually." She shot a meaningful look at him to see if he'd take the bait. Neville kept his eyes on the road. "It's about some missing Columbia professor he knew, so I gotta get into some files. But I don't think they'll let me in."

"Family history, breaking and entering, weird secrets locked up in a Ivy League fortress," Neville said. "Sounds like my kinda mayhem. You got a plan?"

Sierra shook her head. "That's why I brought you along. That and the Cadillac, of course."

"Of course."

It was hard to believe that the wide-open, ultramanicured campus of Columbia University was in the same city as Bed-Stuy. Sierra actually gasped when they walked in through the front gates and stood surrounded by all those pillared temples of knowledge and lush lawns. Summer-term students milled around in small clumps, chatting excitedly.

"So we're on a college visit," Neville said.

"In June?"

"In June."

"Alright," Sierra said.

Neville steepled his fingers. "And you are a bookworm."

"I like books."

"You love books, so you wanna see the library. Got it?"

"Got it."

"Now, get into character, pick yourself a Ivy Leaguer, and ask directions." Sierra took a step toward a cluster of chatting students. "Make it a boy, Sierra," Neville said under his breath. "And smile."

She forced a cheeseball grin across her face and walked

up to an Asian kid in a baseball cap. "Hi, I'm a visiting student and I love books. Can you tell me where the library is?"

Behind her, Neville put a hand over his eyes and cringed.

"Um . . . it's that huge building across the lawn," the kid said, eyeing her.

"That was a disaster," Neville said when she walked back over.

"Look, we found out what we needed to know. I never said I was a good liar. That's your department."

"Fair enough. Lead the way."

"Where's your ID?" the security guard at the library entrance demanded. They were standing in an imposing marble foyer, and Sierra felt tiny, a crumb in a giant, pristine oven.

"I left it at home," she said.

"Then go get it." The guard was about thirty, with greasy black hair slicked sharply against his skull and a shadow of stubble around his chin. He looked as if he had this conversation at least fifteen times a day.

"I can't," Sierra said.

"Why not?"

"I'm locked out my room."

"Then call the main office. They'll send one of our guys to let you back in."

"I can't," Sierra said again. And then her mind went completely blank. "I gotta . . . go." She gritted her teeth and walked outside to where her godfather waited by a low stone wall.

"Didn't think so," Neville said.

"I tried."

"Okay, my turn." He strutted off toward a grassy area where students were gabbing in small groups.

"Where you going?" Sierra called.

"Watch and learn, child." Neville was getting more than a few suspicious glares from the mostly white students. His towering frame, slick suit, and dark skin put him in stark contrast to everyone else around. He carried an old-fashioned leather briefcase in one hand and a smoke in the other. Sierra felt her ears get hot as a wave of whispering and snickers erupted in his wake. She lost track of him for a second, and then caught sight of his bouncing Stetson hat making its way back to her through the crowd.

"What was that all about?" Sierra said. "And where's your briefcase?"

Neville, now empty-handed, walked past her without stopping. "Stay here," he said quietly. "Wait for the right moment. Imma be in the car."

Sierra wanted to go with him. The whole situation was making her more and more edgy, but there was no turning back now. Neville had gone and done whatever it was he'd done, and that was that. Besides, finding Wick was her best clue for figuring out the rest of Lázaro's riddle. She plopped miserably on a bench and waited.

Less than five minutes later, a commotion erupted from the picnic tables. Students scattered hurriedly away and campus police emerged from all directions, faces and bodies tensed for a fight. *Can't take Uncle Neville anywhere,* Sierra thought, but just then the greasy-haired guard came out of the library alongside a few others and ran toward the ruckus on the lawn.

Sierra stood up and poked her head through the glass doors. No one was watching the entrance. Ignoring the tap dance her heart was doing in her ears, she ducked quickly through the low security arch, past the guard post, and into the library.

EIGHT

Sierra had never seen so many books. *Economic Development in the Third World*, one title proclaimed loudly from a display table. *Studies in Puerto Rican Literature* said another. It'd never even occurred to her there was such a thing as Puerto Rican literature, let alone that it would be worthy of a thick volume in a Columbia University library. A smaller paperback was called *Debating Uncle Remus: An Anthology of Essays and Stories about the Historic Southern Folktales.*

Stay focused, girl, she told herself, imitating her godfather's voice. *Do what you came here to do.* She found a sprawling map and ran her finger along it till she found the area called Anthropology Archives. "Subbasement Seven?" she said out loud. "Great." She passed through a loudly clanking doorway and went down two flights of concrete stairs that reeked of clove cigarettes and perfume.

Subbasement Seven looked more like a warehouse than a library. Metal shelves stretched into the darkness of a vast gray hall. Churning machinery hummed somewhere close by. They must've had the AC cranked up all the way, because Sierra had to wrap her arms around herself for warmth as soon as she walked in.

"Can I help you?" said a girl sitting behind a desk. She looked only a few years older than Sierra. She had a scarf wrapped around her neck and a knit cap pulled over her curly black hair. The name tag on her button-up shirt said NYDIA OCHOA.

"I'm doing some research," Sierra said. "For a project I'm doing in anthropology class. For summer session." She fished a little scrap of paper from her jeans pocket and put it on the desk. "I'm studying a professor who used to work here? His name was Jonathan Wick."

Nydia's face lit up. "Oooh!" she said, smiling conspiratorially. "Dr. Wick! Juicy stuff."

"You know Dr. Wick?"

Nydia shook her head. "No, he's been gone since, like, two semesters ago. He, um . . ." She leaned over the desk and lowered her voice. "Well, no one knows what happened to him. No —" She threw herself back into the swivel chair. "Check that. He completely vanished from the known universe. Like, poof. I asked everyone. I can't help it that I'm curious, you know? But Ol' Denton — the guy I took over for when they brought me in to run the archives —"

"Wait." Sierra put up a hand. "You *run* the archives?"

"Well, the Anthropology Archives, yeah."

"But aren't you like . . . twenty?"

Nydia let a warm smile spread over her face. "Thirty-three, sweetheart." She held up a framed photo of two grinning boys with dark brown skin and big afros. "And I got a seven-year-old and a nine-year-old. But thanks for the compliment. Black don't crack, ya know? And anyway, we Boricuas age at our own dang pace. You Puerto Rican, right?"

Sierra nodded.

"I love books and I wanna be around 'em all day, even if it's in some dingy basement at a stuffy old university on the Upper West Side." True to her heritage, the head librarian talked a mile a minute. "Eventually, Imma open my own library up here in Harlem, but like a people's library, not just for academics. And it'll be full of people's stories, not just jargony scholar talk. This is like practice, really, and to boost my standing in the eyes of certain potential funders."

"You have a whole plan, huh?" Sierra said. She'd never met anyone like Nydia before.

"Yeah. Anyway, Ol' Man Denton told me all kindsa mysterious crap about this Wick guy. He was a big anthro dude, specifically the spiritual systems of different cultures, yeah? But people said he got *too* involved, didn't know how to draw a line between himself and his" — she crooked two fingers in the air and rolled her eyes — "*subjects*. But if you ask me, that whole subject-anthropologist dividing line is pretty messed up anyway."

"What do you mean?"

"Ugh, you ask me these questions like it won't end up with me unloading a dissertation into your ear until three o'clock in the morning. Imma control myself, though, because I'm sure we both have other things we need to be doing. I'm just saying: Who gets to study and who gets studied, and why? Who makes the decisions, you know?"

"I don't know at all," Sierra said.

"Right! Most people don't. It's a whole messy bureaucracy of grants and . . . oy, see? Anyway, Wick was sort of beyond that for a while, the way I understand it. Or he thought he was. He'd go in and learn a whole bunch about some group and their rituals, and then, like, disappear for a while and learn actually how to do . . . you know . . ."

"What?"

"Magic. Stuff with the dead. Whatever."

Sierra's eyes widened. "Word?"

"I mean . . . That's what people say, yeah." Nydia shrugged. "Me? I dunno. People side-eye guys like Wick on account of all that old-time medical anthropology type of research way back when, and you know that's some icky ish this grand ol' institution was into, grave robbing and worse . . ."

"Um . . . I didn't know that."

"But Wick was against all that, from what I hear. He was like, down for the cause or whatever. But lemme stop runnin' my big mouth and get you your files." Before Sierra could even digest the avalanche of information she'd just heard, Nydia had turned and disappeared into the stacks.

She came back a few minutes later and placed a thick file of papers on the counter. "Here you go, hon. This'll give you a good introduction to Wick's work. Thing is, you gotta photocopy 'em. You can use the copier over there, just swipe your ID like a credit card."

"Thing is . . ." Sierra mumbled. "I don't have my ID."

Nydia stopped sorting through the file and took a long look at Sierra. "I thought you looked kinda young."

"I can explain."

The librarian held up a hand, which Sierra was grateful for because she really had no idea how she was going to explain. "No need. I see you're up to something interesting. And I'm curious. And I like your style. Here." She fished around in some hidden desk drawer and then handed Sierra a laminated card with a pin on the back. "It's a temporary ID, the one I give to my interns. We can get you a real one later if you wanna keep coming through. You can use it on the copiers and it'll get you past security."

"Wow," Sierra said, admiring her gift. "Thanks. I don't know what to say."

"De nada." Nydia smiled. She separated a smaller file of papers from the rest. "This is the good stuff anyway — his journals and notes. Most of the other crap is like research and equations and blah blah. Anyway, here's my cell." She scribbled a number on a yellow Post-it note. "Lemme know if you find out anything interesting about Wick."

"What was in the briefcase?" Sierra asked her godfather.

Neville either ignored her or couldn't hear her over the old funk song he was happily singing along to as they cruised down the West Side Highway.

Sierra clutched the file to her chest. The world seemed to get stranger and stranger by the hour, but the waning afternoon stayed stubbornly beautiful. The setting sun played hide-and-seek with some purple clouds stretched out along the Jersey City skyline, and a warm summer breeze swooshed in through the open Cadillac windows and made a mess of her hair. "Neville!" she said.

"Get up get up get up!" he yelled, honking the horn on the one.

Sierra clicked off the radio. Neville shot her an irritated glance. "What was in your briefcase?"

"Nothing."

"What you mean nothing?"

"I mean not a damn thing. I emptied it out before we left."

"Why?"

Neville looked proud of himself. "I always roll with an empty briefcase. In case I gotta leave it somewhere."

"Why'd everyone go running and security get all upset?" Sierra said.

"Cuz a black man put a bag down and walked away."

"But . . ."

"It worked, didn't it?"

"But you coulda got arrested, man!"

Neville scoffed. "For being forgetful? For needlessly troubling the good people of lost and found? I wish they would. Did you get what you needed?"

"I mean, yeah . . . But you were sittin' out in the car that whole time. They coulda . . ."

"I woulda left if it got hot and just called you to meet me somewhere else. I do have a cell phone, you know. But it's a good thing things didn't come to that. Got my sawed-off in the trunk."

"Sawed-off shotgun?"

Uncle Neville just laughed and turned the radio back on. Sierra could never tell when he was kidding about things like that.

NINE

Uncle Neville screeched to a halt on Throop Avenue. Sierra thanked him, grabbed a pack of gum and an icey at Carlos's bodega, and then leaned against the wall in the shade of the red awning. She pulled the Wick file out of her shoulder bag. Most of it looked to be journal entries, all scrawled out in elegant script. There were a few pictures and diagrams — a lot of the human body, and some overlapping circles that Sierra couldn't make heads or tails of. She skimmed through some more pages. Somewhere in here was the hidden history of her grandfather's weird secret society, she was sure of it.

Sierra's eyes caught the word *Lucera* and she flipped back to that page. *Back in Brooklyn. Amazed, humbled by the beauty and devotion of this community to its local spirits. The art of commemorative regeneration is strong here, a thrilling collision of artistry and spirituality. The shadowshapers' mythology revolves around an archetypal spirit named Lucera, who apparently vanished mysteriously a few months back, not long after I entered the fold. There are whispers that without Lucera, the murals that are touched with shadowshaper magic will eventually fade and the connection to the spirits will be obliterated.*

"Wow," Sierra said out loud. She bit open the plastic wrapper of her icey and sucked the cool blue slush out of it.

The vacancy has left them struggling, but still one can feel the buzzing of spirits in the air, the power of a collective imagination manifesting its devotion to ancestry across the walls and inner sanctums of the city.

Laz says the secrets of the shadowshapers are not understandable to the outside mind. And I had to suppress that old urge to defend myself, my field, the ugly collective history, you know. He smirked when he said it, as if realizing it would rile my deepest insecurities. I suspect there is some wiggle room in this arrangement. We shall see . . .

Her grandfather's name in this strange professor's journal. She wanted to read more but it was getting dark, and Robbie and the domino warriors were waiting for her at the mural. She shoved the file back in her messenger bag, tossed the empty icey sleeve, and headed off.

Vincent's mural still looked cold and determined. Old Drasco limped past her, mumbling his own endless stream of riddles, and his parade of cats marched along behind him as always. Across the street, some white chicks in bikinis lounged on a billboard for something — maybe a car dealership, or some kind of cigarette? Sierra couldn't tell and didn't care that much either way. Below it, women with big, pastel-colored hats filed in for a night service at a storefront church, and a whole other congregation cluttered into the liquor store next door.

Sierra turned and walked into the Junklot.

In the open, dusty area between wrecked car mountains, Rutilio executed an off-kilter pirouette in time to his own breathy beatboxing. He landed in a squat with both hands out in front of him. He was mostly skinny, which made his enormous beer belly even more alarming. It didn't do much for his balance either. He gingerly eased himself up, exhaling a slew of Spanish curses as he got to a full standing position, then swiveled his hips in a creaky circle, stomping forward arthritically.

Sierra, Manny, and Mr. Jean-Louise applauded. "Worst dance move yet," Mr. Jean-Louise muttered.

Manny frowned. "Ah, come on, it wasn't that bad."

"You haven't seen it with the music on: total disaster. Katastwóf."

"You see?" Rutilio yelled. "So simple!" Then he winced in pain and clutched his lower back. "¡Ay, cojones!"

A monstrous dog — some kind of Saint Bernard mixed with pit bull mixed with Satan-spawn — bounded across the Junklot toward him, its huge tongue flapping to either side.

"No! Not you, Cojones!" Rutilio yelled. "It was an expression! No!"

The dog tackled Rutilio and gave his face a thorough tonguing.

"You really needn't have named your dog that, Manny," Sierra said.

"I know, but I thought it would be fun. And look, it is!"

Sierra nodded, conceding the point, as Rutilio struggled back to his feet and hurled a random scrap of metal for Cojones to chase after. "I hate that perro!" he shouted.

"Well, he loves you," Mr. Jean-Louise chuckled.

"Y'all too much," Sierra said. "Robbie started back in?"

Manny smiled at her. "Yep, and we turned on the industrial lights for you."

"I see," Sierra said. "Thank you."

The domino warriors nodded and toasted one another with the evening's first portion of rum.

"You ready to talk yet, bro?" Sierra said.

They had worked fast for the last hour. Sierra filled the whole dragon wing as the sky became a hazy orange around them. A few birds flitted past, and down below, families meandered by on the way to the park. Robbie had covered a huge chunk of the wall in white paint, and his skeleton now wore an elaborate dress and was grinning wildly. Papa Acevedo's eyes seemed to glare off at some impossible enemy, and his colors had faded into an almost see-through wash since yesterday.

"Robbie," she said when he didn't answer.

"Hm?"

"What are they?"

"What are what?"

"What are the shadowshapers?"

Robbie sighed. The scaffolding shook violently, which meant Manny was on the way up. Sierra spoke fast. "Something's going on and my abuelo was involved, and so is that creepy guy at the party and whoever Lucera is . . . Everybody in on this but me!"

"Oye, chicos," Manny panted, climbing onto the platform with them. "I'm done for the night."

"Manny," Sierra said, "you knew this Ol' Vernon guy that died, right?"

Robbie tensed.

"Yes," Manny said, "a few years back. Those days are over now, Sierra."

"But you and Vernon and my granddad were all close. What was it all about?"

"I'll tell you one thing," he said, looking back and forth as if someone might be sneaking up on them.

Sierra narrowed her eyes. "Yeah?"

"Your abuelo could tell a mean story."

"Oh." She tried not to sound disappointed. "I mean, I knew that. Everyone talks about it. I only barely remember him telling stories, though. Like when we were really little, he used to."

"Oh!" Manny held up one hand. "Let me tell you, este viejo . . . he used to have us *riveted*. Us, a bunch of old men, sitting there silent as a room full of escared children, waiting to see what happens next. The domino game would be on hold."

That in itself was an impressive feat; the domino guys were notorious for continuing games unabated through all kinds of natural disasters and even, infamously, a shoot-out. "The shadowshapers, Manny," Sierra said. "Tell me about the shadowshapers."

The old newspaper man raised his eyebrows. "Ah."

Sierra heard Robbie shifting back and forth on his feet behind her. "Ah what?" she said.

Manny sighed. "It was a social club, Sierra. A boys' club. You know, a place for the guys from around the neighborhood to get together every now and then. Like these guys that wear funny hats and whatnot, except without the funny hats. Thank God."

"But then who's this Wick dude, and why's he writing about it like it's some kind of spiritual fellowship?" Sierra asked.

"That" — Manny smiled sadly — "is a question for another time. It's not something I really talk about. Perhaps your friend Robbie here can explain further." He wiped his hands on his slacks. "Alright, you two." The whole scaffolding convulsed rhythmically as he made his way to the ground. "Buenas noches," he called.

"Good night," Robbie said quietly. His voice sounded a hundred miles away.

Sierra turned around and shot him a sharp look. "You can explain your end of things while you walk me home, buddy."

TEN

"Look, I really don't normally don't talk about this stuff with, like . . . anyone." Robbie had his hands shoved into his pockets. They stood at the edge of the scaffolding where the Tower formed a corner with the back of the old brick building.

"Well, this is a special occasion," Sierra said. "Everything's falling apart."

He laughed weakly. "Well, that is special. It's just that people tend to think you're crazy when you talk about this stuff, you know? And we're, you know . . . sworn to secrecy."

"You're a shadowshaper too? I knew it!"

Robbie smiled. "It's kinda hard to explain."

"Alright," Sierra said. "I can't promise I won't think you're crazy."

"Thanks."

"But I'll still be your friend and help you finish the mural anyway."

"It's your mural! I'm helping *you* finish!"

"Man, I'm kidding! Lighten up, my dude."

Robbie pointed to Papa Acevedo's sad face. "Okay, look. I made this."

"Right."

"Papa Acevedo — Mauricio — he was my teacher before he died. I was just a kid, twelve, when I met him, but he knew I had something in me . . . and he trained me."

"Trained you to what?"

"Both in painting and . . . to work with spirits. Shadowshaping."

About a hundred contradictory confused thoughts crowded Sierra's mind at the same time. She ended up pushing them all away and just nodding. Yes, it sounded crazy. It was one thing when someone was telling her stories about some weird old professors, or even her own family members. But Robbie was only a few months older than Sierra and he was absolutely serious. *To work with spirits.* Something about it sounded so true. Part of Sierra knew he was going to say it, had known it was what he'd been talking about since . . . well, all along.

Robbie exhaled, watching Sierra. "But they're not like evil spirits. These ones aren't, anyway. The ones we work with, I mean."

"Spirits like . . . dead people? Like ghosts?"

"Yeah, some of 'em are the ancestors of us shadow-shapers, some are just other folks that passed on and then became spirits. But they're like our protectors, our friends even. And they just look like shadows, until . . ." His voice trailed off.

"Until what?"

"Until we 'shape 'em. Look." He pointed to the now barely visible face peering out of the brick wall. "Papa Acevedo's spirit is . . . *was* in the painting."

"That's why it was crying!"

He nodded, that slight grin creasing his lips.

"I thought I was losing my mind . . ."

"You're not, Sierra." He was smiling, but he also looked like he might shatter at any second. "It's just that people don't usually see it. Their minds won't let them, so it just looks a regular painting, not movin' or nothin'. Papa Acevedo always used to say people don't see what they're not looking for. It's like that."

Sierra gazed at the old man's sad face. Robbie had captured his essence perfectly: that big nose and the way his salt-and-pepper mustache had turned upward at either end to make room for his old-man smile. He had on the same brown cap Sierra remembered him wearing every time she went to visit her abuelo and the domino warriors at the Junklot.

"Anyway, he started fading — both his spirit and the actual painting — when Lucera disappeared, more than a year back now. It was slow at first, barely noticeable. Then it got faster and faster. And now —" Robbie put his hand on the wall and closed his eyes. "I can't feel him there. Can't talk to him. He knew he was gonna be gone soon. And . . . the last time I talked with him . . ."

"He could talk to you like . . . through the mural?"

Robbie nodded. "He said there were forces gathering against us. He didn't know what, exactly — just that we should paint more murals, even if they kept fading, and that we were in trouble. The shadowshapers, I mean."

He gave the painting one last glance, and then they climbed the rest of the way down the scaffolding. Sierra locked up the Junklot, and they strolled along Marcy Avenue together. "But why'd he fade, Robbie? I don't understand."

"There was a fight. Your grandpa and Lucera. This was before I was coming around. No one knows whatall it was about or what happened, but Lucera disappeared."

"Hold on. Who is this Lucera anyway?"

"Lucera, she was . . . is . . . a spirit." He shot a sideways glance at Sierra. She nodded at him to go on. "But a really powerful one. They say she was the one first gathered the shadowshapers, that her power was in everything we do. But I guess no one realized just how crucial she was until she vanished, not long before your grandfather had his stroke. And then people just scattered. Some moved on to other traditions, some folks just went back to, like, normal, old, non-shadowshaping life."

They passed an all-night hair salon and then a fancy new bakery with dainty cupcakes stenciled on the window.

"Damn. All of you disappeared?" Sierra said.

"Pretty much. 'Cept me, I guess."

"The last shadowshaper."

Robbie laughed, a good hearty chuckle that made Sierra grin. At least he'd lightened up a little. "I mean, you don't have to make it sound like a bad kung fu movie, but yeah, something like that. We been looking for her, but there's no clues, no sign, nothin' . . ."

Sierra dug into her pocket and pulled out the scrap of paper her grandfather had given her that morning. "*Where lonely women go to dance,*" she said aloud.

"Come again?"

"My grandpa gave this to me today." She handed it to Robbie. "Said that's where Lucera was."

"Whoa!" He held it close to his face and squinted at the letters. "We've never had anything to go on before. I don't even know what to say."

"Mean anything to you?"

Robbie shook his head. "Nah, but . . . look, there's more, somewhere." Little lines of ink could be seen at the torn top edge of the paper. "I bet if we had the rest of it, we could figure out where Lucera is."

"Yeah but . . . where we gonna get that? My grandpa ain't trying to give up nothing else. If he even has it . . ."

Robbie handed the paper back to her. "Well, it's a start, at least. Everyone had pretty much given up hope on ever finding Lucera. I'm not even sure where the other shadowshapers ended up. The only one I was tight with was Papa Acevedo. And now things are getting really dire."

"What was up with that guy at the party — Vernon? He was still looking for her."

"That wasn't Vern." Robbie shook his head, frowning. "That was a corpuscule."

"Alright now, Sierra!" a heavyset woman in a colorful dress called. All of Sierra's neighbors were out on their stoops, taking in the warm summer night.

Sierra waved back to the woman. "Hey, Mrs. Middleton." She looked at Robbie. "A corpus-who? What is that?"

"It's . . . it's like, when someone dies, their body is an empty shell with no spirit, right?"

"I guess?"

"A corpuscule is a dead body with someone else's spirit, like, shoved into it."

"A . . . a dead person? Ugh!"

Robbie nodded. "I know. It's not something shadow-shapers would ever do, not the ones I know anyway. Takes someone really messed up to force a spirit into a dead body. I didn't know Vernon well, but whoever did that to his body is controlling him. That's who's looking for Lucera."

They walked in silence, Sierra remembering the corpuscule's icy grip, its foul smell. She shuddered as they walked up to the Santiagos' four-story building. "This is me."

Robbie looked up at it. "I love brownstones."

"So . . . we gotta find Lucera, huh?"

"Only Lucera can turn this around. I didn't even think she still existed, but if someone's corpuscle is out looking for her, man . . . Yeah."

"Alright. Hey, you know some cat named Wick? I picked up some of his files at Columbia today."

"Oh, that random white dude that used to roll with your granddad? I didn't see a lot of him, but I remember meeting him once or twice."

"Yeah, I'll see what I come up with. Maybe he knows something . . ."

Robbie looked up and met Sierra's eyes. "Sounds good. Hey, thank you. For listening, I mean."

"You're welcome. Thanks for telling me all that."

He smiled. "Listen, I could . . . I can show you how shadowshaping works better than I can explain it."

Sierra raised an eyebrow. "Oh?"

"Yeah. Meet me tomorrow night at the Church Ave stop on the Q. If you're free, I mean."

"Yeah, I could do that."

"Cool."

They stood there for a few seconds. Sierra felt an invisible thread of possibility hanging in the air between them, but she didn't know what was supposed to happen next. "See you tomorrow," she said finally, and walked up the steps into her house.

ELEVEN

The next morning, Sierra crept into Lázaro's room. The rising sun played across the Bed-Stuy rooftops, glinted against windowpanes, and cast stark shadows down the avenues and walkways.

Her grandfather lay with his mouth wide open, a trickle of dried saliva crusted against his face. For a second, she wasn't sure if he was even alive. She was about to cross the room to check when the old man's nostrils flared and he let out a colossal snore.

Who was this man? He'd always been sweet to her when she was a little kid: piggyback rides and stupid magic tricks with that cigar-stained hacking laugh of his. But then she entered that awkward preadolescence stage, all pimples and big glasses and brand-new curves, and Lázaro acted like he didn't know what to make of this new creature. Mama Carmen had remained quietly firm and occasionally ferocious, but there was never any doubting her love — it came through in every small move she made, the way she'd absentmindedly adjust Sierra's clothes and do her hair for her, or lay her wrinkled old hand on Sierra's shoulder. She didn't pay much mind to small talk or banter, but when she asked Sierra a question, she meant it. Grandpa Lázaro, on the other hand, just drifted further and further away as time went on, and Sierra had never figured out how to get him back.

Then came that terrible day with the phone ringing endlessly, the police showing up at the door, Sierra's parents hurrying their shoes on and rushing out to Brooklyn Hospital, where Lázaro lay comatose. Liver cancer had taken Mama Carmen a few months before. It had been a sudden and devastating death, and everyone said it was grief that had sapped the old man's ability to make sense anymore.

Sierra had gone to visit him in the hospital the next morning. Her grandfather's face had been frozen into an open-mouthed mask of terror, like one of those poor souls who glimpses Medusa and turns to stone. Tubes and cables snaked across his body, coiled into his flesh, and wound in a tangle up to an incomprehensible mesh of blipping waveforms and drip-dropping fluid pouches. Sierra hadn't found it in herself to cry — the shock seemed to knock away all emotion and just leave her with a dull, vacant throbbing — but her brother Juan had been inconsolable. Lázaro looked only slightly better now, a full year later.

Sierra took a deep breath. She wished she could just stand there and take in the view of the neighborhood, the peacefulness of her sleeping abuelo, the new day. But she was on a mission. She soft-stepped past Lázaro to the wall of photographs. Láz still smiled and Mama Carmen still glowered from their faded Kodachrome world. In the shadow-shaper portrait, Ol' Vernon still had a black fingerprint over his face. Everyone else seemed . . .

Sierra almost let out a gasp. Another face had been smudged out. It was a tall, slender man standing behind Delmond Alcatraz. He had light brown skin and a pin-striped suit on; beside him was written *Joe Raconteur*.

Sierra sat in Lázaro's bedside easy chair and pulled the Wick file out of her bag. She found the page she left off on.

I feel so close to something. Something huge. It's in me, I tremble with it — both the knowledge of what's to come and the power of being so close, so close. Close to what? I don't exactly know, I admit. Is it spirit? Ancestors? The dead? Those quiet murmurs I've heard throughout my life, the ones that I never trusted, buried inside myself, in fact, for all these years? Perhaps.

Sierra sat back. Here was someone, a professor no less, treating her abuelo's crazy ramblings with total seriousness. Lázaro's own daughter didn't want to talk about his secret life, but this Wick guy was all in. She tied her hair back with a scrunchie and kept reading as her grandfather snored on.

One world's schizophrenic is another's medicine man, no? Whatever we shall call it, I want only more. More understanding, more knowledge. More . . . power. Because that's what it is, power. It rises inside me, unabated by the dim pettiness of university politics or mind-numbing every-day rules. I am brand-new. I would never say this out loud, of course, but I think, thanks to my extensive knowledge of other cultures and cosmological systems, I could benefit in far greater ways than anyone could foresee from L's magic. If I can combine the powers I am developing under the guidance of the Sorrows with the shadowshaping magic . . . the possibilities are almost unimaginable. There is no hori-zon. But only if Lucera can be found. Without Lucera, shadowshapers will soon scatter and all their work will fade. The only clue to her whereabouts is this single line:

. . . where lonely women go to dance.

"Where lonely women go to dance," Sierra said out loud. Lázaro had passed on the same clue to Wick.

This comes from an old shadowshaper praise song. Laz becomes almost impossibly disdainful when speaking about Lucera — there was apparently bad blood between them before she disappeared. When I pressed him about the rest of the poem, these were the only other lines he would give me:

Come to the crossroads, to the crossroads come
Where the powers converge and become one.

Two more lines of the poem! Wick had circled the word *one* again and again. Sierra scribbled the lines onto a piece of paper and kept reading.

It refers, I think, to the unified powers within the spirit of Lucera herself. As the keeper of a magic that connects the living and dead, Lucera signifies a kind of living crossroads. Imagine what this means, to hold all these converging powers within a single entity.

Imagine . . .

Sierra's phone buzzed and she almost yelped from surprise. It was Robbie. *We still on for 2night??*

"Crap." She put her palm to her forehead. She'd forgotten all about meeting up with Robbie later on, and she still had to swing by the Junklot to get some painting in. She texted back *Yep*, and stood.

Lázaro wrapped around one of his pillows and snored quietly into it.

"Oh, Abuelo," Sierra sighed. "What have you done?"

TWELVE

Sweat rolled down the back of Sierra's neck and stained the armpits of her gray T-shirt. Juan's band careened into another chorus on her headphones. *"Cuando la luna llena . . ."* crooned Culebra's lead singer, Pulpo. His voice wrapped a perfect velvet strand around Sierra. The music roared to a new height of thrashing, static-laced madness, and then got suddenly extra chill as the syncopated bass tumbao trundled out, followed by the *clack-clack* of the clave and then the swinging horns and warbling keyboards.

The song came crashing to an end and Sierra took the headphones off her ears. She climbed down the scaffolding, stepped back from the wall, and grunted with satisfaction. The dragon was almost done; its wings stretched magnificently over the Junklot, a ferocious middle finger to the seriousness of the Tower. Sierra had given it Manny's smile and mischievous, squinting eyes, and added whiskers in more or less the shape of Manny's big mustache. She chuckled to herself.

Robbie must've come back late at night to work on his side: The skeleton woman had a guitar now, and colorful swirls poured from its strings, forming the beginning stages of a bustling city. Sierra could see how the whole wall would look when it was finished, and it was going to be spectacular.

Manny walked up next to Sierra and put a Malta in her hands. "That's a strikingly handsome dragon."

Sierra laughed. "Thank you, sir. I did my best."

"Robbie's stuff is nice too."

"I aspire to be like him. Everything he draws blows me away."

"Oh, you've got your own style, Sierra. Trust me. You're doing amazing things."

Sierra kicked the ground and shrugged. "Thanks, Manny."

They stood staring at the wall in silence. Then she said, "You know this guy Raconteur?"

Manny shot her a stern look. "Sierra . . ."

"I know! You don't like to talk about stuff from the old days or whatever, but look, this is important. I . . . I'm not sure what's going on, but I think you — we — I think we all might be in danger. The night Ol' Vernon disappeared, I —"

"Sierra." She'd never heard Manny sound so grave. "A lot of things happened in the last couple of years with your grandfather and the shadowshapers. I don't know most of it — I stayed on the sidelines mostly. But there's a lot of bad blood around that. Folks don't like to bring it up, you know? A lot of friendships ended, even families torn apart." Manny looked back at the painting.

"Raconteur was a shadowshaper?"

He nodded.

"Do you know how to reach him? If he's still alive? Anything?"

"I'm a newspaper man, Sierra. I understand curiosity, believe me. But this . . . For your own good, this is something you need to stay out of. Stay far away from it, okay?"

"Manny . . . This is my family. You can't ask me to —"

The Domino King shook his head and walked away without another word.

The second she walked into her house, Sierra was greeted by the heavy, mouthwatering smell of arroz con pollo and plátanos simmering on the stovetop. It never failed; even today, with paintings crying and strangers lurking, the scent of her mom's chicken and rice eased her mind away from all that trouble, at least for a few seconds. It wrapped her up in a fragrant cloud that seemed to carry her into the kitchen, disentangling her cares and worries on the way.

"Sierra, m'ija," her mom said without looking up from the stove. "Your father's leaving for the night shift in half an hour, and your abuelo's acting up. I have to finish cooking and I have about fifteen thousand and a half things to do by tomorrow. Can you please, por favor, mi hija querida, take care of Lázaro's room and whatever it is he keeps yelling about up there? He's scaring Terry."

"You mean Timothy?"

"Look, I'm not in the mood, okay? Too much going on right now. Squeeze this garlic into the mojo before you go, please. Gracias." She handed Sierra a little flowering bulb of garlic, its crackling paper skin fluttering like broken wings onto the kitchen floor. Sierra found the press, stripped two little cloves, and placed them in the metal chamber. The stinging smell of garlic surrounded her, stuck fast to her fingers and nostrils.

"Mami." Sierra used a knife to pry the last strands out of the tiny holes in the press. "Can we please talk about Abuelo and the shadowshapers now?" Her hands shone with the pungent juice and slipped around as she worked the tip of the blade back and forth. "I just want to know what's going on."

María Santiago turned slowly around and glared at Sierra. She almost always flitted back and forth like an anxious hummingbird. Now she stood perfectly still, a little fire glinting in her dark eyes. "Just finish squeezing the ajo for me and go see what your abuelo wants, please."

The front door swung open, and Sierra's Tía Rosa came swooshing in as if pushed by a heavy gust of wind. "¡Buenas noches, familia!" she called from inside a thick cloud of perfume. She doled out sloppy cheek kiss-kisses to Sierra and María, and then settled into a chair at the table. The smells of garlic, well-seasoned chicken, and Rosa's ridiculous lady scent clashed in the steamy air.

"Hi, Tía," Sierra said. "I was just about to go clean up Abuelo's apartment." Her mom shot her a look.

"Mi niña," Tía Rosa snickered in a mock whisper. "I hear you have a little boyfriend?"

Sierra felt her whole face turn bright red. "Who?"

"Ay, Sierra," María chided. "The boy you were talking to outside the house yesterday."

"Who, Robbie? Nah, we're just cool is all. He's helping me with the mural."

Rosa lit up. "Robbie, you say? Ooh! What's he look like? Where's he from?"

Sierra's whole body ached to run out the door. "He's, um, Haitian." For a second, she wasn't sure why she was tensing up. Then she saw her aunt's exaggerated scowl.

"Oh, Sierra, m'ija, what are we going to do with you? Is he, you know . . ."

"What?" Sierra said.

"María," Rosa said, turning in her chair toward the stove. "What did Tía Virginia used to say?"

María shrugged and shook her head.

"If he's darker than the bottom of your foot, he's no good for you!" Rosa let out a shriek of laughter.

María looked horrified. "Rosa . . ."

"Is he darker than the bottom of your foot, Sierra?"

"Tía, really . . . What's wrong with you?"

Rosa rolled her eyes. "See, María, this is what happens. You let her keep her hair all wild and nappy like this . . ."

Sierra's arms twitched with the impulse to swing out at her aunt's makeup-saturated face, but she resisted.

"Rosa, stop it," María said.

"You let her wear whatever she wants . . ."

"Rosa!"

"All I'm saying is, this is what you get."

Sierra stormed out of the room.

In her mostly dark bedroom, Sierra stood in front of the mirror and frowned. She'd been listening to Tía Rosa's offhand bigotry her whole life and mostly learned to just tune it out. Her mom would always chide Rosa lightly, and then the conversation would turn to something else. But the words crept in, made a home in Sierra's mind no matter how much she fought them off. Her *wild, nappy* hair. She ran her hands through her fro. She loved it the way it was, free and undaunted. She imagined it as a force field, deflecting all Rosa's stupid comments.

Still . . . the mirror had never been a comfortable place for Sierra. It wasn't that she thought she was ugly or anything, but it was never the glance and grin that it was supposed to be. Instead, some patch of dry skin on her face would jump out her. Or a shirt that fit perfectly before suddenly seemed a little too tight, or a bra strap would peek out from a wide collar. And now she needed to get dressed for her — date? — with Robbie, and she really wasn't in the mood. He had completely shattered her whole boys-are-cute-until-they-open-their-mouths thing. Not only was he not stupid, he looked at her like she made sense, like they shared some secret language that no one else knew, and that they spoke it even when they weren't speaking at all.

Go casual, she said to herself. *Nothing special. Casual with a touch of cute.* She chose a skirt and a tube top with a loose white blouse over it. But it was hard work making suggestions and not blatant declarations with her ever-changing Puerto Rican body. Some days her butt was too big; on others she couldn't even find it. Was it the way her pants hung? What she ate last night? Her mood? Her period?

She sighed and glanced sideways at herself. Her butt seemed to be cooperating — it made just enough of a bump beneath her skirt to make itself known without being all extra. Alright then. She laced up her tall combat boots and squinted at herself again. Her hair exploded around her face with its usual reckless abandon. Bennie had insisted on Sierra coming by later so she could braid it.

Her skin was another matter. It wasn't bad skin — a zit here and there and the occasional dry island. But once when she was chatting with some stupid boy online, she described herself as the color of coffee with not enough milk. There was a pause in the conversation, and the words glared back at her strangely, like the echo of a burp in an empty auditorium. She wondered if what she'd typed was burning holes in her chat partner too. Then he typed *o thas hot yo* and she'd quickly slammed her laptop shut. In the sudden darkness of her bedroom, the words had lingered as if imprinted in her forehead: *not enough*.

The worst part about it, the part she couldn't let go of, was that the thought came from her. Not from one of the teachers or guidance counselors whose eyes said it again and again over sticky-sweet smiles. Not from some cop on Marcy Avenue or Tía Rosa. It came from somewhere deep inside her. And that meant that for all the times she'd shrugged off one of those slurs, some little tentacle of them still crawled its way toward her heart. *Not enough milk.* Not light enough. *Morena. Negra.* No matter what she did, that little voice came creeping back, persistent and unsatisfied.

Not enough.

Today she looked menacingly into the mirror and said: "I'm Sierra María Santiago. I am what I am. Enough." She sighed. These days were spooky enough without her talking to herself. "More than enough."

She almost believed it. Downstairs, María and Rosa cackled at some inside joke.

Sierra scowled, grabbed her shoulder bag, and walked out of her room.

THIRTEEN

Bennie's corner of Brooklyn looked different every time Sierra passed through it. She stopped at the corner of Washington Avenue and St. John's Place to take in the changing scenery. A half block from where she stood, she'd skinned her knee playing hopscotch while juiced up on iceys and sugar drinks. Bennie's brother, Vincent, had been killed by the cops on the adjacent corner, just a few steps from his own front door.

Now her best friend's neighborhood felt like another planet. The place Sierra and Bennie used to get their hair done had turned into a fancy bakery of some kind, and yes, the coffee was good, but you couldn't get a cup for less than three dollars. Plus, every time Sierra went in, the hip, young white kid behind the counter gave her either the don't-cause-no-trouble look or the I-want-to-adopt-you look. The Takeover (as Bennie had dubbed it once) had been going on for a few years now, but tonight its pace seemed to have accelerated tenfold. Sierra couldn't find a single brown face on the block. It looked like a late-night frat party had just let out; she was getting funny stares from all sides — as if *she* was the out-of-place one, she thought.

And then, sadly, she realized she *was* the out-of-place one.

Bennie jumped up from her bed as soon as Sierra walked in. "Look at you, fly girl!" She squeezed past Big Jerome and the two friends embraced.

"Shut up," Sierra said, giving Bennie a kiss on the cheek and extending a pound for Big Jerome. "Whaddup, man?"

"Is what it is." Jerome shrugged. "Just chilling, you know, hanging with Ms. B. I heard you got a hot date tonight with Weird Painting Dude."

"Bennie!" Sierra hissed. To Jerome she said, "It's not a date, he's not *that* weird, and . . . yes. We're hanging out. That's all."

Jerome rolled his eyes. "Okay, Sierra."

"You ready for *Extreme Makeover*, Brooklyn Edition?" Bennie said. She settled back into the cushiony pillow throne on her bed and picked up a glass of tea-stained ice cubes. "It's gonna be fun! And extremely painful. But mostly fun!"

"Yeah, listen," Sierra said. "I know this is kinda messed up, Jerome, but I gotta talk to Bennie." He stared at her blankly. "Alone."

Jerome pursed his lips and narrowed his eyes. "Oh."

"I'm sorry."

"Nah," he said, tossing a supposedly carefree arm in the air. "No doubt. I get it. Girl stuff."

"Yeah," Sierra said.

"For your date."

"No! Other girl stuff. You do realize girls have other topics of conversation besides dudes, right?"

"I . . . guess."

"Anyway, it's wack to kick you out, I know, but . . ."

"Nah, it's cool." Jerome was up, sliding himself awkwardly toward the door. Sierra felt crummy.

"Thanks for walking me home," Bennie said.

"No thing, B."

"At least you don't have far to go," Sierra said.

"Yeah, just around the corner." He laughed lamely and was gone.

Bennie shook her head. "You're cold, girl. Ice-cold."

Sierra sat in front of her best friend's mirror. "I know. I feel terrible, but . . . I don't know how to explain this."

"What? You nervous about the date?" Bennie stood behind Sierra and began combing out her hair.

"It's not that."

"Then whatsa matter, girl?"

No words came. How to explain it all? Where to even start?

Bennie narrowed her eyes in a pretty good imitation of her mom's suspicious face. "Alright," she said. "I'll just start braiding this fro and tell you random gossip until you're ready to talk." She separated out a large section of Sierra's hair and started braiding it. "Did you know Pitkin dumped Butt Jenny?"

"Already? The party was like yesterday!"

"Seems he moved on to bigger and better things."

"Janice? Oh my God, Bennie! She's like what? Eighty?"

"She's eighteen, Sierra, jeez!"

Sierra laughed and then it happened: She started talking. The whole weird situation poured out of her mouth, all the things she hadn't even known how to express to herself, from the crying murals to Grandpa Lázaro's strange, doomed fellowship to Nydia the librarian and the search for this spirit Lucera.

"Dang!" Bennie said when she'd finished. "That's wild!"

"Pretty much," Sierra said, breathing a sigh of relief now that it was all out of her system and her friend hadn't called her a raving lunatic. Not yet, anyway.

"I've never hearda anything like that in my life."

"Basically."

"But still, there must be some explanation."

"You and your explanations!"

"I can't help it," Bennie said. "I'm a scientist. That's what we do: We explain stuff." Bennie had spent every year of the decade that Sierra had known her obsessed with one branch of the natural sciences or another. She had settled on zoology recently, after having one eye glued to her telescope for what seemed like forever. "I'm just saying not everything is necessarily how it seems. Okay?"

"Okay. Ow!" Sierra wrenched her head away from Bennie's fingers. "Leave it!"

"You can't leave a half-done braid. C'mere." Hands returned to hair, and the yanking and tugging began all over again. "Look," Bennie said, glaring at Sierra's reflection in the mirror, "I know you excited 'bout seeing Robbie tonight, but I really don't think you should be talking to him about everything that's going on."

"What? Why not?"

"Think about it, Sierra." She began wrestling another strand of wily hair into submission. "He's clearly all up in whatever that whole strange world is. Shadowshapers and all that."

"True."

"And he disappeared right when that creepy dude showed up at Sully's."

"Ow! Be easy! Anyway, he was trying to draw it off, I think."

"I'm just sayin': You can't assume Robbie's on our side."

"What side are we on?"

"Our side. We on our side. Just be careful, Sierra. That's all I'm saying. Do what you gotta do, but don't run your mouth about everything. Just keep that stuff to yourself."

Sierra tried to turn her head, but Bennie tugged her back.

"What are we supposed to talk about then? You know I hate small talk."

"Suck it up. What do you think the rest of us normal people do on dates?"

"It's not a date!"

"Whatever." Bennie grabbed another two strands of hair and went to work. Sierra couldn't help but feel that her friend was enjoying herself quite a bit.

"What if he doesn't like my ponch?"

"Your what now?"

"My little belly ponch." Sierra patted her tummy.

"Oh lord, Sierra, really? Everybody has a little gut, and plenty a' dudes go crazy for 'em. Stop fretting."

They sat in silence for a while, Bennie twisting and pulling away as Sierra tumbled the past two days around and around in her head like a load of laundry.

"Ow!"

"Relax, I'm done. How you feel?"

"Like my face is being slowly yanked around to the back of my head."

"Awesome. Well, you look hot, so go get 'em."

Sierra got off the Q train at the dimly lit Church Avenue station in the heart of Flatbush. The platform was deserted, and a gentle rain drifted onto the tracks.

Robbie smiled as Sierra came out through the turnstile. His long locks were tightened and wrapped into a bun behind his head, and he wore a dignified blazer over a T-shirt and whitewashed jeans. He also had on old sneakers, but Sierra decided to let that one go.

"Not bad," she said.

He looked relieved. "Not bad yourself."

"Why, thank you."

He stopped just in front of her, just a little too close, and then leaned in and kissed her cheek.

"Hey, when did you get so slick?" she said, pulling away. "You're supposed to be the quiet, dorky type."

Robbie laughed shyly. "I am the quiet, dorky type," he said. "I'm really, really nervous." Sierra felt her stomach relax a little. "In fact, that move's all I got, really, and believe me, I rehearsed that like six thousand times." He exhaled sharply, and she realized his fists were clenched at his sides.

"Okay," she said, laughing. "You can relax, buddy, you're doing fine."

"Okay," he whispered. "You ready to go?"

"Where we going?"

"It's called Club Kalfour. I painted a mural for them. I want you to see it."

"You've been planning this for a while," Sierra said, her eyes narrowing. "Either that or you take all the girls there."

Robbie let out a nervous burp and then looked more relaxed. Sierra did her best not to burst out laughing again. "No," he said, "I've been planning this a while."

They walked side by side out into the night.

FOURTEEN

Club Kalfour turned out to be a discreet little operation on the corner of two quiet streets in East Flatbush. An ancient marquee announced C UB K LFO R, and threatened to collapse at any moment.

"Nice," Sierra said.

"Listen." Robbie stopped at the wood-paneled door. "I told you I'd tell you what I could about shadowshapers and what we do."

Sierra nodded.

"And Imma do that. Imma show you, actually. All I ask is that you not freak out." The boy's face was serious.

"Look, I'm not promising I'll stay if things get messy, Robbie," she said. "You know what kind of week it's been."

"It won't be no corpuscules, I swear. Just — trust me for a bit, okay?"

Sierra nodded. "I'll try."

"I want you to understand, this isn't something I show people, like, ever. Got it?"

"Got it."

"And I'm only doing it cuz it's easier to show you than explain it and cuz you're . . ."

"I'm what?"

"Cuz you're you, Sierra. Okay?"

Sierra realized she wasn't sure what to do with her mouth. It kept trying to move around to different parts of her face. She clenched her teeth to keep it in line. "Okay," she said tightly.

Inside, a disco ball sent tiny flickers spinning around the dim lounge. The lights passed fleetingly across the faces of couples dancing, teenagers chatting in corners, some old guys nursing drinks at the bar, and waitresses working the floor. A haze of smoke hung in the air; it wasn't the sweet mustiness of her abuelo's Malagueñas but a danker, cigarette smell. Some old swing-style jazz melody with a calypso beat chortled from a jukebox in the corner.

Sierra wasn't sure why, but she felt instantly at home at Club Kalfour. No one turned to glare at them or size them up like at most of the teenage clubs she'd been to. Robbie didn't appear to be in any imminent danger of getting jumped. People of all ages mingled and joked happily with one another, and most shockingly, no creepy guys tried to devour her whole with their eyes. "I like this place," she whispered in Robbie's ear. Then she surprised even herself by leaving her lips by his neck for a sweet moment.

"I was hoping you would," he said, a goofy smile breaking out across his face. "Come with me." He led her over to
the jukebox corner and said, "You see it?"

"Uh, the music box?"

"No, Sierra, the wall."

She had completely forgotten that he'd said he painted
murals for the place. She squinted through the foggy air at
the walls. The light was so dim that at first she could barely
see the images, but as her eyes adjusted, the swirling lines
and figures seemed to jump out from the wall. She followed
a blue pant leg up to find a well-dressed skeleton waltzing
with his skeleton bride. Behind them, palm trees swayed
before a burning red sky, and beyond that churned a wild
ocean full of beautiful dark-skinned mermaids and swirling
dragons.

"It's amazing," gasped Sierra.

"Thank you," Robbie said. "It was even brighter
before . . . everything happened."

It was true — the mural looked as though it had been
around much longer than either Sierra or Robbie had
been alive. Farther down the wall, a tall black man in an
elegant colonial military uniform stood on top of a jungle
mountain. He stared down into a forest full of growling trop-
ical creatures and magnificent birds. The light blue Caribbean
sky was alive with angels of all colors and sizes; they fluttered merrily toward some unseen source of brilliant light.

Sierra spun slowly around. Each wall of Club Kalfour was covered with an epic masterpiece rendered in Robbie's distinctive graffiti-like style. "You see," she said, "you say you're not slick, and yet, here we are, in this romantic little club surrounded by all your hot paintings. I think you might be slick, mister."

Robbie replied with a "Who, me?" shrug. "There's more." It was the kind of line that would have struck Sierra as cocky if he hadn't said it with such a solemn face. He walked up to the wall and then turned to face the club. "Do you see anything around the place? Anything strange?"

Sierra looked around the room. There were a few more scattered couples, a full family of six eating dinner in a far corner, and a pretty waitress in her thirties walking from table to table, putting down silverware. "Not particularly."

"Squint," Robbie said.

"What?"

"Try to relax your vision, if that makes any sense . . ."

"It doesn't."

"It's called 'soft eyes.' Don't look at any one thing. Just sort of squint at the room so it becomes blurry."

Sierra closed her eyes almost all the way, letting her lashes meet across her view. The room became a blur of color splotches and spinning lights. No big deal.

Then something moved across the room toward her. It was tall. It was dark. It was almost invisible against the foggy haze of the bar. Sierra's eyes shot open, but there was nothing there. "What was —"

"You saw one!" Robbie smiled at her.

"One what, man?"

"I knew you could. I knew from way back. Anyway, okay, look at the wall again."

"Robbie, this is no kinda explanation if all I am is more confused *and* freaked-out at the end of it. You realize that, right?"

"You said you wouldn't freak out. Now look at the wall."

Sierra made a face at him, but he'd closed his eyes, his forehead only a few inches from the painted skeleton foot. He raised his left hand and touched the wall with his right. Sierra squinted and then almost toppled over: The tall shadow charged across the club toward them, dove straight at Robbie, and then seemed to vanish into his chest. Robbie barely moved, his hand still on the wall.

Sierra's eyes went to his painting. She couldn't say exactly what, but something was definitely happening to the mural now. It was . . . different, brighter and . . .

The painted skeleton trembled.

"Robbie!"

"Shh."

Sierra watched in awe as the skeleton's painted skull turned ever so slightly as if to regard her and Robbie. It was smiling, but skulls were always smiling those damn death grins, so that didn't mean anything. Then it started tapping its foot. She could see it beating in time with the music.

Sierra opened her mouth to gasp but fought it back. She'd promised not to freak out. And anyway, how different was this from the strange changes she'd been seeing in murals all week? Something about it made some wild kind of sense.

"You run off?" Robbie's eyes were still closed, his hand still touched the wall.

She shook her head, then remembered he couldn't see her. "No. I'm here."

More tall, dark shadows moved across the club. Sierra could sense them flickering along the edges of her eyes, but she couldn't look away from the mural. One by one, the tall shadows approached Robbie and then vanished into him. The painting brightened and then seemed to awaken, each mermaid and monster flexing and turning ever so slightly, as if rising from an epic nap.

"I just . . . I just . . ." Sierra whispered.

Robbie was smiling when he opened his eyes. "Shadow-shaping. The shadows come to me. When they're just in shadow form, they can't do so much in the living world, just whisper and rush around mostly. Some can do other stuff, but it takes a lot of their energy. But when I put their spirits into the painting — a form — they take on way more powers."

"Can other people see it, though?" No one else was looking up, no one gaped. The murals were bursting to life, and everyone around her was like *la di da, another day at the club.*

"Not most of 'em, no."

"Why . . . why not?"

"It's like I said the other night: They're not looking."

Sierra just stared at the churning wall.

"But it's real," Robbie finished. "Anyway, you . . . You wanna dance?"

FIFTEEN

Sierra had to peel her eyes away from the swirl of living paint. "I do but . . . I don't dance Haitian."

"Do you salsa?"

"More or less."

"Then you'll be alright."

A group of older gentlemen in matching white suits shuffled onto a stage at the far end of the club. Most of them looked well past retirement age, and a few seemed ready to check out at any moment. "Don't they have curfew at the nursing home?" Sierra asked.

Robbie rolled his eyes and led her onto the dance floor. The old men all raised their instruments at once, and the room filled with a shock of horns over the gentle footsteps of conga drums. Then the pianist let loose a sequence of rising and falling syncopations and a man's crooning voice stretched over it all. It sounded like some of the old boleros that Lázaro used to put on his phonograph in his house on Myrtle Ave, but the little fellow on stage was definitely not singing in Spanish. Whatever he was saying, though, it was heartbreaking.

"Can we, uh, dance now?" Robbie asked. Sierra had just been standing there staring at the band. She put her arms in salsa position, remembering the feeling in her muscles from weekend after weekend of classes when she was a kid. Robbie took her waist in his hands. They started moving, stumbled slightly, and then caught their rhythm.

"It's salsa!" Sierra laughed, her feet stepping naturally in time with Robbie's.

"Not exactly, but close enough."

The music swirled around them, moved with them, for them. Sierra saw little old couples tear it up, putting some of the awkward younger folks to shame. Two eight- or nine-year-olds spun happily past. The song surged as the crowd swelled, or was it the other way around? Sierra couldn't tell anymore. Didn't even care.

After a few numbers, everyone was covered in sweat and laughing. Some octogenarian politely tapped Robbie on the shoulder, and Robbie offered him Sierra's hand. Sierra smiled down at the old fellow as he wrapped his little arms around her waist and the band glided smoothly into another song. Two middle-aged women blocked Robbie's path to the sitting area and escorted him back to the dance floor.

Something in a far corner caught Sierra's eye and she swung her partner around to get a better look over his head. The vast paintings churned and swayed in time with the music. The elegant soldier leapt from his peak into the sky and found himself a pretty angel to swing with. The classy fellow and his death bride spun wild circles from one wall to the next. The pretty black mermaids formed a dancing ring around one of the dragons, who appeared to be showing off a sultry two-step.

Sierra glanced over at Robbie, who was laughing as he tried desperately to keep up with his two dance partners. The song wound down, and one of the ancient trumpet players announced that they'd be taking a twenty-minute break. When Robbie reached Sierra, he was still trying to catch his breath.

"You alright there, buddy? Gonna make it?" Sierra asked. "I'm sure someone here knows CPR . . ."

"Those two ladies . . ." he gasped, putting his hands on his knees. "No . . . joke . . ."

Before they made it off the dance floor, the room filled with a thundering beat that threatened to blow the rickety old sound system to pieces. Sierra stopped short. "This," she announced, putting a hand on Robbie's shoulder, "is my jam!"

Actually, it wasn't her jam at all. The track was slick, though — a heavy double downbeat you could feel in your gut and *clickity-clack* rim shots bouncing back and forth like two stuttering ghosts. Sierra preferred crazy metal and alternative for relaxing or doing homework, but this would definitely do for the dance floor. She led Robbie back out into the gathering crowd of teenagers. He was smiling, but his eyebrows were raised in concern.

"What?" Sierra laughed. "You don't dance to nothin' made after 1943?"

"I mean . . ."

"C'mere." It was hard not to dance with that beat pounding out into the smoky club. "Just use your hips. Find the one and do what you do." Robbie caught the rhythm quickly and broke into an odd little jig, his long arms swinging wild circles. "That'll work." She smiled.

The floor had filled with dancers grinding up on each other, and the murals, Sierra noticed, responded in kind. All the swirling angels suddenly seemed much closer together; the military man was making out with one of the mermaids; even the palm trees swayed seductively in time with one another.

Sweat poured down Sierra's body, giving her brown skin a shine she could only hope was sexy and not gym-class gross. She looked at Robbie and breathed a sigh of relief: The boy was even more drenched than she was. She caught one of his wayward swinging hands and spun into him, wrapping his long arm across her chest. "Don't get slick now, just be easy with it," she whispered. He laughed and stumbled a little. Sierra rolled her eyes. One of Robbie's hands landed on her hip as he found his way back to the rhythm and fell into step, his body pressed up against hers. The song slammed on; various rappers took turns spitting sixteen bars in different languages. Robbie and Sierra stayed there, bouncing easily against each other's sweat-covered bodies. They let the other dancers, the swirling paintings, the whole spinning city around them fade into a colorful blur.

Sierra turned toward Robbie and found his face startlingly

close. She smiled, her cheek grazing against his, and she felt the little beginnings of stubble, smelled sweat mixed with the musky scent he wore.

A different track came on and folks started heading toward the tables. "Outside," Robbie said, panting. "Let's get air."

The light summer rain cooled them off after the thick haze of Club Kalfour. Sierra and Robbie leaned against a brick wall and watched the cars roll by. "I've never had a night like this in my life," Sierra said.

Robbie's smile spread all the way across his face. She felt him watching her out of the corner of his eye. It would be so simple to just stand on her tiptoes and plant a kiss on his neck. He would look down at her and smile, and then they'd make out all night, and everything would somehow make sense.

"Robbie?" Sierra looked up at him.

"Hm?"

His neck called out to her like the tractor beam in one of those sci-fi movies her brother Juan was always watching. She opened her mouth.

"Shoot," Robbie said, looking over her shoulder. He stepped forward.

Sierra growled. "What is it?"

"Someone's coming. You see?"

At the far end of the block, a tall corpuscle stood in the shadows, staring at them.

SIXTEEN

"Run, Sierra!" Robbie said. "Go! I'll handle him. Just get out of here."

"You said that last time and a damn corpuscule guy grabbed up on me!"

Robbie ran past her toward the figure in the shadows. "Go!" he yelled back at her. "Get out of here!"

Then another corpuscule rounded the corner at the other end of the block and burst toward them. It was Ol' Vernon, or Ol' Vernon's poor, abused corpse anyway. Now Sierra and Robbie were trapped between them.

"Run!" Robbie yelled again. He was almost to the corner. The first corpuscule looked back and forth down the block.

Ol' Vernon's corpuscule stopped in the middle of the street and stared directly at Sierra. Sierra wasn't sure if she was breathing or not. She took a step backward. The corpuscule walked toward her.

Somewhere, Robbie yelled unintelligibly. It didn't matter. Ol' Vernon wasn't interested in him. Sierra ducked into

the alley alongside Club Kalfour, came out on a large avenue and sprinted across it, turned a corner, and ran as hard as she could.

She had never been to Flatbush before, so she didn't even bother trying to figure out where she was heading. When you're lost in Brooklyn, the next corner store should only be a block or two in any direction, and they'd always be able to point the way to a nearby train. But somehow Sierra had stumbled into a quasi-suburban enclave of stand-alone houses, complete with front lawns and porch swings. It was creepy. The southern-style mansions glared out at her, making sure she had no designs on the untold secrets and treasures hoarded within. She turned corner after corner, panting as she hurtled through an endless night maze of sleepy, tree-lined streets.

The rain was falling heavier now. It cascaded over the shiny streets, drummed the tops of cars, and pooled in dark curbside gullies. Sierra ran until her chest was on fire, and when she stopped, there was no corpuscule in sight, but something . . .

Something else was following her.

The knowledge of it was as clear as if she could see the thing, but when she squinted her eyes into the dim, soaking suburban streets, there was nothing there.

"Dude stays disappearing when things get tight," Sierra said under her breath. "I swear Imma kill Robbie the next time I see him." She rounded a corner and walked halfway up the block. A raspy intake of air hissed all around her. She spun around. Some tall shape flitted away just as she turned — now nowhere to be seen.

Alright, she thought. *Robbie said the spirits were his friends and teachers. That they protected him.* "Here I am," she said to the empty street. "So protect me." She was proud of how calm she'd managed to make herself, standing there without even a tremble, waiting for some unfathomable wraith to come and deal with her. "Bring it."

The rain fell around her. In the big mansions, behind those darkened windows, happy well-to-do white people snuggled in their cozy beds. Maybe some were peeking out, wondering what that crazy Puerto Rican girl was doing in the middle of their block.

Another cluttered, seething breath sounded over the endless rain splatter. Sierra squinted her eyes the way Robbie had said to and let her vision go soft. At first she saw just falling rain and the glint of streetlights. Then a shadow loped out from behind a car without so much as a sound. It was massive, bulkier than the spirits in the club, and its shimmering darkness seemed to churn endlessly like black lava. It limped toward Sierra, thrusting one long dark appendage forward and then fluidly gliding ahead on the other like a wounded giant.

All that composure Sierra had been so proud of dissolved instantly. Her eyes went wide; the shadow vanished. By the time she got hold of herself to soften her vision again, it was just a few feet away. She barely stopped herself from crumpling onto the street as the giant shadow creature dragged itself forward, towering over her. A sharp, tangy smell flooded her nostrils — an ancient stench that told her whole body to run as far away as she could — but Sierra held her ground. The phantom's infinite emptiness expanded and contracted in long, rattly heaves. It wasn't the warm darkness that the spirits in the club had been — more of a void, like she was looking into the depths of a black hole.

A mouth, wide open in a silent scream, emerged along the sleek emptiness of the shadow creature and then sank back in. Sierra caught her breath. Another mouth appeared along the creature's shoulder; this one blubbered and gnashed. Two more came when that one was gone. Soon the whole creature bubbled and churned with silently screaming mouths.

Sierra. It wasn't one voice but many layered on top of each other to form a hideous dissonance. It sounded like when Juan hit a bunch of piano keys at the same time that were too close together. *Let's see.* The mocking chorus grated the inside of her brain. *What have they made of you, hmm . . . Come, let me see.* It reached for her, agonized mouths blossoming along its long arm.

She turned. Ran. Stumbled over her own feet and then achingly clambered back up. Tried to run again but found herself barely able to move. It felt like an invisible net had been cast over her body, dragging her down. She turned back and caught a glimpse of the towering creature taking a slow, ungainly step in her direction. She couldn't think. Everything inside her concentrated on breaking out of whatever was holding her fast. She thrust one leg forward, groaning from the effort, and then the other. Her insides burned. The thing shushed and crunched as it moved. It sounded as if it was right behind her.

Sierra yelled and managed to make it another two steps, but had to stop and catch her breath. Panting, she turned around.

The shadow lunged forward and grabbed her wrist, and every cell in Sierra's body caught fire at the same time. Its cool, horrible presence crawled under her skin along her left arm. Then her breath seemed to have been whisked away entirely. She collapsed into the rain-drenched street.

Sierra, the many voices said together. *Ahhh . . . You hold many secrets. Now tell us: Where is Lucera?*

Darkness wrapped around Sierra. Her scream caught in her throat as the shadow overtook her.

SEVENTEEN

"What the hell?" The voice sounded miles away. "What's going on out there?"

Gradually, Sierra found she could move her body again.

"Who's there?" Another voice, a little closer.

"It's a Spanish girl. Looks like she's bleeding."

Everything around her was tinged with a golden haze. Sierra lifted herself from the street but stayed in a crouch. Her wet clothes clung to her. "Lucera? Is that you?"

"Did someone call the police?" a voice asked from up the street.

"Lucera?" Sierra whispered. Her vision began to clear, but the world still seemed bathed in that golden glow.

"I already called," a man's voice said. He sounded irritated about it, whoever he was. Sierra fought gravity and managed to stand.

A few feet away from her, three towering golden shrouds stood glowing in the middle of the street. They looked like hooded giants; somewhere within their haze, Sierra could make out the edges of long robes draping down from hoods that hung over their faces. They must've been eight feet tall.

"Lucera?"

She knew the shrouds weren't Lucera, they couldn't be. Something huge stirred in the air, and the ground rushed up at Sierra again. She looked up, squinting with pain, and saw that the shadow creature was back. It lunged toward the shrouds, momentarily eclipsing the stunning golden light.

"Get that girl out of here!" a woman's voice demanded. None of them could see the shrouds or the shadow creature.

The golden shrouds spoke as one: *It's too late for that now.* Their shrill whisper was an explosion inside Sierra's aching head. *You have failed.*

Screaming mouths opened all over the hulking shadow. *NO!* It swung a long arm toward the shrouds.

"Well, isn't anyone gonna help her?" someone yelled.

The three shrouds raised their arms at the same time. The creature howled, stumbling back toward Sierra, and then it fled down the street and disappeared into the night. The shrouds turned to Sierra, seemed to stare at her for a moment, and then vanished.

All the colors went back to their dull darks; the streetlights glinted off car hoods. The shrieking shadow creature was nowhere in sight.

"She must be another OD from that damn Dominican club over on Flatbush!"

"Someone do *something*!"

Sirens wailed not far away, and a delirious panic welled up in Sierra's chest. What had that shadow thing been? And those shrouds? And now the police . . . She had to make her exit quickly, but she could barely stand. The rain had slowed to a steady drizzle.

"You there!" someone called from the house to her left. "Girl. Get out of here! Go on!"

"What's wrong with you, Richard? She's obviously hurt . . ."

Sierra placed a shaking hand on the slick SUV beside her and steadied herself. Someone was coming toward her on a bicycle, pedaling through the puddles. She squinted through the rain. It couldn't be . . .

"Sierra!" her brother's voice said.

"Juan?"

She almost broke down in tears at the very idea of him being there, and then there he was, soaking wet and grinning like a fool in front of her. His grin faded when he saw her frightened, tearstained face.

"Jesus, Sierra, what the hell happened to you?"

"Can't . . . explain . . ." she sighed, throwing herself into an awkward embrace around Juan and his little stunt bike. "Let's get outta here."

"No problem, sis. Hop on."

It had been years since Sierra had ridden the pegs on the back wheel of her brother's bike. They'd been cruising down

DeKalb one bright summer afternoon, he was talking trash with some girl from around the way, he hit a pothole, and they'd both ended up at Kings County, Sierra with a concussion and a permanent scar across one eyebrow and Juan with a fractured wrist and wounded pride. That was that, Sierra had declared as they lay side by side on the hospital stretchers. No more stupid peg riding.

But it was strangely comforting on this dreary, haunted night, standing behind Juan with her hands on his shoulders, watching his spiky head bob up and down as he pedaled along Ocean Avenue, and the manicured suburbs gave way to the twenty-four-hour vegetable stands and roti spots. Even the rain was a soft blessing against her face, and the warm June wind brushed away some of the terror of what had just happened. The gloomy darkness of Prospect Park loomed ahead of them.

"Juan," she said, squeezing his shoulders. "How'd you know to find me? You never bike around Flatbush. And you're s'posta be in, like, Connecticut or something with the band."

He didn't say anything.

"Juan?"

"I just popped back through to check on things."

"Juan. You suck at lies. Just skip it."

"The shadows led me to you."

Sierra dropped her foot to the street and the bike almost tipped over.

"What the hell?" Juan yelled, screeching to a halt.

"What do you know about the shadows?"

He looked away. "A thing or two, I guess."

"Juan." Sierra got off the bike and walked around to glare at her brother, full in the face. "What's going on?"

"Look, you being shady too. You tell me what happened to you back there, I'll tell you what I know about the shadows."

"Deal. You first."

Juan scrunched up his face and exhaled irritably through his nose — the same frustrated tic he'd been doing since his whole life. "It was Grandpa Lázaro first told me about all of it."

"When?"

"When I was like, I dunno, ten."

"When you were ten?" Sierra crossed her arms over her chest. "Are you serious?"

"Dead ass. Said he was passing on the legacy or something."

"Legacy of what?"

"It's like a whole spirit world in Brooklyn that Abuelo was in touch with. He was deep with them. Came over from PR with a buncha spirits, I guess, and then kept it going the whole time he was here. Right up till his stroke."

Sierra just stared blankly at her brother. The rain was a misty sprinkling on her skin. Cars honked and shoved busily past, sending out fleeting excerpts of whatever hot new single was getting overplayed on the radio. All these years, she'd blamed herself for having a shallow relationship with her aging grandfather, and now it turned out he'd had an entire supernatural universe he shared only with Juan.

"Did Gael know?"

"I think Abuelo tried to tell him before I was born, but Gael wasn't trying to hear about it."

"Why . . . why didn't he ever tell me?"

"I dunno." Juan shrugged. "You know Abuelo was all into his old-school machismo crap. He probably just didn't think you'd get it." Sierra stopped herself from slapping her brother across the face, but only barely. He recognized the violence dancing in her eyes. "It's messed up, I know."

"Why didn't *you* tell me?"

"I figured you'd just think I was crazy. Plus, the ol' man made me swear not to tell nobody. Said it'd be dangerous."

Sierra watched the speckles of precipitation jangle and spin beneath a lamppost. Sorrow and rage combined, and Sierra had to push back a wave of tears. This was not the time.

"Can we, uh, get back to heading home now?" Juan asked. "I'm pretty wet. You can tell me what happened on the way."

EIGHTEEN

Later that night, Sierra stood frozen at the foot of Lázaro's bed. The rain sang its gentle song against his wide windows, and outside, the lights of Brooklyn made a blurry haze in the night. She studied her sleeping grandfather's withered face, his gaping toothless mouth and flaring nostrils bathed in the warm glow of the reading lamp.

"Why?" she said, watching the emaciated chest rise and fall beneath his sheets. "Why'd you never tell me about all this stuff?" She sniffled and let a single tear slip down her cheek. "And you still won't tell me what's going on, viejo."

Lázaro stirred slightly but didn't wake. Sierra stared down at him, her heart pounding.

"I almost died tonight, Abuelo. And why? What boys' club did I nearly get killed for? Did you think you were . . ." Her voice faltered, but she refused to cry in front of him. "Did you think you were protecting me by keeping me in the dark all this time?"

She walked out, slamming the door behind her.

In her room, Sierra unraveled her braids and stared at

herself in the mirror. Her newly freed fro still bore the traces of Bennie's handiwork, but Sierra didn't feel like combing it out. Good hair, bad hair. Such nonsense. She blew herself a kiss, flipped off an invisible Tía Rosa, and stomped downstairs.

Juan looked up from his sticker-covered acoustic guitar. He sat at the kitchen table with an open bag of chips and a liter bottle of soda in front of him. "You done pouting?" he asked. "Because we need to have a serious conversation about what happened tonight."

"You're damn right we do," Sierra said. She swung a chair around and sat backward in it, glaring at her brother.

"And you can start by thanking me for saving your ass."

Sierra shrugged and looked away. "Thanks," she said quietly. "How'd you know to come find me anyway?"

"You hungry?"

"Juan, it's like midnight!"

"I know." He jumped up and started rummaging around the cabinets. "Perfect time for midnight breakfast!"

"Alright, but don't think this'll get you out of telling me how you showed up in Flatbush tonight."

Juan cracked some eggs into a bowl. "So, we were couch-crashing at this dude's spot upstate."

"Upstate New York? People there listen to Culebra?"

"What? People all over this nation listen to us."

"But . . . are there Puerto Ricans in upstate New York?"

"I dunno, Sierra, probably. But I'm talking about white people!"

"Shut up."

"I swear to God! White kids come out and eat our music up. They crazy about us. Sing along to our lyrics and everything."

"Half your songs are in Spanish."

"I know. Go figure. Can I finish what I was saying now?"

Sierra busied herself clearing the table of María's loose paperwork and some ad catalogs. "By all means."

Juan opened the refrigerator. "Mom made yucca! Sweet!" He retrieved a ceramic bowl with plastic wrap over it and tossed several white cassava chunks onto the frying pan. "Anyway, we were at this dude's spot, partying, whatever, hanging out earlier today, and I felt something. I mean, I got the shadowshaping skills — Abuelo initiated me, but I don't really use them a lot, so it's all still kind of wild to me, to be honest. But this was like a fluttering in my chest, and then I could just feel the room get crowded. Suddenly there were, like, six spirits in the place."

"Whoa. Did you have to squinch up your eyes and whatnot to see 'em?"

"Oh, so you *do* know a thing or two about all this, huh?"

Sierra looked away again. "No thanks to you."

Juan poked the simmering egg and yucca mix with a spatula. "Anyway, nah, after a while you learn to just see 'em without the squinty thing. They were murmuring, humming to themselves in that way they do."

"They can talk?"

"Kinda. It's like you hear it in your head. But it's not your thoughts. It only makes sense once you've felt it."

Sierra remembered the creature's awful voice echoing through her and shuddered. "I think I know what you mean."

"Anyway, the spirits said you were in trouble. Like bad trouble."

She sat down at the kitchen table, feeling like someone had splashed cold water down her insides. She knew she was in trouble, and tonight, for the first time in her life, she'd felt like death itself was staring her in the face. But, somehow, hearing that these strange shadows thought so too made it even worse. "I don't know what to say."

"So I got on the next bus here."

"Didn't you have Culebra gigs?"

"Yeah, I canceled them."

"Wow . . . Thanks, Juan."

"You're my sister and you were in trouble. And there'll always be other gigs. I told Gordo to see if he could set us up a acoustic show over at El Mar for tomorrow night. You know, for old time's sake or whatever." Gordo was a big ol' Cubano cat who had been teaching Juan music since he was little. He sat in with Culebra when they played New York gigs. "So what happened to Robbie?" he said, prodding his spatula into the yellow, lumpy concoction. A pungent garlicky aroma filled the kitchen. "He just up and disappeared? That kid's always been a weirdo."

"Imma slap him next time I see him," Sierra said. "Leave a girl alone like that when there's all kindsa phantoms and thugs around."

"Yeah, that ain't right. Can you get me two plates?"

Sierra suppressed a smirk — it still gave her a little glint of pleasure to be taller than her older brother. "So lemme see if I have this right," she said, setting down two plates. "From what Robbie said, the shadows are spirits wandering around, and then a shadow*shaper* comes and gives them a form, yeah?"

"Right." Juan set out the silverware and got Sierra a glass. "Like a painting or a sculpture."

"And the shadow spirit goes *through* the shadowshaper *into* the form, yeah?"

"And then the shadows become more powerful and can do cool stuff and whatever."

"That what the official manual says, Juan? They can do cool stuff?"

"You know what I mean!" Juan shrugged and heaped a few lumps of steamy egg and yucca scramble onto the plates.

"What was Abuelo's form that he did, though?"

"He was a storyteller, remember? Apparently that's pretty rare and powerful. Usually it's painting, like Papa Acevedo."

"A storyteller? I mean, he always told us cool bedtime stories, but . . ." Sierra sighed. The list of things she didn't know about her grandfather seemed to get longer by the minute.

"Yeah, he was bad with it. I mean, from what I hear. Never saw him in action. But I heard if someone was coming at him, he'd just stand there all quiet-like and mutter to himself, right? And then whatever it was he was mumbling about would literally take shape around him, like materialize from the ether and go after the bad guys or whatever. The shadows would do what he wanted them to do. Abuelo was a straight G with it."

And now Lázaro couldn't even form words, Sierra thought. She sighed again. Too many thoughts crowded her head, and all of them were tainted with the image of that shadow creature lurching toward her and the golden shrouds' inhuman laugh.

"So, you don't know what that thing was?" Sierra asked.

"The mouthy thing that jumped you? Never heard of anything like that. Or the golden things. That's on some other level. All I ever seen is the tall, lanky shadow dudes. Sorry, sis."

Sierra shook her head. "It's fine." She ate quickly, said good night, and hurried upstairs. Someone was after her, after all the shadowshapers. Maybe Wick had the answers. She climbed into bed and spread the professor's file out in front of her.

Alas, I cannot create. I am a man of science. My only powers are those of observation and analysis. I cannot conjure something out of nothing like the painter Mauricio Acevedo or Old Crane, the metalworker.

The spirits, for reasons still unclear to me, shun my every attempt to channel them into my unfortunate sketches. I can send them into others' work, even enliven some inanimate objects, and once that's done, the results are brilliant. But they will not come to my own work.

There is a power vacuum now with Lucera gone. But here I am, a stranger as skillful as any of the old-timers, more so considering how recently I was initiated, and ever faithful to Lázaro. . . . Yes, the Sorrows have advanced me in ways that L need not know about. But they are my powers now, part of me.

The Sorrows. He'd mentioned them earlier. They sounded like some other secret cult thing. She scribbled the words on a scrap of notepaper.

And yet, when I ask Lázaro about filling the void that this overbearing spirit woman left behind, all I get in response are murmurs and shrug offs.

This weekend I will approach Laz one more time about assuming the role that Lucera has vacated. As I understand it, only she can pass on the powers she holds. Surely he knows where she's gone. She will listen to reason, and if not, surely Lázaro will help me convince her. She must understand one can't simply abandon all that power, all these souls depending on her . . . No. She must share her power. She will be swayed, if not by my logic, then by the sheer fact that already the disastrous effects of her exile can be seen: Shadowshapers slip away daily. Lázaro has no sons to inherit his legacy and his daughters reject it outright. (He does have three grandchildren, perhaps a new generation of shadowshapers that must be looked into . . .) All over Brooklyn, the murals are fading. It is slow, the process, but the fact that it has begun so soon should convince her of the urgency of this matter. The shadowshapers must be saved! Lázaro must speak! Tonight, I will convince him.

The entry was dated March 16 of the year before, just three days before Lázaro's stroke. Had Wick had something to do with that? What had he done?

NINETEEN

Many hands tugged at Sierra's clothes. More hands held her up, keeping her from floating off into an endless ocean of nothingness, and she knew they would help her get to the surface, if she only could figure out which direction it was. For a minute she allowed herself to hang deep underwater, floating somewhere bet before she passed out. Night was a thick blanket around her. Only the little red broken-line numbers on her alarm clock cut the darkness. It was almost one.

Clack.

Outside her window, Sierra could just make out the dim haze of the neighbors' backyard lights. Who was lurking behind her house? She crossed the room at a bound and laid her back flat against the wall, commando-style, then reached one hand across and forced open the screen. "You gonna show yourself or just break my window?" she hissed into the darkness.

"It's me!" someone whispered loudly from down below.

"You're gonna haveta be more specific than that."

between utter desolation and euphoria, all alone and yet surrounded by the hands of a million murmuring ancestors.

Then something flickered at her from far away. It was a soft yellow glow, rippling like a flag in the summer wind. She concentrated on it, mentally letting the ocean hands know where she needed to get. Then she relaxed into the tremendous upsurge as huge torrents of water heaved her toward the surface.

And then something clacked sharply against her windowpane.

Sierra sat up in bed. The fury and fear that'd coursed through her earlier had simmered to a dull headache. She was sweating into her clothes, hadn't even taken them off

"Robbie."

Ah, there came that rage again, along with some other strange rumblings deep in her tummy. "Oh, c'mon up," Sierra called, trying not to sound angry.

The fire escape clanged and quivered. and then Robbie's smiling face appeared in Sierra's window. "Hey," Robbie said.

She slapped him as hard as she could. His cheek had a soft layer of fuzz on it, a world away from her dad's sharp scruffiness. Robbie pulled his head back and almost lost his balance.

"What was that for?"

"You don't leave a girl behind when there's bad guys on the loose, asshole!"

"I . . ."

"No. You just don't. You effed up. Period."

"But I . . ."

"If the next thing you say to me isn't *I'm sorry, Sierra, I messed up,* Imma toss you right off this fire escape, Robbie, I swear to God."

They stared at each other for a full twenty seconds. Sierra watched his tense face soften. "I'm sorry, Sierra," he said slowly. "I did mess up."

"That sounded genuine," Sierra said.

"You sound surprised."

"Apologies made under threat of bodily harm usually aren't."

"Can I come in?"

"Nope."

"Do you want me to leave?"

"Not really."

"Well, then, what am I supposed to do?"

"Hang out out there, I guess." Sierra sat cross-legged on her bed and rested her chin in her palms. Slapping Robbie had given her a whole new outlook on this otherwise grim night. "Now what's your big fancy excuse for being a complete barbarian to me?"

"I thought," Robbie said carefully, "that the guy was only after me."

"That's what you get for being self-centered."

"And then when I saw the other one, it was too late to double back. When I got away, I came to look for you and you were gone."

"I thought I was gonna die tonight, Robbie."

"I'm sorry. I'm really sorry."

The lump was back in Sierra's throat. It was the shadow creature barreling toward her with that uneven gait. It was those laughing golden shrouds. It was her grandfather's secrets. It was everything. "How do I know you're not with them?" She narrowed her eyes at him. Bennie had warned her . . . "Every time you come around, something bad happens and you disappear. How you think that looks?"

"Sierra, I know it doesn't look good." Robbie began pulling himself through the window.

"Back. Get back," she said. "I don't trust you. I don't know you. You're just some stupid painting kid. You've brought me nothing but trouble."

"I didn't . . ."

"Shhh."

"What?"

"I'm thinking," Sierra said.

The horror of running from that creature in Flatbush kept coming back to her, but so did the look on Robbie's face both times they had been interrupted by corpuscules. He had seemed terrified, genuinely so. The kind of terrified you can't fake.

"I'm very trustworthy," he said.

"Be quiet. Now you're trying too hard. It was going better for you when you weren't talking."

"Oh, sorry."

She stood up and took a step toward the window, watching him carefully. Robbie was biting his lip, obviously trying very hard not to talk.

"I've had . . ." She rubbed her forehead, trying to stop overthinking and let the words come out on their own. "I've had a very, very bad night, Robbie."

"Do you wanna talk about it?"

"Yes. No. I don't know. Something attacked me in Flatbush after you left, and . . ."

"I'm sor —"

She cut him off with a raised hand. "Shh, don't. Just let me talk. My brother Juan showed up and brought me home. The creature didn't hurt me, I don't think — I mean, nothing permanent. But . . . I've never felt so close to death, so at the mercy of something so huge and terrible. And no one in that neighborhood would help; they just thought I was another drunk Puerto Rican from the club. And Juan said he's known 'bout the shadowshapers his whole life and Abuelo never even mentioned it to me, Robbie, not a thing, and now he's a babbling vegetable and my mom won't talk about it, denies what's right in front of her face, like she's ashamed, and here I've been trying to get to the bottom of something that doesn't even have anything to do with me really, that —"

Her voice quivered; a deep sob lingered in her throat, ready to gush out. Robbie looked at the ground.

Sierra took a deep breath, steadied herself. "That's just for the boys, I guess, and I'm just tired and afraid and sad all at once, Robbie, and I don't know which one I'm more of because I'm all those things so much."

"Sierra . . ." He was inside the room when she looked up, standing a few inches away from her.

"And then you go and disappear, the one person that I thought I could maybe trust in all this, who also knows what's going on."

"Sierra."

His arms wrapped around her, and it felt good, right. She put her head on his shoulder. "I didn't say you could come in, you know."

"I know."

"You can, though."

"Thanks."

They held each other for a few minutes, their breaths rising and falling as one, their bodies rocking gently to the rhythm of whatever silent music the night was playing for them.

"I'm sorry," Robbie finally said. His hands slid up and down her back, and she wondered how far he might let them wander, imagined him tilting her chin up so that her mouth met his, and she really didn't know what she'd do if that happened.

"You said that already," she said.

"It doesn't ever seem like enough, though. What . . . what was it? That attacked you tonight, I mean."

"I don't . . . I'm not ready to talk about it." She held him for a few quiet moments, letting her fear dissolve beneath Robbie's fingertips. "Come, show me that little Haitian dance you do again."

He took her arm, raised it up, and placed his other hand on her hip. "Ooh! I love a little belly fat on a girl."

"Shut up!" Sierra laughed and felt the blood rush to her face. "No one asked for your opinion."

"I'm just saying."

She pulled his arm in front of her face and eyeballed his extensive tattoo work. "A-dayum, son, that's a lotta ink."

He smiled. "Wanna see the rest?"

Sierra nodded. Robbie pulled his T-shirt off, and she gasped. "Mmhmm," he said.

She narrowed her eyes. "That was about the paint job, a-hole, not your skinny-ass chest."

"Oh, right."

It was miraculous work. A sullen-faced man with a bald head and tattoos stood on a mountaintop that curved around Robbie's lower back toward his belly. The man was ripped, and various axes and cudgels dangled off his many belts and sashes.

"Why they always gotta draw Indians lookin' so serious? Don't they smile?"

"That's a Taíno, Sierra."

"What? But you're Haitian. I thought Taínos were my peeps."

"Nah, Haiti had 'em too. Has 'em. You know . . ."

"I didn't know."

The warrior gazed out across a teeming cityscape that crossed Robbie's abdomen and wrapped around his back. It was Brooklyn, Sierra realized, spotting the clock tower from downtown. The moon hung low over the city, just below his nipple, and was stained with a strange splotch.

"Whatsamatta with the moon?"

"That's Haiti," Robbie said. "See how one side's flat? That's where it borders with the DR."

"Ah. Of course."

Across from the Taíno, a Zulu warrior–looking guy stood at attention, surrounded by the lights of Brooklyn. He held a massive shield in one hand and a spear in the other. He looked positively ready to kill a man. "I see you got the angry African in there," Sierra said.

"I don't know what tribe my people came from, so it came out kinda generic."

"Oh, this is . . . all your peoples?"

Robbie nodded. "For me, they're like the most sacred kind of mural. My personal source of power — ancestry."

Sierra remembered staring at the sprawling art peeking out of Mauricio's sleeves when Grandpa Lázaro would bring her around the Junklot. "Turn."

Just by Robbie's armpit, a little man in a three-pointed hat and a colonial jacket stared suspiciously off to the side, one hand gripping his sheathed sword. "Got a little French in you too, eh?"

"*Oui*," Robbie said. "Just a leetle beet."

Sierra rolled her eyes. The Brooklyn Bridge swooped up from the cityscape toward Robbie's neck. Stars scattered across his shoulders. A few swirling lines suggested a rush of wind and some clouds. It was a breathtaking piece of body art.

"Not bad," Sierra said. "Let's dance."

"Alright." Robbie slipped his shirt back on, then took her hand again and placed his other hand on her hip. "Watch my feet." He backed up a little so she could see his steps. The moves came quickly, just like in the club — a simple and beautiful strut, ancient but casual, like walking down the street. Sierra found her footing, then put her hips into it.

"Uh-oh," Robbie said, breaking out his big grin again. "Lemme stand back so you can do your thing." He sat on the bed. Sierra kept her sweet rumba up, imagining congas winding beneath a softly humming voice, letting Robbie's eyes take her in fully. She spun, felt the moment push her along, guide her steps, and then caught a glimpse of herself in the full-length mirror hanging on her closet door. For the first time in a while, Sierra was struck by how much her face resembled her mom's: that sharp chin, her full lips. The thought was somehow exhausting and beautiful at the same time. She closed her eyes, swinging her hips slowly, and then the shadows burst into life, reaching out from the corners of the room with long, pulsing claws and screaming faces.

"Ah!" Sierra gasped and spun, throwing her back against the closet.

Robbie jumped to his feet. "What happened?"

They were alone. No shadow claws, no screaming wraiths. Sierra shook her head. "Waking nightmares," she said.

"What was it?" Robbie asked. "The thing that attacked you?"

"I don't know," Sierra said. "It was like . . . it was like the shadow I saw inside Kalfour, but bigger and with long horrible arms and . . . there were mouths all over it. Screaming faces." She shook her head. "And when it spoke, it was like a dozen voices speaking together, but all off-key and awful. Ugh."

Robbie looked pale. "A throng haint."

"A what?"

"It's like a . . . It means . . . wow."

"Make sentences, man. Complete ones."

"I've just heard about them in rumors and lore and stuff, but a throng haint is when someone — someone powerful — uses binding magic to enslave a group of spirits and then fuses them together into one huge shadow. From what it sounds like, the one you saw tonight was still a shadow, right? But if it ever gets into an actual form, I mean . . . if someone shadowshapes it . . . I can't even imagine."

"What you mean, binding magic?"

"See, shadowshapers, we work in tandem with spirits. We unify our purposes with theirs, and it's like a give-and-take, a relationship. When we're creating, we attract spirits that are like-minded. And then when we shadowshape: They align with us."

"I think I get it."

"But with binding magic, you're basically enslaving a spirit. Like the corpuscules? Someone with binding magic captured a spirit and then shadowshaped it into Ol' Vernon's corpse and sent it to do their bidding. And the person binding can see and speak through the spirit and its form. With a throng haint, it's like that times ten."

Sierra started pacing across her room. "So it would have to be someone who could shadowshape . . . and how does one get this binding magic?"

"It would have to be given by a more powerful spirit worker . . . or spirit."

She looked at Robbie. "Ever hear of the Sorrows?"

Robbie cocked his head. "Once or twice, I think. They're some old crew of powerful phantoms. Supposed to have, like, a golden glow. No one knows too much about 'em. Why?"

Sierra stopped pacing. "Golden glow?"

"Yeah, why?"

"There were three other spirits there tonight when the throng haint attacked me. They glowed — made the whole world glow golden, actually. And they told the throng haint that it'd failed. Said it was too late."

"Sierra, you *saw* the Sorrows? And you're still alive . . . Do you even know —?"

"Could they give someone the binding magic?"

"From what I've heard, absolutely."

Wick. He had wanted to save the shadowshapers by taking over Lucera's powers. Sierra could understand it now: A few days after the last journal entry she'd read, Wick had gone to talk to Lázaro about finding Lucera. But something had gone wrong, and Lázaro had never been the same again, rendered useless when Wick tore his power of telling stories from him. Wick was a shadowshaper, but the powers he received from the Sorrows had given him a one-up over the others.

This man had come in and destroyed everything. Everything.

"Sierra," Robbie said. "What is it? You're just walking back and forth and squinting at nothing at all. You okay?"

She stopped right in front of Robbie and looked him in the eyes. "You remember I told you I was researching that guy Wick?"

"Yeah. Like I said, I only saw him a few times. Seemed like a nice enough dude. Had a lotta questions about shadowshaping."

"I bet he did," Sierra growled.

"You think he's mixed up in this?"

Some stranger had shown up and gotten inducted into a family legacy that Sierra herself had been kept from her entire life. And now he wanted to destroy it, and he had almost killed her abuelo to do it. Joe Raconteur, Vernon Chandler . . . who knows who else? All wiped out at the whim of this one man. "Robbie?"

"Yeah?"

"I want you to make me a shadowshaper."

Robbie shook his head. "I don't know how."

"What?" Sierra stepped back from him and crossed her arms. "But I thought . . ."

"I mean, I can do a lotta stuff. But initiating someone as a shadowshaper, that's like . . . that's on the heavy-duty elder tip. I'm just not there yet."

Sierra's shoulders slumped. "This is some . . ."

"But . . ."

"But what?"

"I wonder. There's a chance that . . . You know what? Lemme see your hand," he said. "Your left one."

She held it up, and he put his against it and closed his eyes. He smiled.

"What? What'd you do?"

"I can feel it," he whispered. "It's alive in you. The shadow-shaper magic. You've already . . . Someone already gave it to you."

"But . . . how?" Sierra looked at her hand. It wasn't glowing or anything.

"Does it matter?" Robbie grabbed her hand and pulled her along beside him. "C'mon."

"Wait . . ." Sierra remembered the impossible nothingness of the throng haint rearing up over her, blotting out the suburban Flatbush streets, all those screaming mouths and the searing iciness creeping along her left arm. "What you just did there — the thing tonight did it too."

"What?"

"The throng haint. I felt it inside me, inside my left arm." She shuddered. "It was checking. It wanted to know — *Wick* wanted to know — if I can shadowshape."

Robbie nodded. "It makes sense in a horrible way."

"Wick knew about my powers before I did." She shook her head.

"Sierra. Come with me." He shoved on his shoes.

"Where we going?"

"You're a shadowshaper, Sierra! We gonna try it out!"

TWENTY

"Okay," Robbie said. "Try to relax and take some deep breaths."

Sierra closed her eyes. They stood at a bend in the paved road that wound around Prospect Park, directly beneath a lamppost. Around her, the urban wilderness churned with cricket calls and the gentle swoosh of trees. Somewhere, a river flowed. The park was like a wooded city inside a much larger world of concrete. The sun wouldn't be up for a few hours yet.

"Okay?"

Sierra opened her eyes and nodded. "I'm ready."

"Look," Robbie said, "it all starts with an act of creation." He pulled a piece of red chalk out of his pocket, crouched, and started to sketch out something on the ground.

"Do you always walk around with chalk in your pockets?"

"Of course. I mean, think about it."

"Wait . . . that why Mr. Aldridge stays whining 'bout he ain't got no chalk in the classroom?"

Robbie stopped drawing and shot Sierra a sly smile. "I plead the Fifth. Now look." He returned to his picture, a rough sketch of a mean-looking guy with a metal pipe. "It doesn't have to be perfect, okay? You just want some semblance of what you're thinking."

"Does it have to be me that draws it? Can I . . . shadowshape your drawing?"

"The magic is stronger if you draw it yourself. Because you're like, more connected to your own picture, and the spirits grow strong off that connection."

"I think I get it. Kinda."

"In shadowshaping, two things matter most: material and intentionality."

"Feel like I should be taking notes," Sierra said.

Robbie laughed. "I'll try and keep it simple." He pulled out a stub of blue chalk and shaded in some areas of his drawing. "A painted mural is gonna be a more powerful vessel than a little chalk sketch."

"Got it."

"Both because the material itself is stronger — chalk is just dust, right?" He blew away a section of the guy's pipe to demonstrate. "And because a mural is generally gonna be a higher quality of work. Gives the spirit more to play with." He redrew the part he'd scattered. "Like, you're going to a knife fight — do you wanna show up with a toothpick or a machete?"

He filled in the last section of the guy with the pipe, then added some wings and sharp teeth. "Intentionality matters because that's what the spirit connects to, what attracts them. I'm drawing this so you can shadowshape it. If I wasn't drawing it for you, you could still use it, but it wouldn't be as strong. The spirits respond to emotion. Since we're friends, they'll react to that when they enter the drawing. If I was scared of you and I was drawing it for you, it'd be powerful too, but a different kind of power. The strongest is when I draw a picture of the spirit that's going in it, like the mural I did for Papa Acevedo. But you can't usually do that; it's hard if you didn't know the person in real life. So we get creative with it."

"Like the mermaids and them at Kalfour."

"Right!"

"So it doesn't have to be, like . . . *my* dead relatives that go into my pictures, right?"

"Nah, it can be any spirit. Like I said, you'll attract like-minded ones with your intentionality. Anyway, since this is just practice, all the details don't matter much. You wanna get a feel for it. Now, you see any spirits around?"

Sierra looked up and down the two-lane road. The forest stretched along either side of it. A little farther along, the road sloped up into darkness. If it wasn't for the sounds of traffic whooshing down Flatbush, you could almost pretend you were deep in the wilderness. "There were a bunch around at the club earlier," Sierra said. "Man, don't tell me spirits are like cops . . ."

"Look again. Sometimes you gotta go all soft eyes to see 'em, even though you've already seen 'em."

She let her vision blur and almost immediately saw a tall figure slow-stepping toward them down the path. "Whoa . . . Yeah, one's coming." Sierra tensed. It didn't look anything like the throng haint, but still . . .

"It's okay," Robbie said. "It's not going to hurt us."

"You say that," Sierra said. She concentrated on relaxing as the shadow loped closer.

"Now, look." Robbie held up his left hand.

"There's your hand."

"Thank you, Sierra. I realize that. Now you do it."

"Oh. Wait, you want me to. But . . ."

"Sierra."

Sierra shuffled her feet and looked up at Robbie's determined face. "Alright, alright." She put up her left hand. The air shimmered where the spirit had been; she squinted her eyes. The shadow was barreling toward them. "It's . . . Robbie, it's running."

"I know. Touch the picture."

"But how do you know . . ."

"Do it, Sierra. Now."

Sierra dropped to one knee and touched her right hand to Robbie's drawing. She closed her eyes, bracing for the spirit to dive into her.

"Don't move," Robbie whispered.

A rush of coolness burst through her; it streamed along her raised left arm, past her chest and down to her right hand. Sierra's eyes flew open as the chalk man shuddered against the pavement and then scattered into nothing.

"Whoa!" Sierra stood. "That's not what's supposed to happen, right?"

Robbie was smiling. "It's alright, you're just starting out." He took a step toward her, closing the distance between them. "You'll get it. Try again."

"What happened to the spirit that tried to get in there?" She scanned the forest.

"Prolly wandered off," Robbie said. "You'll see — different spirits show up, and most are real down for the cause, because that's why they here, you know?"

"Not really."

"I mean — it's an exchange. You give them form, they work for you — *with* you, ideally, toward your goal. And they know that, so they show up ready to work. But sometimes you might come across some that just wanna be a nuisance, jump in whatever form you got for 'em, and do what they feel. Just ignore 'em and keep it movin'."

Sierra tried not to gape. "Okay, man." She took a piece of green chalk from him, crouched, and sketched a girl in a ninja outfit.

"Nice," Robbie said, peering over her shoulder.

She pushed down the flush of pride at his compliment,

closed her eyes, and then opened them halfway. A small shadow glided across the path toward her. She raised her left hand and waited a beat, and just as the shadow reached her, she smacked her drawing with her right hand. The coolness slid through her faster this time, a rushing stream that burst out her fingertips. Then the ninja girl shivered and stretched.

"I did it!" Sierra yelled. The drawing twirled a circle in the pavement, bowed to Sierra and placed one gloved hand at her feet, then danced off. "Robbie, did you see that?"

Robbie smiled. "It was saluting you."

"C'mon, man! I wanna see where it goes!" She jogged along the road, watching the glint of green dash in and out of sight.

"Where do you want it to go?" Robbie said from behind her.

"Up a tree!" Sierra said. The green ninja slid off the road and disappeared in the dark grass. A second later, it flashed along the trunk of a nearby oak tree.

"Robbie, this is amazing!"

Robbie was laughing. "That was great, Sierra. You don't have to say what you went 'em to do out loud, though. You're connected. It'll respond to your thoughts."

She turned and found Robbie a few paces behind her. Her smile felt like it was going to burst off her face and float away. "Do they always stay close to the ground like that, flat? Or can they lift up and be 3-D like us?"

"They can," Robbie said. "But it takes a lot of work to get there. And it takes a powerful shadowshaper. The spirits only have so much energy, so you wanna use it wisely. Gettin' all 3-D like that drains 'em." He took a step toward her.

"Can other people see them? Like . . . regular people?"

"If they look."

She took a step toward him. "They usually don't look, do they?"

"No."

The park suddenly seemed very quiet. Sierra wasn't sure if all the cars had just vanished from the road and all the night animals had agreed to shush at exactly the same moment, or she was making the whole thing up. Robbie's face was very close to hers. She felt his breath on her forehead. He wasn't smiling anymore; he looked serious, almost sad. She felt like if she put her hand against his chest, his heart would be beating a thousand times a minute and so would hers and maybe they'd both explode.

She opened her mouth to speak, and then something rustled in the tree branches above them. They both looked up. A few stars twinkled beyond the leaves. A bright green shape flashed past, and then the branch shook again and a flurry of leaves cascaded in a slow, circular downpour around them.

Sierra looked back at Robbie. She took in all the little details of him: the beginnings of a beard reaching down the line of his jaw, his wide nose and long eyelashes. For a few seconds, there was no Wick, no phantoms, no weird family history, no murals. Just Robbie's peaceful face and the leaves on their gentle night sojourn, buffeted by the summer breeze.

She opened her mouth again, but whatever was going to come out got caught in her throat.

"What?" Robbie asked.

"What happens now?"

He closed his eyes and slowly opened them again, now grinning. "We practice."

"Practice shadowshaping?"

"Combat 'shaping," Robbie said. He walked past Sierra down the path and then broke into a run. "Come get me."

"Robbie, what? Wait!"

But he was gone.

TWENTY-ONE

Sierra swallowed a wave of panic and squinted at the dark trees around her. "This dude just *loves* disappearing," she muttered, crouching. She placed the green chalk against the pavement, took a deep breath, and drew three sets of eyes. Then she looked up. The road was empty. "Come on, spirits. I know you out here." She squinted, and for a few seconds all she saw was the muted star shine of the night lanterns. Then three small, plump shadows emerged from the darkness and swayed toward her. "There you go." She steadied her trembling hand, raised it to the air, and gulped as the figures launched into a run. The icy swirl poured through her; Sierra slapped her right hand against the eyes, and they sprang to life, each set swerving across the pavement into the night.

Sierra smiled. "Find Robbie," she whispered. All three pairs of eyes swung off the path into the forest. She rolled her own eyes. "Really, dude? You just had to go right into the creepy forest, huh? Ugh." She steeled herself and stepped into the woods.

Sierra had never known such total darkness. She put her hands forward and moved quickly between the trees, trying to ignore her thundering heartbeat. A flash of green glinted across a tree stump a few feet ahead, and she made her way toward it. "I'm seriously going to have a talk with Robbie when I find him," she growled. "Seriously."

When Sierra first heard the humming, it wasn't because it had just started then; it sounded as though it had been going on for a while. It was like when she'd be sitting in class for forty-five minutes and finally get so bored she'd notice the stupid heater had been clacking and smashing away the whole time. The voices grew around her in a cloud of sound.

Ooooooooooooooooooooooooooooooooooooooooooh . . .

It sounded like the choir at Bennie's church — both beautiful and haunting. The voices ranged from low and mournful to high and exultant; they blended together in rising and falling harmonies that filled the night. Sierra stopped walking and glanced to either side, but the forest's darkness was unyielding. She wanted to yell out "Who's there?", but that was too much like what the chicks in horror movies did right before they got ate, so she kept quiet and stayed perfectly still as the hum rose and fell in harmonious waves.

It was too late to turn back. The noise was all around her, seemed to well up from inside her. "Nice," Sierra said. "Got myself lured out here to this stupid forest." She took a step back toward where she hoped the wide-open field was. "In the middle of this stupid, stupid situation." Another step. The humming kept getting louder. "After this stupid week full of stupid weirdo things happening."

She couldn't take it anymore. The drone seemed to be covering her, bursting through her.

Raaaaaaaaaaaaaaaaaaaaaaaaaaaaaaaaaaaaaaaaaaaaaaaah!

Sierra ran. She didn't care about what she might run into or what direction she was going — all she wanted was to get away from that noise. But the sound kept with her, burned incessantly through her ears, trailed her like a stalker around every turn. Branches slapped against her face and arms, biting into her skin. She saw a log up ahead, planted one foot hard on the ground, and threw her body into the air.

It was only after she'd sailed over the log and landed several feet past it that she realized something was different. First of all, she'd *seen* the log lying there right across her path. It wasn't just her eyes adjusting to the darkness: She could see everything around her in crisp detail. And then there was the jump. She'd been airborne for five or six seconds, easily. She had basically glided along until she felt ready to land.

For a flickering moment, Sierra saw herself as if from above, bounding through the forest in long strides, nailing each leap. It was terrific and terrifying at the same time — like she was some kind of superhero. And then she was back, without having lost a step.

She hadn't escaped the voices. In fact, they were louder, and now she could make out dark shapes moving along the edge of her vision. She turned, her suddenly spectacular eye-sight capturing every nook and nub of each tree, and she realized that there were indeed tall shadows rushing along on either side of her. They emitted a slight, pulsing glow, a single, illuminated heart beating through each one. A jolt of terror coursed from her throat to her stomach and sent tremors up and down her arms and legs.

The humming, once a deep baritone, was becoming higher pitched.

OOOOOOOOOOOOOOOOOOOOOOOOOOOOOH!

She bounced from rock to rock up a steep hill, grabbed a hanging branch, and hurled herself toward the top. Everything seemed to slow as she burst through the night air. The shadows flitted and swarmed around her, reaching out.

Sierra saw a cement walking path ahead, aimed for it, and came down running. Something about these spirits buffered her, kept her afloat. She was protected. She could feel it all over her body, like the same faint glow the spirits emitted radiated from her too.

She shot forward, barely conscious of her feet moving at all. The path led to a clearing, and beyond that would be the Long Meadow and then Grand Army Plaza. She pumped harder; the trees became a blur on either side of her.

Where was Robbie?

As if in answer to her silent question, a pair of green eyes flashed past her along the tree trunks and then whizzed off toward the Meadow. Sierra kept her course along the edge of the woods, the shadows swirling and dancing around her. He'd said "combat 'shaping," and he would be ready for her, wherever he was out there. She couldn't just roll out empty-handed or with a bunch of unformed shadows. Without losing stride, Sierra pulled out her chalk, now only a stub, and dragged it along the trees she passed. When she'd tagged more than a dozen trunks, she doubled back, the spirits still storming along with her in long strides. She raised one arm and then retraced her steps, tapping each chalk mark as she passed. The shards of green burst to life as spirits danced through her.

Now, Sierra thought, and she felt her small battalion of green projectiles fall into formation around her. Once again, the night seemed to hold its breath: a blessed moment of silence. Then Sierra pivoted off a stone and burst out of the woods. Shadows and green spikes unfurled around her like a crashing wave. She landed in an open field and raised her head just in time to see a splash of bright red flush across the dark grass toward her. Sierra leapt toward the nearest tree, caught a branch and swung up onto it as Robbie's red tide passed.

Where is he?

The three pairs of green eyes flew out into the field and converged at a darkened area at the far end of the park. *Go,* Sierra commanded her shards. She leapt out of her tree and hit the ground running, flashes of green flitting along at her side. *Go!* They burst ahead, racing across the field. Robbie's red tide swept out again, but this time Sierra was ready. She leapt up into the night sky, surrounded by the pulsing lights of the shadows, and landed far outside of the tide's reach.

"Whoa!" Robbie yelled from his hiding place.

Sierra smiled and dashed into a dark grove of trees as another red tide swept past. She crept through the underbrush, finished off her chalk on a nearby tree trunk, and shaped four more spirits into the jagged lines. *Eyes,* she called silently. The six eyes appeared on the ground before her. *Lead the way.* They sped off.

Shards, when the eyes find him, strike. She walked briskly through the woods as the shards dashed ahead. *But be gentle.*

Sierra strode out into the field toward the darkness, watching the bursts of light as her spirit soldiers converged on Robbie. Something red flashed, but then vanished.

"Ow!" Robbie yelled.

"What happened?" Sierra called.

"Ow! Call them off! Dang, Sierra, you won! I get it!"

Back! Sierra thought. *Fall back.* "Sorry, I'm still getting the hang of it! You give up?"

"Yes! Jeez!" Robbie stumbled out of the darkness, his face smudged with green streaks. "Where'd you learn to do all that?" He was smiling in spite of himself; Sierra could tell it was one of those smiles that couldn't be held back or tempered.

She shrugged. "It just . . . seemed natural, I guess." She wasn't really sure what had happened. Had all that flying through the air just been her excitement at being part of this magical new world? Or was something else at play? Either way, she felt amazing. "Let's do it again!"

TWENTY-TWO

Underwater again. The hundred million souls reached their long shadowy fingers up from the depths of the sea. It was a stretch that lasted centuries. A calming, uplifting, terrifying, sorrowful kind of movement, gentle and deadly like the tide. Sierra drifted somewhere in the middle of all those souls — a flash of living flesh amidst so much death. They wrapped around her, poured into her nostrils and became her blood, sanctified her spirit with their longing. She inhaled and the world caught its breath; exhaled and a tidal wave of space emptied out around her.

A hundred hands held her, released her, brought her close, sent her spinning away.

Sierra.

The souls whispered songs about their lives and deaths, a swirl of loves lost and remembrances, hymns and murder ballads.

Sierra. Wake up.

They were so full of life it was easy to forget they were

dead. They pulsated with the love of all things alive, a powerful yearning that Sierra could taste.

Sierra!

Sierra opened her eyes reluctantly, releasing the soothing ebb and flow of the spirit world.

M'ija, you need to focus.

It was a faraway echo, that voice. Barely there. The early afternoon sun painted sharp geometric designs across Sierra's room. She'd gotten home at sunrise and slept all morning. Had she dreamed the whole night? No. Echoes of it seared through her mind: the haint attacking, Robbie's tattoos, the tingle of spirit as it passed through her into the chalk.

She sat up and rubbed her eyes. Wick was out there, plotting, sending these dead things to ruin her life. She shuddered, flung herself out of bed, and stumbled into her clothes. Her notebook lay open on the desk; lines she'd jotted down from Wick's journal criss-crossed the pages. She shoved it in her shoulder bag. Today she would solve the riddle.

When she opened her bedroom door, Tía Rosa's cackle echoed through the house.

"What is that noise?" Timothy's face poked over the bannister from the floor above her.

Sierra smiled. "My stupid tía. Sorry. I'm pretty sure she's proof my family has hyena blood."

"Oh, ha!" Timothy blushed. "Right. Okay, just wanted to make sure everything was alright."

Alright wasn't the word she would use, but Sierra kept up her smile and waved as she headed down the stairs. "Right as ever!"

María Santiago looked exhausted; the lines etched across her face had suddenly grown sharp and pronounced. "¿Pa' dónde vas, m'ija?"

Sierra stopped at the door and rolled her eyes. "Out."

The coffeepot let out a gurgle. "You want a cafecito, sweetie?"

Sierra turned. "No, Mami, I want to talk about what's been going on around here."

"What do you mean?" Rosa asked.

Sierra didn't take her eyes off her mom. "I'm pretty sure I wasn't talking to you, Rosa."

Rosa gasped.

"Sierra," María snapped. "Don't talk to your aunt like that."

"I want to talk about what's been going on around here for years now," Sierra said again. "I want to know the truth about Abuelo and the shadowshapers."

Sierra's words hung in the air for a moment.

"The truth," Rosa said, "is that your grandfather is crazy. He was crazy before the stroke, and now he's just more crazy. You hear me? He's lost his mind. He lost it a long time ago. I don't remember a time when Papi made sense — do you, María? He's been babbling about spirits as long as we've been alive. He's the shame of the family, he almost got himself put away because he wouldn't shut up about it, and —"

María slammed the coffeepot down. "Ya. Enough, Rosa."

Rosa sighed and fiddled with her long painted nails. "She asked for the truth."

"I said enough. We don't speak of this. Sierra, are you happy now? Is that what you wanted to hear?"

Sierra shot a stony glare at her aunt. "No wonder you're miserable."

"Sierra!" María gasped.

"What are you talking about, child?" Rosa said, squinting across the room at Sierra. "Oh, are you still upset about your little hissy fit the other day over that Negrito you're dating?"

"Negrito? He's taller than you. And we're not dating! Mom, really, are you gonna let her talk like that?"

"I'm just saying . . ." Rosa began. María sat there with her eyes wide.

"I don't wanna hear what you're saying. I don't care about your stupid neighborhood gossip or your damn opinions about everyone around you and how dark they are or how kinky their hair is. You ever look in the mirror, Tía?"

Rosa turned bright red as her face scrunched into a fist.

"You ever look at those old family albums Mom keeps around?" Sierra went on. "We ain't white. And you shaming everyone and looking down your nose because you can't even look in the mirror isn't gonna change that. And neither is me marrying someone paler than me. And I'm glad! I love my hair. I love my skin. I didn't ask your opinion about my life and I don't wanna hear it. Not now, not ever."

"W-well," stammered Rosa, her face the picture of flabbergasted.

Sierra's voice went calm. "What are you running from?"

"I . . ."

"What are you afraid of?" She turned to María, whose mouth hung open. "What are *you* running from?"

"I don't see what that has to do with your crazy grandfather," María said weakly.

Sierra turned around and stormed out of the house.

TWENTY-THREE

Sierra headed quickly down Lafayette, pulling out her phone as she walked. If she couldn't get wisdom from the women in her family, she'd find it elsewhere.

"Hello?" Nydia the Columbia archivist sounded stressed.

"Hey, it's Sierra. Sierra Santiago, from Brooklyn? Is this a bad time?"

"Oh! Hey, Sierra! Not at all, wassup?" Total transformation.

Sierra let her shoulders drop and exhaled. She stood in front of Carlos's Corner Store, a few blocks from the Junklot. Yelling at Rosa had felt amazing, like releasing a thousand years of pent-up steam, but her body was still shaking from it. "I mean . . . everything." Where to even begin? "I got . . . something chased me? I'm not sure how to —"

"What?"

Sierra started walking again. Her thoughts wouldn't congeal into sentences that would make sense. "I don't know, Nydia. It's really hard to explain."

"Are you in danger?"

"Not right now." She looked around. "I don't think."

"That doesn't sound good, Sierra. Do you have people who can help you?"

"I think I do, yeah."

An SUV slowed nearby and a window rolled down. "Ay, girl, c'mere! Lemme talk to you a sec!"

Sierra rolled her eyes and kept walking. "I mean, my friend Robbie is helping me. And my brother Juan."

"Why you frontin', girl?" another voice yelled. "Come back here."

Sierra raised her middle finger overhead and turned a corner, making sure to go down a one-way street so the car couldn't follow her. "Oh damn, I see how it is," the guy called after her. "Nobody wants your ugly ass anyway." The engine growled and the SUV screeched off.

"Sierra," Nydia said. "What's going on over there?"

Sierra shook her head. "Same BS as always, don't worry about it. Listen, have you ever heard of the Sorrows?"

A few seconds of silence passed. Sierra looked at her phone. "Hello?"

"I think Wick mentions them in his notes," Nydia said. "Right?"

"Yeah. He said he got some extra powers from them."

"There's not much out there about the Sorrows," Nydia went on. "It's all just whispers and myths. Supposedly they haunt some ol' broken-down church uptown by the river.

The story goes that they're devotees of some shrine up there — some kinda ancient magic. It's all very creepy, to be honest. And, of course, just stories."

"Of course."

Another strange silence passed. "I can look into it more," Nydia said slowly. "If you want."

Sierra's hand was shaking again. "Thanks, Nydia."

"Keep me updated, Sierra. And . . . stay safe."

The Junklot was all locked up, which was almost unheard of. Sierra looked around to make sure no one was following her, unlocked the gate with the key Manny had given her, and slipped inside.

"Manny?" Sierra called.

No one was around, not even Cojones, the way-too-friendly Junklot dog. She made her way through the trash heaps and then caught her breath when she reached the Tower wall. Robbie must've been there earlier to put some work in: An entire city had sprung up from the music swirling out of the skeleton woman's guitar.

Sierra's dragon was almost done and looking fierce. She got out her painting supplies and went to work. Now that she knew she was a shadowshaper, the painting took on a whole new life for her. She was a part of the image somehow, and she knew that when it was finished, the bond between her and the colorful, towering figure would literally be sealed by spirit. It would become part of this wild family legacy she was only beginning to understand. The whole thing still seemed like some mythology or ghost story, but the more she thought about it, the realer it became. Someone had initiated her long ago; some mysterious shadowshaper had brought her into the fold, even against the wishes of her own grandfather. She smiled against the turmoil of emotions.

She was a shadowshaper. Just like Robbie. His smile flashed in front of her mind's eye, the sheepish one on his chalk-covered face when he stepped out of the shadows of Prospect Park. He admired her. She could see it all over him. It was the strength of her shadowshaping, yes, but it was something else too. He respected her strength, her mind, her power. She'd never felt that from a boy before.

"Sierra!"

Sierra took off her headphones and looked down at the Junklot. Tee stared up at her, arms akimbo. "You really deep in that thing, huh? We been tryna get your attention for, like, ten minutes." Izzy stood off to the side, her mouth opening and closing silently around some new rhyme she was working on.

"Yeah, sorry," Sierra said.

"Come down! We brought you some iceys and we headin' to one'a them new coffee joints Izzy loves so hard. Bennie and Jerome meeting us there later."

"Alright, y'all, be right down!"

"Whatchy'all gettin' into tonight?" Tee asked as they walked toward Bedford Avenue, slurping flavored ice out of plastic sleeves.

"My brother's band is playing," Sierra said. "You guys should come through."

"That's that thrasher salsa joint, right?" Izzy asked.

"Yeah," Sierra said. "Culebra. But they playin' a laid-back unplugged kinda set at this Dominican restaurant that Gordo hangs out at."

Izzy let out a belly laugh. "Gordo, that huge Spanish dude that taught us music in the fourth grade?"

"Yeah," Sierra said. "He's Cuban, though."

"Oh, I'm definitely goin' then," Izzy said. "I usedta love that dude. Any time you ain't do the homework, you just hadta go, 'Oh, Señor Gordo, tell us about when you met Beyoncé or whatever.'" Everyone was giggling now.

"It's true," Sierra laughed.

"And he'd be all, 'Well, we were playeeng un concierto een the palacio weeth Esteban and Julio, and then we estopped when thee pretty lady came een.'"

"He didn't really let you call him Señor Gordo, did he?" Tee asked.

"I swear to God!" Izzy chuckled.

"Yep," Sierra said. "He insisted on it."

"Here go the spot," Tee said. They'd stopped in front of a storefront that Sierra could have sworn had been empty and disheveled as recently as last week. Now freshly painted wooden beams framed an elegant stained-glass window design. In the display area, potted plants and old books were arranged on a burlap coffee bag.

Sierra scrunched up her face. "You sure about this, guys?"

Tee nudged her. "C'mon, silly. It'll be . . . fun!"

TWENTY-FOUR

Tee sipped a tiny mug of flavored coffee. "One thing I'll say for these yuppies . . ." she said with a grin.

"Jesus, babe!" Izzy put a hand on her forehead. "You have to be so loud? We're surrounded in here. Besides, these ones aren't yuppies, they're hipsters."

Sierra looked up from her iced tea. "What's the difference, anyway?"

"Far as I can tell," Tee said, "hipsters are basically yuppies with tighter pants and bigger glasses. Whatever they are, they make a mean mochaccino."

"The hellsa mochaccino?" Sierra demanded.

"It's chocolate and espresso, I think. You wanna try it?"

"Oh my God, she's crossing over!" Izzy squealed.

Sierra shook her head. "I'll stick to Bustelo. This iced tea is just brown water. Blegh."

"It's three dollars and twenty-five cents' worth of brown water," Tee reminded her. "So you better enjoy it."

"You guys are ridiculous," Izzy said, looking around. "Utterly ridiculous."

Everyone else in the little wood-paneled coffee shop was studying quietly or whispering into cell phones. Splotchy brown-and-gray paintings covered the walls, and a chalkboard behind the counter listed a whole slew of colorfully named overpriced beverages.

Where lonely women go to dance . . . Beyond Wick's ramblings about "crossroads," the line was still the best clue she had that would lead to Lucera, and it still meant absolutely nothing to her. She had scribbled the words in her notebook at least twelve different times in various handwriting styles, from bubbly to elegant. It hadn't helped. Lonely women. They went to dance clubs. Parties. Weddings. "Weddings?" she said out loud. "No, right? No."

Tee and Izzy rolled their eyes. "No," they said at the same time. Sierra had explained everything to her friends as best she could, leaving out all the actual supernatural stuff she'd seen. She could tell they weren't really convinced, but they played along anyway.

Funerals. No one danced at funerals. Or did they? Sierra had a vague memory of Gordo going on in music class about how, in certain parts of Africa, they used to throw big parties and parade through the streets when someone died. The tradition had carried on to the Caribbean — the Haitians would march in wild circles with the coffin so that the spirit wouldn't be able to find its way back home to bother everybody. And New Orleans . . . Something about New Orleans . . .

"Imma write a book," Tee announced. "It's gonna be about white people."

Izzy scowled. "Seriously, Tee: Shut up. Everyone can hear you."

"I'm being serious," Tee said. "If this Wick cat do all this research about Sierra's grandpa and all his Puerto Rican spirits, I don't see why I can't write a book about his people. Imma call it *Hipster vs. Yuppie: A Culturalpological Study*."

"But there's black and Latin hipsters," Sierra said. "Look at my brother Juan."

"And my uncle is most definitely a bluppy," Izzy put in.

Tee rolled her eyes. "There'll be an appendix, guys. Sheesh."

"What the hell is culturalpological anyway?" Izzy demanded.

"It's like the slick new term for cultural anthropology."

"You made that up!"

"So what? I'm on the forefront. If I say it's slick and new, then slick and new it is."

Sierra burst out laughing. "You two need to stop distracting me!"

The wind chimes jingled against the glass door as it swung open. Big Jerome came in, still wearing his church suit and looking quite dapper. "Whatsup, ladies," he said, leaning over to plant cheek kisses on Sierra, Izzy, and Tee.

"Lookatchu all cleaned up," Izzy said. "And same old

same old over here: Tee bein' ridiculous as usual, and Sierra nerding out over there on some riddle."

"As it should be," Jerome said. "I'm getting a coffee."

"Bring your life savings!" Tee called after him. Izzy cringed.

Where lonely women go to dance . . . Costume balls. Nightclubs. Churches. No. Sierra's mind wandered back to the image of her chalk ninja shooting up a tree. She wondered what other spirits watched over her. "Hey, you guys know where your people are from?"

"Of course," Tee said, looking up from her comic book.

Jerome placed his coffee cup on the table and pulled up an easy chair. "You Haitian like Robbie, right, Tee?"

"Actually . . ?"

Izzy sighed loudly. "Everybody think that just 'cause her name's Trejean and she black, she gotta be Haitian. There's other French-speaking islands in the Caribbean, you know."

"Izzy . . ." Tee said.

"She's actually Martinique . . . Martiniquian. Whatever — she's from Martinique."

"But Izzy, you said the same thing when you first met me." Jerome snickered.

"Yeah, well, that's not the point," Izzy insisted.

"But yes, Sierra, to answer your question," Tee continued, "I was born in Martinique, and my parents were too. My mom's parents were from Martinique, and my dad is half French, half Nigerian, from the Igbo people."

"Sheesh," Sierra said. "You weren't kidding about knowing your people."

"What about you, Sierra?" Jerome asked. "You just Spanish, right?"

"If she's Spanish, I'm French," Tee said.

"Yeah, but you know what I mean."

"You're Puerto Rican, right, Sierra?" Tee said.

Sierra was beginning to wish she hadn't brought up the topic. "C'mon, Jerome, you know it ain't as simple as Spanish."

"Yeah, but we just *say* Spanish. Like Spanish food. Whatever, that's just what we say."

People around them were starting to look up from their books and take their headphones off. Sierra felt her ears get red.

"I doubt her African and Taíno ancestors feel like it's 'whatever,'" Tee said.

Sierra was stunned. "Tee, since when you start talking 'bout ancestors?"

"You think Puerto Ricans' the only ones got ghost stories? Please. My uncle Ed's been tellin' me 'bout his ghosts since I was tiny. Said they wouldn't come up to New York with him, though, that it was too cold or something. And now he all depressed and won't leave his room. Half my family got ghosts."

"Whadup, y'all!" Bennie burst in. "Who buying me coffee?"

Everyone looked at Jerome. "What?" He scowled at them.

"Never mind, I got it." Bennie went to the counter and came back stirring milk into a paper cup. "What we talkin' bout?"

"Tee's jacked-up uncle," Jerome said.

"Shut up," Tee said.

"Sierra was asking us about our ancestors," Izzy said. "And trying to figure out some dumb riddle. And Tee is acting the fool and making the rest of us cringe as per standard operating procedures."

"I don't like any of you anymore," Tee announced.

Bennie smiled and sipped her coffee. "Sounds about right."

"Hey," Jerome said, "did anyone else notice the *Searchlight* didn't come today?"

"Oh, yeah," Izzy said. "My mom was like all freaked-out about it, said Manny'd never missed a day since 1973."

Sierra's stomach plummeted. No *Searchlight*? And Manny hadn't been at the Junklot. And he was in her abuelo's photo of the shadowshapers. . . . She stood and made her way around the other chairs. "C'mere a sec, Bee."

"Where you guys going?" Izzy demanded.

"Private conversation," Bennie said.

"Something about this isn't right," Sierra whispered once they were a few steps away. "Manny wasn't at the Junklot either."

Bennie furrowed her brow. "And now the paper ain't

come? I don't like that. You think maybe something happened to him?"

Sierra had been thinking exactly that, but trying not to say it out loud. She rubbed her eyes. "I don't know. But there's only one way to find out."

TWENTY-FIVE

The B52 bus was taking forever, but there was still really no quick way to get to certain parts of Bed-Stuy. "Just wait till they get a couple more bakeries and boutiques stuffed in here," Bennie said as they started and then ground to a stop for the four hundredth time. "New train stations'll be poppin' up real quick."

"True story," Izzy said.

"What you talking 'bout, Izzy?" Tee said. "All you do is sit around in those bakeries and write poetry."

Izzy looked truly offended. "That's not the point, jackass!"

Big Jerome rolled his eyes. "Here we go. They been like this since school got out."

"The hell we have!" Izzy and Tee said together.

Sierra was in no mood for the banter. She watched Brooklyn pass as the achingly slow city bus lurched ahead. The past three days replayed over and over in her mind, but nothing made any more sense than it had before. She couldn't get rid of the feeling that Manny was in serious trouble and it was somehow her fault.

"You alright, Sierra?" Bennie said quietly. Sierra nodded, but her friend's face was suddenly elsewhere. Then she realized: They were passing Vincent's mural.

Bennie looked like the wind had just been knocked out of her. "You can barely even see it anymore," she said under her breath. Sierra took Bennie's hand in hers and squeezed.

"It's back here, ain't it?" Jerome called.

They were standing outside a broken-down church. It looked as if it'd been hit by a couple of hurricanes and left for dead. Weeds posed grotesquely in the side yard. Jerome had ventured through the fence and was peering around back, but everyone else waited safely on the curb.

Jerome came back to the group. "Manny's spot is around the other side and down some stairs to the basement, if I remember right."

"When were you here?" Tee asked.

"Mr. Draley took us here to see the *Searchlight* offices on one of those get-to-know-your-neighborhood trips in the sixth grade. But they coordinated wrong and Manny was out making a run, so we never got to see the printing press or nothing."

"Nice."

"You see the entrance back there?" Sierra asked.

"I think so. C'mon."

The four girls followed Jerome gingerly into the side yard. There was no way to walk without the icky weeds brushing up against you like greasy old men in the street, so Sierra just gritted her teeth and kept moving.

"God," Izzy said, "imagine the rats that must hang out here."

"You're always so grim," Tee said.

"They probably play dominos and whatnot too."

Sierra was about to shush them, but then they rounded the corner and everyone got quiet and serious.

"This don't look good," Bennie said.

The trapdoor entranceway to the basement was wide open. Cement stairs led into the darkness.

"Not like him to leave it open, I suppose," Sierra said.

"Maybe he went for some coffee and forgot to close it," Jerome tried.

Sierra braced herself and then stepped forward. "I'm going in."

"You're crazy," Izzy said.

"I'm going in too," Bennie said.

"You're both crazy."

Tee frowned. "Ugh. Me too. I hate you guys."

Izzy sighed loudly. "Fine," she said, taking Jerome's tan hand in her small brown one. "But I'm taking the big guy with me. C'mon, Jerome."

Once Sierra went down the first few steps, the darkness surrounded her completely. She pawed blindly at the wall inside the doorway but found no switches. "Cell phones out, people," she said, flipping open her own. The dim blue glow didn't do much, but at least she knew there weren't any walls in front of her as she moved deeper into the space. Izzy cursed as she tripped over some debris at the bottom of the stairs.

"Can you make anything out?" Bennie said from just beside her. Sierra could see her little phone light dancing through the darkness.

"Nope." Sierra reached out a hand and touched a cool brick pillar. Lava-lamp color splotches spun in the darkness around her and gradually faded as her eyes adjusted to the dark. Every tick and tremble was a towering throng haint lying in wait. For all she knew, they were surrounded by the things.

Sierra thought she heard something scraping along the ceiling and stopped walking. At first, there was nothing. Then it came again: a raspy exhalation. After a pause came another breath. *Something is down here.* The breathing continued, sickly and uneven, but Sierra couldn't pinpoint where it came from. She swung her phone around in front of her, but there was only darkness. "You guys hear that?"

"Aw, c'mon, Sierra!" Izzy whined. "Don't be that jerk."

"I'm not!" Sierra tried to keep her voice from getting all high-pitched. "I just . . . you really didn't hear anything?"

Had she made it up? For a second, there were no noises at all. Then it came again: a horrible rattling breath. The same one she'd heard the night before in Flatbush. It was all around her.

"Ahhh!" Bennie yelled.

"What happened?" Jerome called from behind them.

"I'm alright," Bennie said. "Just stubbed my toe on something."

Sierra stepped carefully toward Bennie and then watched her friend's phone light illuminate the ancient, rusty gears of Manny's printing press. "The dude do it old-school style for sho'," Bennie said. Its great metal arms stretched into the darkness, and the silver turning rod shone with the ghostly reflections of the phone's glow.

"You guys," Izzy whimpered, "I don't like this at all."

"Neither do we, dodo," Tee said. "But we gotta find out what's going on. Something ain't right here."

Sierra couldn't hear the breathing any more. She inched along past the printing press, keeping one hand on it to steady herself. Her left foot bumped something just as her phone light decided to blink off. She clicked one of the buttons and swung the blue glow down to the ground to see what she'd hit. It was a boot. In her surprise she toppled forward, dropping her phone, and landed on something a few feet above the ground. It felt like a man's fleshy belly.

"Oh my God!" Sierra yelled, scrambling madly away

from the hideous cold flesh. Footsteps came toward her from all around.

"What happened?" Bennie yelled.

"Where are you guys?" Izzy said. "What's going on?"

Sierra flailed along the ground till she found her phone. "I'm okay, but someone's here. I think it's Manny." All she wanted to do was run as fast as possible out of that basement and far away, but she had to know what was going on. She raised her glowing cell phone in front of her.

It was Manny, sitting up in a chair, his mouth twisted open in terror, his eyes staring emptily into the darkness. Sierra gasped. Then Bennie was beside her, grabbing her arm, sobbing silently.

"Guys!" Jerome called from across the room. "I think I found the" — bright fluorescent lights blinked on along the ceiling, making everyone squint — "light switch."

Izzy screamed at the sight of Manny. Then Tee turned around and started screaming too. Jerome ran past them toward Sierra and Bennie. "Oh my God," he said, gazing over the bloated, sprawled-out body.

Manny was in an old-fashioned barber's chair, the one folks said he sat in to brainstorm the next issue of his paper. His guayabera hung open, splayed to either side of his gigantic belly. His big arms hung limply at his sides. Sierra had seen dead bodies before, had been to more than her fair share of open-casket funerals, but this was something entirely different. His body looked as lifeless as the chair he was slouched in — an empty vessel.

But it was Manny's pale face that really got to Sierra. His mouth seemed inhumanly huge, like his jaw had twisted itself out of place to allow for a wider expression of fear.

Izzy was crying. Tee wrapped an arm around her girl-friend's shoulder and sniffled quietly. Jerome stood completely still, as if any movement might make everything suddenly even worse.

"We gotta get outta here," Bennie said, her voice shak-ing. "Whatever it was did this might still be around."

Sierra nodded, but it didn't seem right, just leaving Manny like that. She had known Manny practically her whole life — they all had — and now he was just a heap of lifeless flesh and bones slumped in a barber's chair. All around them, the image of the Domino King grinned out of shiny, scribbled-on photographs with various celebrities and back-in-the-day civil rights leaders. Stacks and stacks of old copies of the *Searchlight* were scattered haphazardly around the giant metal printing press.

"Sierra," Bennie said, from what seemed like miles away.

It was those eyes, those unseeing, terror-stricken eyes, fixed on the ceiling. Without thinking about it, Sierra reached over and closed his lids.

Manny groaned.

Sierra stumbled backward as all five teenagers screamed at the same time. He'd barely moved — just the slightest twitch swimming across his tormented face — but the sound had unmistakably come from him.

"He's not . . . dead?" Sierra gasped. She wasn't sure whether to turn and run or try to help him. She took a step closer to Manny.

"Sierra, what are you doing?" Izzy said. "Let's get out of here!"

"But . . ."

"*SIERRA!*" Manny gasped. Except it wasn't Manny's voice, it was the hideous cacophony of voices from the throng haint.

Panic swept over the group. They dashed up the cement stairs and out into the dimming afternoon light, then bolted across the street.

"What . . . was that? What the hell was that?" Izzy kept sobbing.

"I don't know, I don't know," Tee moaned. "What's going on, Sierra?"

"I don't know, but we can't leave Manny there, you guys. He's still alive! Even if he's . . . whatever he is."

"You gonna go back in?" Bennie demanded.

Sierra glanced warily at the vacant lot and dilapidated church. "No. We gonna get someone else to do it."

TWENTY-SIX

Fifteen minutes later, Sierra and Bennie strolled back around the corner, trying to act as casual as possible. Police cars and ambulances filled the street, their angry red lights pulsating against the brick buildings.

"What happened?" Bennie asked an ornery-looking paramedic with a potbelly and salt-and-pepper mustache.

"Nothin'," he grunted, tossing his equipment into the back of his truck. "Another prank call. Stupid kids."

"What do you mean *nothing*?" Sierra demanded.

"I mean" — the medic lit a cigarette and glared at her — "some kids called up and said there's a dead guy in the basement. But there ain't. So nothing. Nada."

"Are you sure? Did you check the whole place?"

"Who do you think you are, kid?" the medic growled. "You made the call? Huh? You know it's illegal to prank call 911, right? Lemme see if I can get one of the cops to come and have a word with you."

As if on cue, a police officer walked out of the basement.

He was young, with startling blue eyes and a severe frown. "What's the problem?"

Bennie grabbed Sierra's wrist. "Sierra, come on!"

They fast-walked around the corner. When they made it out of earshot, Sierra threw her hands up in exasperation. "It doesn't make sense! You think Manny could've walked away in the state he was in?"

"I don't know," Bennie said, gazing back toward the flashing police lights.

They rejoined the rest of their group in a small park and told them what happened. The late afternoon turned to gray dusk around them as Brooklyn settled into another summer night.

"What do you mean, he wasn't there?" Izzy demanded. Tee put a calming hand on her girlfriend's shoulder.

"I mean," Sierra said, "for the fifteenth time, that's what the angry EMT guy said. And then some young-ass cop started looking a little too interested in us and we split. What else can I tell you?"

Izzy stood up and paced a small circle around them. "It's not like he could just stroll off! He was, like, ninety-eight percent dead!"

"True," Sierra said. The trees around them rustled, and she had to squint to make sure no shadows were loping out toward them. She looked around at her friends' worried expressions. The smudged faces in the photograph. The shadowshapers. Sierra looked at her hand. Wick had figured out she was a shadowshaper before she'd even known.

"What are we gonna do?" Izzy moaned.

Wick had sent corpuscules after Sierra and Robbie, and they'd failed. He would probably try a shadowshaper he'd be more likely to catch next — someone who wasn't aware of the danger. . . . *Perhaps a new generation of shadowshapers that must be looked into* . . . , Wick had written.

Sierra stood up suddenly.

"What is it?" Bennie asked.

"Juan!" Sierra threw her shoulder bag on and started heading for the bus stop. "I gotta warn him. Y'all coming?"

TWENTY-SEVEN

On a normal night at El Mar, a few chubby couples would swing around the dance floor to the strains of a local bachata band or some overdressed drunk guy with a keyboard and drum machine. Old-timers would lean against the corny papier-mâché coral reef, sip their drinks, and mutter about the jóvenes. Occasional cops and paramedics would pass through to grab their superstrong cafecitos and flirt with the decadent waitresses. The night would pass with that cool, slow-stepping rhythm that allowed folks to believe for just a few hours that they were still back in the embrace of a warm Caribbean island.

But Culebra was in full swing when Sierra walked in, and instead of the usual laid-back El Mar scene, a sweaty mass of punks, teenyboppers, and hipsters pulsed and churned to the music. The tables and chairs had all been cleared out, and the crowd was throbbing against the coral reefs, hanging from the mounted captain's wheel, dancing along the hallway to the restrooms. Sierra tried to peek above the swarming bodies and see if there were any corpus-cules lurking, but it was too dark to make anything out.

She glanced around, trying to keep sharp while Culebra's lush sound washed over her. Playing acoustic always freaked Juan out; he'd get unbearably talkative and jittery and then pass out for an hour before the show. But the results were mesmerizing, and tonight was no exception. His old Spanish guitar spat out a series of warm, labyrinthine phrases that wrapped melodic vines around Gordo's fierce piano hits. As the two instruments wound intricate loops, Pulpo, the tall, dark-skinned bass player and lead singer, unleashed a torrent of feverish, pounding notes from his stand-up, throwing his head forward in an avalanche of braids on each downbeat.

The music grew like a fog around the crowd, and then, with only a sly rim shot for warning, the drums kicked in full thrust. Ruben, a lanky, light-skinned Dominican with a finely trimmed goatee, rained thundering blasts down on the kit, while his brother Kaz came in with a suave *tuk-tuk-tuk*ing on the congas. The crowd exploded. Sierra let herself get swept up in it, let go of the fear and sadness that had been haunting her limbs since their visit to the printing press, and danced. Ruben's driving beat moved inside her, shoved her lovingly into motion.

Sierra closed her eyes, then let them open ever so slightly. There was no mistaking it this time: Tall, long-armed shad-ows high-stepped in a flowing circle inside the club. When her eyes opened wide, everything went back to normal. She willed herself to calm down, felt the excitement of the crowd, the wild thrash of her brother's music. Closed her eyes again. Much to her own surprise, she felt safe. The whole room was so full of life, and those shadows — she squinted her eyes open again, gazing through her lashes — they were dancing too.

The whole band moved as one now. All five heads thrashed up and down as the song kept swelling to more ridiculous heights. The shadows spun faster, their long strides reaching over the heads of the writhing crowd. The spirits were protecting Juan, Sierra realized. He didn't need her warning about Wick; he was safe. She exhaled and let the moment sweep over her. It was like being inside the most beautiful car accident in the world with all your best friends and a bunch of total strangers and knowing you couldn't get hurt.

Then, just like that, it was over. The room let out a collective sigh of satisfaction and then burst into cheers. Juan looked up from his guitar with that smug smile and nodded at Gordo, and the band whirled into another number.

"We're going to eslow it down a little for you now," Gordo's voice boomed out.

"Thank God!" Bennie gasped, collapsing against Sierra. "Hey, you alright?"

The shadows had retreated some; they stood swaying in the dark corners of the room as the song spun to life.

Manny's face lingered in Sierra's mind. "Nothing," She blinked her eyes all the way open. "Just . . . Manny."

"We'll find him."

"I know. I'm alright."

"Good for you. I'm a sweaty wack disaster up in this mess."

"You were doing alright, B," Jerome said.

"Actually," Sierra said, "Sweaty Wack Disaster was their first band name."

"Shaddup," Bennie panted. "Too winded . . . to laugh."

The music wound along gently, a stroll in the park, but occasional drum bursts and off-kilter chimes from Juan's guitar gave a sinister edge to it. *"Cuando la luna llena,"* crooned Pulpo in a rich, haunting vibrato.

"I always had a thing for Pulpo," Sierra said.

Bennie nodded. "Voice like that — who wouldn't?"

"Mata al sol anciano . . ."

"Word," said Tee, who'd come up behind them with Izzy when the music slowed. "I don't even like dudes, but that dude's fine."

Izzy shot Tee a pained face. "What kind of a lesbian are you?"

Tee shrugged. "One that can appreciate a beautiful man with a beautiful voice."

". . . Ven a los cuatro caminos a los cuatro caminos ven . . ."

"Singing a beautiful-ass song," Tee continued. "I don't

even know what he's saying, but I know that's gorgeous. Who wrote this, Sierra?"

"Juan did, I guess. He writes all their stuff."

"... *Mujeres solitarias* ..."

"I think it's on their last album," she said slowly. "It sounds kinda ..."

"... *Van a bailar* ..."

"Wait a minute!" Four sets of eyes swung around to Sierra. "Did he just say 'mujeres solitarias van a bailar'?"

"Sounded like 'ban the bar bar' to me," Izzy said. "So yeah, he probably did."

"Ban the bar bar, babe? Really?" Tee laughed.

"What about it?" Bennie said.

"It's the poem!" Sierra gasped. "The song! 'Mujeres solitarias': lonely women. 'Van a bailar' is they go to dance!"

"You mean the poem you were trying to figure out at the coffee shop?" Tee said.

"Yes!" Sierra yelled. "The one that tells us where Lucera is!"

"*Soy el susurro,*" Pulpo sang, "*que oyes ...*"

"I can't believe it," Sierra said. "It's been in my ears all this time. I had it on my headphones while I was painting yesterday. I just couldn't hear the lyrics, because on the studio version, it's much —"

Before she could finish her sentence, the band exploded into another thundering onslaught of metal drums and speed guitar. The crowd burst back into motion. Pulpo was still singing, but his words were lost beneath the clashing layers of music. Tee and Izzy had already disappeared into the thrashing masses.

"Something like this?" Bennie yelled into Sierra's ear. "That would explain why you had no idea what they were saying! We can ask Juan after the show."

That was true, of course, but those few words, that taste of the answer, was teasing Sierra. She kept perking up her ears, catching little glimpses of phrases here and there and working them through her head. "... *mata al sol anciano* ... *cuando las sombras* ..." A writhing body surfed along the top of the throng up ahead. People pushed and shoved all around. "... *como la bala de una pistola* ..." *Like a bullet from a gun.*

It wasn't just a game anymore, Sierra thought angrily, as dancing limbs and torsos slammed against her and fell away again. Manny had vanished. Corpuscules and throng haints were popping out of the shadows. She had to find Lucera if she wanted to stay alive and get to the bottom of all this. And to find Lucera, she'd have to figure out whatall Pulpo was screaming up there . . .

Something was wrong. People rushed around her, not in the rhythmic chaos of a mosh pit, but in true desperation.

Bennie grabbed Sierra's hand. "C'mon, space cadet, we out."

"What happened?"

"Fight," Tee said, running past with a wily grin on her face. Izzy came next, holding tight to Tee's hand and cursing out someone behind them.

"Yo, you need us to mash someone up for you?" Sierra said, catching up with Tee.

"Nah, we got that covered," Tee said. "Let's just, uh, get some fresh air."

TWENTY-EIGHT

CULEBRA was scrawled in ridiculously large and colorful letters across the tinted windows of El Mar. The club sat squished in between a barbershop and one of those odds-and-ends stores that sells everything from 3-D Jesus pictures to porn to pogo sticks. A train rattled along the ancient metal caterpillar over Fulton Street and sent a cascade of rainwater onto the exiting crowd.

"What'd you guys do?" Bennie said when they regrouped outside the front door.

"This grease-stain cornball in tight pants thought he was gonna get slick with us," Izzy said. "Asked us which one was the girl in the relationship."

Sierra put a hand over her eyes. "Oh lord . . ."

"Tee told him, 'You are,' and broke his nose."

"Damn!" Big Jerome said. High fives and back pats were doled out lovingly to Tee. She blushed and waved them off, but you could tell she was flattered.

"That's my baby," Izzy said, nuzzling her way under Tee's arm.

"Did you figure out the song, Sierra?" Tee asked.

Sierra shook her head. "I couldn't hear a thing once it got crazy. I guess I'll just ask . . . Juan!"

As if on cue, Sierra's brother had strolled out of El Mar with a big, tired grin on his face. He looked even tinier than usual next to Gordo's ginormous lumbering bulk. Sierra ran up to Juan and hugged him as tightly as she could. "That was amazing! I'm so proud of you!"

"Uh . . . thanks, sis."

She held him at arm's length and glared into his eyes. "Now, where'd you get the lyrics to that last song?"

"It's a poem Abuelo usedta always —"

"I knew it!"

"What's going on, Sierra?"

"The riddle! Didn't I tell you 'bout the riddle that says where Lucera is?"

"Uh . . . no."

"I must've forgot with everything going on. Doesn't matter. The text of the riddle is in those lyrics! You have them memorized by heart?"

"Yeah, but would you let go of me now? People are staring."

Sierra didn't let go. "Tell me, man!"

Gordo was doing what he always did: smoking the same thick, musty Malagueña cigars that Grandpa Lázaro favored and chuckling like a big Cuban Santa Claus. "*Donde las mujeres solitarias van a bailar,*" he sang softly.

"Yes!" Sierra said, releasing Juan. "That's the one. You're the best fourth-grade music teacher ever!"

"Actually, I teach fifth grade now too."

Sierra pulled a blank sheet of paper from her bag. "Can you write the lyrics out?"

Juan scowled. "Now, sis?"

She got up in his face and walked him forcibly away from the others. "Listen to me," she growled. "Manny's either missing or dead or I don't know what —"

His eyes widened. "What?"

"I got chased by a soul-sucking phantom the other night, in case you hadn't noticed, and who knows what other creepiness is about to go down. I have no idea where this Lucera is, and she's the only one who's gonna be able to get us out of this mess. So if you really came back to Brooklyn to help your little sister, please, Juan, write me out the damn lyrics to the song and stop being Crown King Jackass."

"What happened to Manny?"

"He was in a coma or something," Sierra said. "We found him at the printing press and we called 911, but when they got there, he was gone. I think . . ." How to explain? She shook her head. "I don't know."

Juan looked pale. "Damn . . ."

"Please, Juan . . ."

He nodded. "I'm on it. You okay?"

"I don't know," Sierra said as they walked back to the

group. "I'm worried. This guy Wick . . . I'm pretty sure he's trying to wipe out the shadowshapers."

"Wipe out like *kill*?"

"Yeah," Sierra said. "He's turned at least two into corpuscules already. That's what Abuelo was trying to warn me about the other day, and why the shadows sent you to keep an eye on me. We're in danger, Juan. All of us."

Juan frowned. "Wow . . . Alright. Gimme the paper, Sierra." He furrowed his brow and went back to consult with Gordo. They worked quietly for a while, scribbling little notes. Tee, Izzy, and Jerome were still joking about the grease stain with the new nose job.

"Oh!" Gordo perked up suddenly. "I love this part: 'Por el carnaval rodeado de agua del destino y chance.' That's 'the water-bound carnival of destiny and chance.' ¿Sí?"

"The water-bound carnival of destiny and chance?" Bennie said. "What the hell does that mean?"

"No idea," Juan said.

"It's your song!" Sierra said.

"Naw, it's Abuelo's song. We just turned it into a death metal salsa ballad and threw on some lyrics at the end about a guy who kills his parents, and boom! Hot number-one underground hit in Wisconsin!"

"You're insane."

"No," Juan said. "I'm a rock star." He passed the paper back to Sierra. She stared down at the full, translated poem:

When the full moon kills the ancient sun
As the one lures the other who in turn lures the one
When the shadows swarm
Take hold in their form
And burst through the borough like a bullet from a gun

Come to the crossroads, to the crossroads come
Where the powers converge and become one
See my enemies fall
As my spirit voice calls
And the energy surges like a thousand suns

At the water-bound carnival of destiny and chance
I'm the whisper you hear as you enter the trance
When the lanterns go dead
I'll light the path ahead
From where lonely women go to dance.

"What's it mean?" she asked.

Gordo and Juan shrugged simultaneously. "But it sounds hot, right?" Juan said.

"Well, we gotta figure it out," Sierra said. "This is supposed to tell us where Lucera is."

"I mean, *'the whisper you hear as you enter the trance,'*" Tee said. "Maybe she at the club, listening to trance music, and some hot girl is like, whispering in her ear? Right before she goes into the club?"

"The bouncer!" Bennie yelled.

Tee burst out laughing. "Oh my God, yes! Lucera is a fine-ass bouncer at a dance club. Yo, Sierra, why didn't you say that before? Let's go find her!"

Sierra laughed with the rest of them, but she was trembling inside. The shadowy back alleys seemed to be closing in around her, long, clawed hands reaching out from the darkness, that horrible breathing. Manny's tortured face, his mouth opening wider and wider until it took over the whole world.

"And which crossroads she mean, yo?" Izzy asked. "I'm sayin', there's what, eighteen eleven billion crossroads in Brooklyn alone, right?"

"Word."

The answer dangled in the air right in front of Sierra. She could almost taste it. *Come to the crossroads, to the crossroads come / Where the powers converge and become one.* But Izzy was right; the crossroads could be anywhere. It might not even mean an actual crossroads.

"I mean, they probably mean where Eastern Parkway hits Atlantic Avenue, though," Jerome said, like it was the most obvious thing in the world.

Tee gaped at him. "Really, my dude? You wanna explain that magnificent feat of poetic analysis for us?"

"Yeah, I mean Atlantic and the Parkway are like the two major-major streets in Brooklyn, really. And plus, that's right before Atlantic gets all bridge-like and goes past that hotel."

A vigorous shouting match ensued. Sierra felt that if she could just be alone for a few seconds to clear her head, maybe she could make sense of the poem. She mumbled something about having to pee and walked back into El Mar. The waitstaff were all busy cleaning up and putting the tables back in order. Sierra slipped past them and into the dingy ladies' room.

Wick's final, frantic journal entry still echoed through Sierra. He had wanted spirit powers he'd kept secret from Lázaro — whatever creepiness those Sorrows had taught him. And he thought he should get Lucera's role. Sierra gazed into the murky mirror over the sink, past all the hearts and names etched into the glass. How could something as sacred and beautiful as shadowshaping get twisted to make corpuscules and haints? The thrill of watching her chalk creations come to life in the park had been the most amazing thing she'd ever felt.

Robbie. She felt calmer just thinking about him. At least she had a partner in this madness. She smiled. That moment in the Club Kalfour came swimming back: the swirling paintings, the old-man band busting out that sweet Caribbean soul music, Robbie's hands wrapped around her . . .

Sierra opened her eyes and realized she was swaying back and forth, a slow salsa step with an imaginary Robbie in her arms. She was dancing. She watched the reflection of her body move in the smudged glass. Something inside her head clicked. She was lonely. She was a lonely woman dancing.

"The mirror!" Sierra shouted, bursting out of the bathroom. A room full of irritated waiters turned their curious stares in her direction. She ignored them and busted outside to see her friends. "It's the mirror!" she said again.

They gawked at her.

"Uh . . . care to explain, crazy lady?" Izzy said.

"Where lonely women go to dance. We dance in front of the mirror. When we're lonely."

"Really?" said Jerome. "Is that what ya'll do?"

"That's what I just did."

Bennie scratched her chin. "It does sound right, somehow."

"Of course it's right!" Sierra said. The rest of the answer was so close, she could feel it all about to fall into place. "But which mirror?"

"What's the line before it?" Tee asked. "About the carnival?"

"*The water-bound carnival where destiny meets chance.*"

"Love that line," Juan said. "No idea what it means."

"Well, since we're speaking of water and such . . ." Izzy said.

Tee adjusted an invisible pair of glasses and stuck out her front teeth. "Yes, professor?"

Izzy punched her shoulder. "I'm saying: The water is a mirror. You can see the lights of the city reflected in the East

River. It's like the corniest poetry cliché ever. Oh, the moon, reflected in the sea, blah blah blah, blee blee blee."

"Oh my God," Bennie said. "She's right."

Izzy shot Bennie a look. "Why you sound so surprised?"

"Brilliant!" Tee said. "But still . . . We're on an island. There's water all around us."

"It's Coney Island!" Sierra yelled.

"Huh?"

"What else could it be?" She started walking toward the train. "The games, the rides — it's the carnival of destiny and chance. The moon reflected on the water."

"You going there now?" Bennie said. "It's late."

"Of course," said Sierra. "Who's with me?"

TWENTY-NINE

Getting to the Q train didn't take too long; it was waiting on the Prospect Park station platform that seemed endless to Sierra. Everything was fine as long as they were moving, but standing still was making her anxious. She kept trying to imagine some scenario where Manny was okay, walking around somewhere, joking with the domino guys about whatever had happened, but all she could think about was the throng haint looming in the shadows of the printing press. Had it been there? Was that its ragged breath she'd heard as they made their way toward Manny in the darkness?

Izzy and Tee were sitting on a bench, Izzy splayed out in Tee's lap like an old sweater, and they were talking quietly. Big Jerome was telling Bennie some story about getting picked up by the cops on Marcy Avenue. Bennie nodded and said "Oh, wow" occasionally, but her eyes wandered up and down the subway map, and Sierra could tell her thoughts were elsewhere. Juan sat against a pillar, his head locked between his arms and bent knees like some surly, spiky-haired statue. He probably understood better than any of them what all this was about, having grown up in it and never let on to Sierra . . .

An angry flame surged inside of her. Juan and her grandpa, talking endlessly about all these deep spiritual things, whole other worlds that Sierra had been completely excluded from. How could they? She breathed in and tried to let the anger go. She stared impatiently into the dark, empty tunnel. *This has to end*, she thought to herself, *and this is the only way I know to do it.*

Lonely women dance in the mirror, she texted Robbie. *the mirror = the ocean –> coney isl. we on the way. c u there?* Then she put her phone away, trying not to wait for a reply. Who else should know? Certainly not her mom. María would just bug out and tell them not to go. She speed-dialed Nydia's cell instead.

"Sierra? Are you okay?"

"Hey, Nydia! Listen, sorry to call you so late," Sierra said. "You know that whole thing I'm researching 'bout Wick?"

"Of course, hon. Whatsup?"

"We're following up with something out in Coney Island. I think . . . I figured something out."

Nydia chewed gum for a second. "You sure you okay out there? Coney Island at night? Not so much."

Apparently all Puerto Rican moms were the same, even if they weren't your mom. Sierra rolled her eyes. "It's fine, Nydia. Thank you. But don't worry about me, okay? I'll be careful."

"Alright, I'm at the library if you need anything. They got me keeping crazy hours."

"Thanks again. I'll call you tomorrow."

After what seemed like forever, but was really only fifteen minutes, the bright train lights finally came flooding around the corner. Sierra felt a flush of excitement. Whatever happened, this train would bring them that much closer to Lucera.

A scruffy homeless guy was laid out across four seats, stinking up the whole car. They sat on the opposite end. A few seats over, two well-dressed Russian guys slept with their heads on each other's shoulders, sure to wake up in a concerned flurry at their stop and pretend it had never happened.

Sierra was staring out the window, trying not to see Manny's endlessly open mouth in the flickering darkness, when Bennie leaned over to her. "Sierra?"

"What is it?"

Juan sat off to one side, still deep in his own world, but Izzy, Tee, and Jerome were all in seats directly across from Sierra, looking right at her.

"You gotta tell 'em," Bennie said. "They coming all the way out here with you and they don't even really know why. It ain't right."

"Yeah, wassup, Sierra?" Izzy said.

Sierra rubbed her face. "I know, I'm sorry, I just . . . I don't know how to tell you this. I've wanted to since it started."

"Well, tell them how you told me," Bennie said. "Just start from what you found out about the freaky corpsy thing and the shadowshapers. They'll believe you."

Sierra wasn't sure if she would even believe herself, but she started talking, tentatively at first and gradually with more confidence. Juan put in little annoying factoids here and there, but mostly Sierra had the floor. One of the drunk Russian guys woke up and sat listening intently too.

"And that's . . . that's about it, I guess," Sierra said. It felt like she'd just told her life story, but, really, only a few minutes had gone by. She looked at her friends' faces, all wide eyes and mouths hanging open. "Um . . . hi?"

"Whoa," Jerome said.

Tee nodded. "Yeah. I don't even know what to say."

Sierra scrunched up her face. She hated having to explain something so huge in such a hurry, and hated even more that she felt so dependent on what her friends thought about it all. She sat back.

Izzy had been shaking her head the whole time. "I just . . . It creeps me out."

"What does?" Sierra asked.

"The whole thing! The haint creature that came at you in Flatbush, the thing with Manny, all the shadowshapers getting corpusculed. I mean . . . I don't even know what to say. I'm freaking out right now." Tee rubbed soothing circles on her girlfriend's back, but Izzy swatted her away. "No, stop. I'm serious. What if, Sierra, you're wrong about all this stuff? We're doing a whole lot right now, going all the way out to Coney Island, and I'm not saying you're crazy per se but I'm saying —"

"What are you saying?" Sierra asked. "That I made all this up?"

"I don't think she's saying that," Jerome said. "But there's gotta be some other explanation."

"I mean, you don't *know* that's what's happening," Izzy said. "All these ghosts and things. It just seems like it right now."

Tee scooched a few inches away from Izzy. "Are you serious, babe?" she said. "You saw Manny today. Can you think of some other explanation?"

The train screeched to a halt at Avenue J and the doors swung open.

"I'm sure there's plenty of possibilities," Izzy said as the doors slammed shut and the train started back up again. "I mean, I'm sure I'm not the only one that thinks this whole thing sounds completely cra —"

"No." Sierra's voice sounded cold and faraway, even to herself. *Crazy.* It was the same word María and Tía Rosa flung at Grandpa Lázaro. The same word anyone said when they didn't understand something. *Crazy* was a way to shut people up, disregard them entirely. She shook her head. "Don't do that. Don't try to . . . Don't. If that's what you think, then go."

"Sierra, I didn't mean . . ."

"I know what you meant. You said what you meant. Fine. Get off at the next stop. Go home. And take anyone else with you who thinks I should just sit back and chill because I'm crazy." She scanned the startled faces of her friends. Juan stared glumly out the window.

Izzy stood up as the train slowed into another station. Tears threatened the edges of her eyes. "I didn't say I thought you were crazy. But fine. Honestly, I think this is ridiculous and probably dangerous. Tee?"

Tee shook her head. "Sorry, babe," she said matter-of-factly. "I'm with Sierra on this one. I said I'd have her back and I do. I can't run home now. Besides, I wanna see how this plays out."

Izzy looked like she'd been slapped. Her glossy lips quivered and her eyes narrowed into furious slits.

Jerome stood up. "I'm out too," he said. "I'm sorry, Sierra. This all just creeps me out. I can't . . . I can't do it. I'm not saying I don't believe you, I just . . . I can't." He shrugged, looking infuriatingly blasé about the whole thing. "I'll make sure Izzy gets home okay, though," he said, looking at Tee.

"Such a gentleman," Tee said, rolling her eyes.

Sierra turned to Bennie. She didn't want to look desperate, but she'd never felt like she needed her best friend so badly in her entire life.

"What?" Bennie said. "You think if these two losers leave, I'll leave too?"

The train stopped and the doors slid open. "I don't know, B. You think I been makin' the whole thing up?"

Jerome and Izzy looked expectantly at Bennie. Bennie showed them two fingers. "Peace, my people." She turned to Sierra. "No, Sierra, I do not."

Sierra smiled, ignoring Izzy and Jerome's glares as they watched from the platform. "Thank you."

They pulled out of the station. Sierra and Bennie fist-bumped.

"Alright then!" Tee yelled, disturbing the old homeless man from his slumber. He pulled his filthy baseball cap farther down his face and grumbled. "That was awkward. Now can we go get this Lucinda chick out the sea or whatever?"

"It's Lucera, Tee," Sierra laughed.

"Oh, shoot!" Bennie yelled. "The poem!"

Sierra stared at her. "What?"

"*The one lures the other who in turn lures the one.*"

"So?"

"The full moon killing the sun . . . . I'm just saying here we are, being lured out to some creepy place, basically chasing the moon, right? Or its reflection anyway."

Sierra's heart sank.

"Either way," Bennie said, "it does speak to Izzy's whole theory that we just walking into a great big trap, doesn't it?"

No one answered her.

THIRTY

"Last stop," the conductor's voice garbled over the intercom. "Coney Island. Everybody off."

"Where to now?" Bennie said as they walked onto the platform. Juan trailed a few paces behind the girls.

"The beach, I guess," Sierra said.

None of them had been to Coney Island in years, and it looked more like an alien planet than their childhood stomping ground. Trash trundled past like tumbleweeds in old Western movies. The streetlights were dim, leaving most of the corners and alleyways shrouded in darkness. All the pizza spots and souvenir stores hid behind graffiti-covered metal grates. Off to their left, massive housing projects cut into the night sky. No one was around. Sierra wasn't used to seeing any part of the city so deserted.

"This sucks," Bennie said. "What happened to happy-happy Coney Island?"

"I think that's a daytime thing," Tee said. "After midnight it's grim tower-of-terror Coney Island, apparently."

"Apparently."

Up ahead, the ancient Wonder Wheel hung over the sprawl of carnival that hadn't been torn down or converted into fancy shops. Farther off, the shinier Luna Park cast its orange haze into the dark sky. The wind whipped down the open walkway, through various sideshows, fun houses, and arcades, all grated over and shut down for the night. On the other side of the Wonder Wheel was the boardwalk, and beyond that the beach. They'd have to cross through the darkened carnival area to reach it.

"Something doesn't feel right," Sierra said.

"Well," said Bennie, "we're chasing ghosts into an empty amusement park. How's that for starters?"

Sierra clenched her teeth. "When you say it like that . . ."

"I know, I was trying to be funny, but it backfired."

"That's for damn sure," Tee said.

"Alright then," said Sierra. "Let's go." No one moved. "Okay, I'll start." She stepped forward. "See, it's fine." She took a few more steps, felt the chill ocean breeze. "C'mon, guys."

Bennie and Tee walked to where Sierra stood, and then the three of them fell into stride together, heading toward the beach. Juan still trailed morosely behind. Grotesquely painted signs announced that the Human Cat and the Living Cyclops lurked nearby. Some kind of hunchback with three eyes and a long tongue gawked from a banner stretched over the street. The air stank of fried food and salt water.

"What do we do if we bump into creepy pale guy and them?" Bennie said.

Tee shushed her, stopping suddenly. Nobody moved for a few seconds.

"Maybe . . . just the wind," Bennie said very quietly.

All the darkened inlets and corridors that stretched into the carnival's back alleys seemed to writhe and simmer. Each scurrying rat and windblown soda can racked up Sierra's growing nervousness. "We're so close," she whispered. "The boardwalk's just up ahead."

Then why did it seem so far away?

A cloud bank drifted slowly by above them, and for the first time that night, the nearly full moon made a timid appearance. Sierra looked up and felt a wash of relief at the sight of that somber, shining face looking back at her.

"Do you know how we're gonna find Lucera once we get to the beach?" Bennie asked.

The boardwalk stretched dark and empty to either side. Occasional lampposts opened up dreary patches of light.

"Uh-uh," Sierra said. "But we're gonna figure it out. Look!"

As they stepped onto the boardwalk, the whole ocean seemed to spread out before them. It looked like it went on forever; both the sky and the sea were so dark you couldn't tell where one began and the other ended. The moon hung huge and low over the water, sent ripples of light dancing along a pathway toward the shore. "That's it. The mirror," Sierra said. "I know it."

Something was pulling her toward the water. All she wanted to do was beeline for the waves. The beach before them was empty except for a few bums sleeping in little huddled circles. Their bodies were splayed out at odd angles amidst candy wrappers and empty beer bottles. Sierra felt a familiar edginess creep over her.

"Oh, great, here we go," Bennie was saying. "Can't go nowhere in New York without some bum tryna get fifty cents off ya. I swear."

One of the drunken slumberers had risen from the pack and was stumbling toward the boardwalk. He was wider than the others and lumbered with an unsteady gait. Sierra caught her breath as a scratchy, familiar-sounding voice blasted through her mind: *Sierra!*

Everyone squinted into the darkness.

"Who is that?" Bennie said.

Two other figures were standing now, walking toward them.

"I don't know," Sierra said. "But I don't like it. Let's get . . ."

Sierra! Sierra! The raspy whisper kept burning through her thoughts. It was the throng haint, she was sure of it. She didn't know where it was, but it was approaching fast.

She froze, transfixed by its beckoning.

Then Bennie screamed as the figures coming toward them broke into a run. Bennie and Tee shot down the boardwalk toward the Wonder Wheel. Juan grabbed Sierra and yanked her toward one of the shuttered-up fried-food stands.

"What's wrong with you, sis?" Juan panted as they dashed down a greasy alleyway and stopped to catch their breath.

"That voice, calling my name," Sierra said. She rubbed her eyes, trying to clear her head. The gravelly voice spoke her name like a native Spanish speaker would, a light roll of the Rs leading into the clipped A. It didn't matter. The beast could be Puerto Rican all day long, it was still a horrible, lurking, festering . . .

"What voice?"

Footsteps clomped toward them. Terror exploded through Sierra. She couldn't think straight, couldn't slow her heart, could barely breathe. She closed her eyes.

"They're coming," Juan whispered. "We gotta do something!"

"How many?"

"Two."

"The bigger one?"

"No. They're both skinny. Sierra, we need to —"

"There's . . . something else . . ." Waves of nausea crashed over her. She fumbled in her pockets, praying her fingers would miraculously close around some chalk that Robbie had snuck her when she wasn't looking. Instead, she found the pen Juan had used to scribble the words of the song. It would have to do. Somewhere beyond it all, the ocean was still beckoning, a distant and urgent cry, but the terrible voice saying Sierra's name drowned out almost everything else. The throng haint was getting closer. She knelt down.

"What are you doing?" Juan demanded.

"I'm . . . trying" — Sierra scratched furiously at the wooden boardwalk with the ballpoint pen, but only a few broken lines came out — "to make something I can shadow-shape with."

In the corner of her eye, Sierra could see Juan pulling on his fingers and shaking his head at her. "Sierra, we ain't got time for that right now. C'mon."

She finally put together some semblance of a figure and raised her left hand in the air, trying to ignore how much it was trembling.

"Sierra!" Juan whispered.

She touched the drawing and closed her eyes. Nothing happened. A few seconds passed. The footsteps came closer.

"I gotta do something," Juan said. "Can't just wait here for them to come get us." Before Sierra could stop him, he pulled out his pocket blade and ran onto the boardwalk.

"No!" Sierra slammed her hand on the drawing and felt the jolt of spirit flood through her. The figure bolted from beneath her fingers and skittered out on the boardwalk.

The whisper got louder. *Sierra! Sierra!* The throng haint was coming.

On the boardwalk, two corpuscles barreled toward Juan. Sierra recognized one as the guy from outside Kalfour. The other she hadn't seen before. Juan crouched, blade ready. Just before they reached him, Sierra's shadowshaped figure slid across the planks and then up the first corpuscle's pant leg. It etched itself like a sudden scar across its face. The corpuscle reared back, hands splayed, and Juan took the opportunity to shoulder-check it. It collapsed backward, but the second corpuscle lurched toward Juan.

Juan stopped in his tracks. "Mr. Raconteur!" he gasped. "I . . . What are you . . . doing?"

"No!" Sierra yelled. "Juan, it's not him, it's a corpuscle! Run!"

Sierra. The throng haint's voice sent spasms through her stomach. She looked up; the corpuscle swung at Juan. A flash of bright color splattered across its face. The corpuscle let out a guttural cry and toppled over, clawing at his eyes. The first corpuscle rose from where Juan had shoved it, just as Robbie stepped out from a pile of old boxes and raised one hand in front him, palm out.

Juan looked stunned. "Robbie, what are you . . . ?"

Robbie yelled, and Sierra saw the tattoos surge forward along his arm and flash through the air. The corpuscle stumbled backward, waving his hands in front of his suddenly color-stained face, then fell to its knees, screaming. Robbie's ancestors swirled viciously around the neck of Raconteur's corpuscle. They were a colorful blur against the pale flesh, a raised ax, a swinging machete. The corpuscule scrambled to its feet, took two steps, and then dropped.

SIERRA!

Sierra almost collapsed from the sudden ferocity of the voice. The ocean, the perfect endless ocean, was her only hope. She didn't understand that thought, couldn't even think logically anymore. All she knew to do was get away from that horrible voice and make it to the water.

The corpuscules lay still. Robbie turned around and smiled at Juan and Sierra.

"Not bad," Juan said.

Robbie nodded, and then his eyes met Sierra's. "Sierra, what's wrong?"

SIERRRRAAA!!

The throng haint was upon her. About to pounce.

Sierra broke into a run and burst across the boardwalk, out onto the milky darkness of the beach.

THIRTY-ONE

Sierra's feet pounded over the sand. The crashing waves grew closer, and yet the throng haint stayed tight behind her. She could hear its heavy footfall and ragged breath, even more real now than it had been that night in Flatbush. It was a hulking monster and it was only a few feet away. Her own breath came shorter and shorter, a knot tightening inside her chest.

"Sierra! Sierra, it's me!"

She would keep running, into the ocean if necessary. She thought maybe, just maybe, she had gained some distance on it.

"It's Manny, Sierra! Wait!"

Sierra stopped, the crashing waves only a few feet away. She turned around. Manny the Domino King stood about ten feet away, panting. He looked like hell — his mouth half open as he gasped for air; dark, yellowish splotches beneath his eyes; and a few days' worth of stubble crescenting the lower half of his face. Worse, his normally brown skin had faded to dull gray, like he'd been underground for months. Sierra shuddered.

Manny took a step toward her, and she took a step back. "Sierra." He looked hurt. "It's me! Don't . . . Just calm down, please."

Sierra shook her head. Tears poured out of her eyes before she could stop them. "I know what you are, Manny. I know that thing is inside you."

"I know, Sierra. Just give me a chance to explain, please." Another step forward. Sierra held still, narrowing her eyes. "I'll explain everything."

Everything. Just the idea of someone explaining everything made her slightly delirious with hope. If someone could explain everything, that meant that everything actually had an explanation. Even if the answers came from a creepy, corpselike version of her friend. "What do you know?"

"There's so much, Sierra. Your family, old Lázaro . . ."

"Now you wanna talk, Manny? After everything?"

"He . . . was a powerful sorcerer, Sierra."

"Stay back!"

Suddenly, Manny was much closer to her than she had realized. It hadn't even seemed like he was moving. "And you've led us right to Lucera, haven't you?" His voice was different now, all hints of Spanish gone. Sierra realized something was dancing in Manny's eyes besides his usual mischievous charm. Something . . .

"Such a shame," many voices sobbed mockingly from Manny's bluish lips. His thick fingers wrapped around her left wrist, pulling her forward. "You'll have to join the rest of them." Tiny screaming mouths erupted along his gray flesh like welts.

Sierra's breath caught in her throat. Nausea flooded up inside her, and then the pain, the searing burn that shredded up and down her body that she remembered from Flatbush. Everything started moving slowly. She was vaguely aware of swinging her right fist at Manny's face as she wrenched her other arm free. Her punch found its mark but barely seemed to daze him. His skin was cool and rough to the touch.

There was no plan, just sheer terror. The only thing left was the ocean. The crashing waves were only a few feet away. Sierra threw her body to the side just as Manny lurched toward her. She almost fell, put one hand on the beach to steady herself, and then sprinted forward.

With her first stride, she felt the spirits surround her. Her second stride seemed longer; she hovered in the air for a split second before landing and then hurtling toward the sea. Tall, long-armed shadows sprinted alongside her in a thick, humming crowd — the same spirits from the park the night before. Their song rose and fell in gentle crescendos that matched the waves lashing along the sand.

Oooooooooooooooooooooohhhhh!!

Sierra became acutely aware of a gentle harmony rising among her racing heart, her footsteps thumping along the

beach, the swirling tide, the chorus of spirits, the moon . . .
A whole symphony of escape took shape in the night.

Okay, she thought. *I know what I have to do.*

As if in response, a surge of energy welled up inside of
her. She imagined a bright light flashing from some hidden
chamber of her heart, pulsing in time with the spirits' lights.
Without thinking about it, she pivoted off her left foot and
threw herself out over the water.

THIRTY-TWO

She didn't realize her eyes were squeezed shut until she opened them. Then there she was, gliding along three feet above the ocean, spirits all around her. She opened her mouth and screamed as loud as she could, releasing the great wave of joy and exultation that was bursting inside of her, but the wind swallowed up her voice. The spirits' song had become laughter, or some joyful hymn, and the shadows swooped and dove along beside her. Some of them sped across the waters like rain clouds on the way to work. Others were taller and human-shaped; their long arms swayed to either side of them as their legs shot out in fast arcs over the waves. Each pulsed with the same glowing light that they had in the park. The lights grew brighter as they sped away from the shore.

Up ahead, the moonlit patch of water seemed to froth with anticipation. Sierra could almost hear it calling as they raced along. Then, all of a sudden, they were hovering over the shimmering moon's reflection, waves thundering around them. The shadow procession formed a wide circle around Sierra, their dark faces turned expectantly toward her.

"Lucera!" Sierra called into the water. "I've come for you! I need your help!"

Some seagulls flew past, cawing in the dark sky above them. The ocean thundered on, oblivious to Sierra's plea.

"Lucera!" she called again, her voice barely audible in the wind.

The water might have been getting brighter; it was hard to tell. Sierra squinted into the shifting luminescence of the moon's reflection, trying to adjust her eyes, and then she was sure of it: A glow was rising beneath her. "Lucera." This time, she said it quietly.

A bright circle of light beamed out of the ocean, filling her with warmth and energy. Still hovering over the crashing waves, Sierra reached down toward the water. All around, the spirits hummed their harmonious spirituals and murmured quietly to one another, their glow pulsing in time with the shimmer growing in the dark waters.

When a sparkling hand emerged from the ocean, Sierra nearly toppled over with surprise. The hand surged upward, finding Sierra's, and wrapped around it. It was warm to the touch and seemed to buzz with a gentle electrical charge. Sierra pulled. The light grew stronger and then erupted in a bright flash.

Sierra felt her body fly upward. She heard herself scream, and then that was drowned out by the shriek of the wind as she soared even higher. Something very warm was pressed up against her back, a golden glow wrapped tightly around her waist. She closed her eyes as they slowed.

"Open your eyes." Lucera's voice was warm and scratchy, as if she was smiling.

Sierra shook her head. "I'm good."

"Sierra."

She cracked one lid open. Darkness and a few sprinkles of light. She opened both eyes all the way.

Sierra gasped. Brooklyn stretched out before her. in blinking avenues and cross streets, interrupted by the thorough emptiness of the East River and then the New York Bay. Whatever spirit magic had heightened her senses in the park the night before must've been in full throttle now: To her left, Manhattan was a mess of rising and falling towers, crisscrossing spotlights, traffic signals, and blinking advertisements. Farther up, the Bronx and Queens dwindled into the northern suburbs. Coney Island twinkled beneath them, and behind them, the Atlantic Ocean reached its vast darkness into the night.

They spun in slow circles, giving Sierra the full panorama.

"Look at me, m'ija."

M'ija? Sierra turned and gazed up at Lucera.

"Mama Carmen?" she said. The skin around the old spirit's eyes creased as she blinked away sparkling tears. Lucera was, without a doubt, Sierra's grandmother. "You . . . you're . . ."

They began descending in a slow spin toward the shore, the shadow spirits forming a graceful entourage. Sierra opened her mouth but nothing came out. All her questions, all her hopes and fears — they were all gone, scattered in the salty night air. For a few seconds, the two just stared at each other as the shadows danced around them.

"Sierra . . ." Carmen said it slowly, as if she didn't want the name to crumble on her lips. "Sierra María Santiago."

Sierra nodded.

"You have come. I knew you would."

"Abuela."

Mama Carmen's face opened into a stunning smile. It burned out at Sierra through a golden haze of light.

"You're Lucera."

The old woman nodded; shiny tears streamed along the lines of her face.

"All this time and . . . all my life . . ." Sierra's voice trembled. She felt her own tears coming and forced them back.

Carmen raised one of her hands, gliding toward Sierra. "Let me see your left hand, m'ija."

"No!" Sierra drew back. The spirits stopped their circles and watched.

"What is it? I want to see . . ."

"No," Sierra said again, quieter this time. She stared into her abuela's ancient face. "You're no better than Lázaro. You . . . just left me out in the world with no idea about all . . . all this. All my life . . . I have to get back. I have to help my friends."

Mama Carmen nodded, her face tightening into that stern glare Sierra remembered so well. She turned to the retinue of shadows around them. "A la playa," she said softly. They descended faster now, the wind wailing around them. The spirits all pulsed in time with the same glowing rhythm. It surrounded Sierra, lit up the entire night. Mama Carmen was literally the beating heart of the shadowshaper world. A few shadows flitted ahead toward the shore.

"I'll get you to your friends," Mama Carmen said. "But the spirits will get there first, to help them. Now, Sierra, m'ija, please. Let me see your hand."

Sierra shook her head. "Why didn't you ever tell me about the shadowshapers? And then you just disappeared — you abandoned us. All of us."

Carmen sighed. "No, m'ija. I wanted so badly to . . . You don't understand."

"You're right. I don't understand. Not at all. And no one seems to want to tell me, Abuela . . . Lucera."

"You can call me Abuela. I'm still your abuela, Sierra."

"And I'm out here and I have no idea how to help my friends or myself or anyone else. Because you never told me! You just got mad at Abuelo because he initiated Wick, right? And then you took off?"

Carmen closed her eyes and lowered her head. "No."

Sierra tried to hold her face tight, but tears kept teasing the edges of her eyes. "What do you mean?"

"The fight wasn't over Wick. Of course, I was furious that he'd done it, especially after I'd told him again and again not to trust that man. But that wasn't why I left. That fight was over *you*."

"Me?"

"Of course, m'ija. I wanted to bring you into the fold as soon as you were born, but Láz refused."

"Why?"

"Because we'd already tried once with someone else and it hadn't gone well . . ."

For a few seconds, all Sierra heard was the wind whipping around them as they slid gracefully through the sky. She closed her eyes. "Mami."

"Yes, your mother." Carmen shook her head. "Maybe I started her too young, who knows? She was fourteen. We stood on that very shore, all the spirits of our ancestors dancing around us like they are now. I know she saw them — I watched her eyes chart their dancing paths over the water. But she turned her back on me. She called me crazy, said she never wanted to hear about it again. You know how folks just want to fit in, to be *normal*. I think she held me and Láz at a distance ever since that day."

"No wonder she gets so tense when I bring up shadowshaping."

Mama Carmen sighed. "I can only imagine. And Rosa was even worse — we didn't even bother trying."

"Good," Sierra growled.

"When you were born, I . . . Of course María wouldn't hear of me bringing you into it, and Lázaro was dead set against it too; by that time he was convinced shadowshaping was for men. Never mind that he was saying that to *me*, of all people."

"So what happened?"

"After Láz brought in Wick against my advice, I was through with all of it. He was more than ready to initiate this stranger and keep his own granddaughter in the dark about our family legacy. This was after my physical body had already passed, mind you. So I went into your room late one night, and while you slept, I gifted you the power to shadowshape, m'ija."

Sierra couldn't stop the tears flowing down her face. She nodded slowly, felt her abuela's words seep inside her, settle in her bones. Finally, the truth. "And Abuelo found out?"

"Found out? Ha! I told him. He was beside himself with rage, and he banished me." Carmen rolled her eyes.

"Banished? But . . . you're more powerful than he is, how could he . . . ?"

"Ah, Sierra. You can't heal someone who doesn't want to be healed. Maybe I should've stayed and fought, but . . . it would've been terrible. Imagine a shadowshaper civil war with a husband and wife heading up each side." She shook her head. "The tradition never would've survived. He grew so stubborn in his old age, your abuelo. So hardened. So I came here; the ocean is a sanctuary for all ancestral spirits."

"Where lonely women go to dance."

Carmen smiled the saddest smile Sierra had ever seen. "I used to sing your mother to sleep with that every night when she was a child, just like my mother, your great-grandmother, Cantara Cebilín Colibrí, used to sing to me, and her mother, María, whom your mom was named after, sang to her. It's an old shadowshaper prayer. The details change from generation to generation, across time and place, but its deeper secret stays the same."

"They were all shadowshapers? All the women in Mami's lineage?"

"Not just shadowshapers. The role of Lucera has been passed down the line. The song is a lullaby we gift to each new generation, a riddle. If something ever happened, I knew the sea was where I'd end up."

Sierra imagined her mom as a young girl, sleeping as Mama Carmen sang the shadowshapers' riddle to her. When had María let her heart push all that magic away? All those walls she built . . . "I never knew."

"Of course you didn't — she would never speak of it. The night I left, I put a spell on that silly group photo your abuelo took of the shadowshapers after he'd made it into his own little boys' club."

"The fingerprints?"

Mama Carmen nodded. "It's called photomarking. When anyone in the picture is murdered, their face gets smudged out. Wick hadn't started on his crusade yet, but I saw it in him, I knew it wouldn't be long." She wrinkled her brow at Sierra. "How . . . how many has he killed?"

"At least four so far," Sierra said. "Counting Manny."

Mama Carmen closed her eyes and shuddered. For a moment, Sierra thought her grandma was about to burst into tears. "That was one thing Jonathan Wick never could understand. He thinks he can wipe out the 'shapers and keep the power to himself, that the power comes from me."

"It doesn't?"

"Without Lucera there's no shadowshaping, but without shadowshaping there's no Lucera. We are entwined. I drew power from the spirits and spirit workers and I returned it to them tenfold. The true source of shadowshaper magic is in that connection, community, Sierra. We are interdependent."

"*Donde los poderes se unen y se hacen uno,*" Sierra sang.

Mama Carmen unleashed a wide smile. "Right, m'ija! Not one and only, one as in togetherness." She rolled her eyes. "I wrote out a copy of that poem and made Lázaro swear he'd pass it on to you when the fingerprints started appearing."

Sierra dug in her pocket and retrieved the scrap of paper Grandpa Lázaro had placed in her hand. "You mean this? He must've torn it up."

Mama Carmen shook her head. "Comemierda."

"No wonder he kept apologizing." Sierra traced the wrinkles etched across her abuela's face. She took in the old ghost's quiet ferocity and found that it was deeply familiar — a certain glow that in better times she occasionally found looking back at her from the mirror. "It falls on me next, doesn't it?"

Mama Carmen smiled sadly. "Hold up your hand, m'ija."

They'd stopped moving. Sierra could just make out the dark shoreline ahead of them and now hovered just a few feet above the waves. She closed her eyes and lifted her left hand to her grandmother, palm out. A warm tingling sensation enwrapped it. She heard Mama Carmen chuckle under her breath. "You have tried shadowshaping already, have you?"

Sierra nodded. "It was fun." A smile found its way to her lips.

Suddenly the warmth was all around Sierra. A burning glow infiltrated her eyelids. "My child," Mama Carmen whispered in her ear. "I am so proud of you."

"But . . ."

"So proud."

Something inside of Sierra was melting inside that embrace — a gentle tide of acceptance flooding through every corner of her body. It was all real, every moment of it, and it reached deep into the heart of her own family. Her abuela — that same old face she'd feared and loved as a child — was Lucera, the exiled sun of the spirit world.

Sierra made a noise that was somewhere between a sob and laughter. Her grandma squeezed her tighter, patting her on the back. "Hush, mi niña, shhhh. Está bien."

When Sierra lifted her teary face from Mama Carmen's shoulder, she saw that the spirits had circled closer. She thought she could glimpse the hints of faces on some of them, open mouths and eyes both sad and inspired. She wondered what secrets they carried, what powers. They spun in slow orbits around the two women, singing their spirit songs and watching, always watching.

They would help her, these spirits. They would rise up against Wick beside her. And Mama Carmen would lead the charge.

"So, c'mon," Sierra said. "Let's go back there so we can be Luceras together and whup Wick's ass."

"I can't."

"What?"

"I cannot return."

Sierra pulled away from her grandmother's embrace. "Why not?"

"Once a spirit enters this realm, it is for good. I'm no longer of the living world, Sierra. I held on this long only so you could reach me."

"But I just found you, Abuela . . . I just . . . found out who you really are. The murals are fading . . . Wick is killing the shadowshapers off. Who will . . . ?"

Mama Carmen's face hardened. "You will, Sierra."

"But you can't . . . I can't . . . I'm just . . ." Sierra looked around. She couldn't say she was "just" anything; she was, after all, floating a few feet above the crashing waves off the southern tip of Brooklyn. But still . . .

"Of course you can," Mama Carmen said. "You are a brilliant young woman: brave, passionate, adventurous."

"But I don't —"

Carmen's voice turned sharp. "Sierra, stop second-guessing yourself. There isn't time for all that. You made your way here, just like I'd hoped you would. You followed each hint. You've earned this; you almost died for it. I won't see my legacy destroyed after we've given up so much to keep it alive. No. You will be Lucera now, Sierra. You will come to understand everything that means in time, but for now, you have to make a stand against Wick."

"I can't do it alone, Abuela!"

"Who said you had to do it alone? There are those around you well qualified to help you through. And yes, you will need the help. I don't know what exactly Wick is up to, but I have no doubt that whatever he has in mind involves the complete annihilation of our family, all of our spirits. You understand?"

"No, Abuela. I barely understand what we *are* . . ."

"You will. Be careful, m'ija."

The old spirit wrapped around Sierra, and suddenly the entire world was full of blinding light. The brightness seared into Sierra's eyeballs, coated the inside of her brain, and burst like a languid, slow-motion explosion down her spine and through her entire body. Light, invincible, unstoppable, infinite light flooded through her veins, filled each of her organs, poured out of her mouth, covered her skin. And it *pulsed*, Sierra realized. The same gentle, relentless rhythm that surged through the shadows and Mama Carmen surged through her now. The spirits' hymn grew louder and louder, erupted from inside her, but somewhere beneath it all she heard a voice singing softly. She could barely make out the words.

And then everything stopped: the crashing waves, the singing spirits, the wind. Sierra floated in an infinite sea of light. The only sound she heard was the old woman's song:

Cuando la luna llena . . . mata al viejo sol . . .

It wasn't Mama Carmen's voice; it was someone else, even older than her. Sierra inhaled; the smell of fresh soil and recent rain surrounded her. And something else: garlic. Garlic simmering on a stovetop nearby.

. . . a los cuatro caminos . . .

The rush of wind and crashing waves returned gradually, drowning out the old woman's trembling voice.

When Sierra opened her eyes, Mama Carmen was gone.

"Don't go," Sierra whispered. "I'm not ready."

THIRTY-THREE

Back on the shore, Sierra trudged toward the blurry board-walk lights. With Mama Carmen gone, she didn't know how she'd learn about her powers, how she'd defeat Wick. But if she kept moving forward, eventually she'd get there, and then she would find Bennie and Juan and . . . Robbie!

There are those around you well qualified to help you through. Robbie was a powerful spirit worker. The image of his swirling tattoos sliding up the corpuscle's legs during the fight on the boardwalk danced through Sierra's mind. He'd saved her life then, even if he'd blown it the first few times with the corpuscles. He knew all kinds of secrets, understood the depths of this mysterious new world. He could help her. They could do it together. And once she got her bearings and they'd dealt with Wick, she could see what all this being the shining center of the shadowshapers business was about.

Sierra quickened her pace, her eyebrows arched, mind racing now. She was a shadowshaper, one who had the power to transfer spirit into form. It all seemed so new, yet the power had been with her all along. Power. It was an odd thought, the idea of some strange magic coursing through her veins. Robbie had used his tattoos as weapons earlier . . . What more could be done?

There's so much to talk about with him, she thought, breaking into a light jog. Long nights staying up late figuring out new ways to channel spirits together. Someone who understood her.

Sierra stopped in her tracks. Up ahead, the streetlamps of Coney Island twinkled in the night sky. She wanted Robbie. She wanted him by her side, wanted his smell all around her, his goofy smile pressed up against hers. She wanted to sort through clues with him, figure out this terrifying supernatural puzzle with him, laugh about it all when it was over. She wanted him right then and there. Nothing felt more true.

She was so close now. Her feet plodded over the sand. She felt light suddenly, free of the terror that she was all alone in this maze. She would find Robbie, tell him what she learned, kiss him full on the lips. She wasn't even concerned about whether or not he'd kiss her back — of course he would. She was his match: a child of spirit just like him, a fellow traveler in this mystical Brooklyn labyrinth. He hadn't said it, but he didn't have to — he told her with his eyes every time they met up. They would make out, and then they'd go ahead and figure out how to get rid of this Wick madman, together.

She charged up the stairs onto the boardwalk, skipping every other step. Bennie was talking to Tee and Juan beneath a lamppost. They all turned as Sierra hurried toward them. Bennie's tearstained face, clenched with fear, told Sierra all she needed to know.

"They took him," Bennie sobbed. "They took Robbie."

THIRTY-FOUR

The subway ride home was a blur. Sierra tried to explain the gist of her encounter with Lucera, but her heart wasn't in it. Juan sat with his mouth gaping open at the thought that their grandmother had been Lucera all this time without telling him, and Sierra was too tired and afraid to throw the irony in his face.

Bennie and Tee gave a play-by-play of what had happened back on the shore. Robbie had tried to go after Sierra when she took off, but more corpuscles had come out and surrounded him. Juan said at least four of them had been caught in the colorful web of his tattoos before they finally grabbed Robbie and ran off with him. Tee had tried to sneak after them to see where they were headed, but they'd disappeared quickly into the darkness of Coney Island. It had all happened so fast, and the shadows had swept in from the beach just a few minutes later, too late to help Robbie.

Tee shook her head. "I'm so sorry, Sierra."

Sierra gave a half-hearted "Don't be," and then everyone

fell into a gloomy silence as the Q train rumbled toward Prospect Park.

"Juan," Sierra said as she and her brother walked up Lafayette Avenue toward their house. "Do you remember anything at all that could help us figure out where Wick might have taken Robbie?"

Juan shrugged. "I dunno, sis. I'm still reeling from the fact that Mama Carmen was a part of this all along and no one told me."

"Hmph. Now you know how I feel."

"Fair point."

Sierra was getting impatient. Robbie could be a corpuscule already. "What if someone is helping Wick . . . another shadowshaper maybe?"

"I mean, who would do that? Most of the shadowshapers don't 'shape anymore, otherwise I'd say we should track them down to help us. Even the ones that do — I wouldn't know where to look for 'em. And I don't think we have time for all that anyway."

They walked up the front steps. Sierra stopped Juan from opening the door.

"What?" Juan demanded.

"I need you to think, Juan."

"I *am* thinking!"

"Were there any of the 'shapers that struck you as weird or off?"

"Not that I remember."

"Any that seemed jealous of Abuelo?"

"How are you so sure it was a shadowshaper, Sierra? Coulda been one of your friends helping Wick."

Sierra opened her mouth to argue and then closed it again. Juan had a point.

"Think about it," Juan said. He opened the front door and walked in. "Did anyone else know you were heading out to Coney Island?"

Sierra growled and followed him inside.

"Wassup, young'uns?" Uncle Neville sat at the kitchen table, his long legs stretched out in front of him, a cup of steaming coffee in his hand. "How the night treatin' you?"

Sierra had no answer for that. Grandpa Lázaro's heavy, impossible presence seemed to cast a shadow on her all the way from the fourth floor.

She stormed up to his apartment. A slew of furious demands, accusations, and complaints for him burned on the edge of her tongue. But when she opened the door, Lázaro slept peacefully, splayed out across the bed. She shook her head and marched past him to the photographs.

Sierra gasped. More than half of the faces had been smudged out now. Manny's, of course, and Raconteur and Ol' Vernon, along with four other guys Sierra didn't know. Besides Papa Acevedo, the only shadowshapers left unsmudged were Caleb Jones, a tall, light-skinned guy in his thirties with a bright red fro and tattoos creeping up his neck; Theodore

Crane, a shriveled-up old man with his arms crossed over his chest; Delmond Alcatraz and Sunny Balboa, the two guys who ran the barbershop over on Marcy; and a thick, frowning guy in a tracksuit and Stetson hat named Francis True.

None of this helped. If someone was helping Wick, it could be one of the surviving shadowshapers, but how would she find out which one? Sierra shot one last angry look at her grandfather and went downstairs to her room.

She didn't know what to pack, didn't even know where she was going. All she knew was that she had to get out of the house and start looking for Robbie. She started putting random things into her courier bag: a flashlight, batteries, some rope. A vague notion began swimming through her mind; an answer. She couldn't put her finger on it yet, but it was there. It was there and it was uncomfortable — something that was throwing off everything else in her calculations. Someone who knew about Sierra's every move.

Why? Because every time she made one, no matter where she went, those corpuscules were there waiting. Like there was an all-seeing eye glaring at her from above. Or a spy.

A spy . . .

"Sierra?" Her mom's voice was still grating from three floors away. "¿Dónde estás, m'ija?"

Someone she trusted.

"¡Aquí arriba!" Sierra called, not bothering to hide the irritation in her voice. She sat at her desk and rubbed her face. Tension pulsed angrily through her tired body. The answer was flirting with her, staying just out of her mind's eye but making itself known around the edges. María Santiago's footsteps came up the creaking stairs. Sierra wanted the answer to show up before her mom did.

"Sierra?" A gentle *tap-tap*. María always started extra meek when she was really upset about something. It had been years since the technique had thrown Sierra off guard, but it was still unnerving. María eased open the door and poked her head in. She looked exhausted. "What's going on, baby? Can you talk to me, please?" She walked in and stood at the foot of the bed, looking like she didn't know what to do with her hands. "You're going and coming at all kinds of strange hours. You're yelling at Rosa. You're not your-self, m'ija."

Sierra stared into her mom's dark, severe eyes. "I . . . it's . . ." None of the possible lies made any sense. "I can't . . . talk about it."

"Sierra, are you taking drugs?"

"Mom!" Sierra slammed her fist on the desk, maybe a little harder than she'd meant to. "I said I don't want to talk about it. You keep pressing the issue. Sound familiar? How do you like being on the other side? I'm learning from my elders how to be nice and quiet when the situation calls for it."

María's exhaustion turned quickly to anger. "How dare you pull attitude with me right now, with all that's going on? How —"

"How dare I? How dare I?" The dam that had been holding back Sierra's rage collapsed. She stood up so forcefully the chair almost fell backward behind her. "You've been keeping things from me about my own family for my entire life! How dare *you*?"

"Sierra" — María switched into wise-old-mother mode — "now is not the time to get into all that."

"Now is exactly the time to get into it. You think if you don't talk about something, it just goes away? You think you were . . ." Sierra felt herself swinging dangerously close to tears and slowed her breathing, keeping an icy stare on her mom. "You think you were protecting us? Well, look where that got us. Manny . . . Robbie . . ." She couldn't find the words to explain without breaking down.

"What did you want me to say?" María yelled. "That your abuelos were crazy magicians? That they thought they could communicate with the dead? Es una locura, Sierra, family eccentricities. It has nothing to do with you."

"Nothing to —"

"It's insanity!"

Sierra realized her hands had been trembling, clenched in tight fists. She relaxed them. She had thinking to do; the possibility of someone helping Wick still danced just out of sight. It was time to go. She took her bag and walked calmly toward the door.

María exploded into a fury. "Don't you dare walk out on me, Sierra María Santiago!"

Sierra turned suddenly, catching her mother off guard. "You wanna know how I know that you believe in our power more than anyone? I can see the terror in your eyes. You're afraid. You been scared since I mentioned it. You're afraid of me finding things out, but more than that, you're still terrified of your own parents. Because you know they were powerful. You know they had it, that magic. And you see it in me, don't you, Mami? And it terrifies you."

María's eyes were wide and watery. She must've been working hard for years to convince herself that both her parents were completely insane, Sierra realized. She must've fought to believe that she was a normal person, just like everyone else, and not a gifted spiritist, linked to a legacy of magic.

"And you know what else?" Sierra continued. "I know you got it too. You got that magic touch, Mami, but you too afraid to use it. Too afraid that the other teachers at your school or Tía Rosa might find out, or that it'd be more power than you knew what to do with. That's probably it — you're afraid of your own power." Sierra was sniffling, but she refused to let the tears out. Her jaw was set, her eyes narrow. "Well, I'm not afraid, Mami. I'm not scared of my power. I'm not ashamed of what I got. Not ashamed of my history, and I'm not ashamed of Abuela. You hear me?"

Ever so slightly, María Santiago nodded. For a second, Sierra thought her mom might shatter into a million pieces right then and there.

A door opened in the hallway above them and Timothy poked his head over the banister. "You want me to call the police?"

"No!" Sierra and her mom yelled at the same time.

Something in María's eyes relented. Tears still teased their edges, but they held a peacefulness that hadn't been there before.

Sierra turned and started down the stairs. She felt like she'd lost about twenty pounds just by speaking.

She walked out into the hallway. The answer was coming, she was sure of it. Wick had known they'd be at Coney Island. That meant someone had to have . . .

She froze in her tracks on the second-floor landing. In her mind's eye, she saw, or felt, a flurry of movement, a shadow that flickered away just before she could see it. Besides her friends and Juan, only one other person knew she was going to Coney Island.

Sierra's feet barely touched the steps as she raced down them.

"Neville!"

Her godfather smiled up from his coffee mug. "Sierra, I thought you were turning in, girl."

"Neville, can you be that cool godfather that does his goddaughter a solid without asking too many questions?"

"Conspicuous and Ridiculous are my middle names."

"You mind giving me a ride uptown again?"

Neville's grin got bigger. "You know I love an adventure."

THIRTY-FIVE

It made some kind of creepy sense. Why had Nydia been so helpful anyway? Sierra was just some kid from around the way; why was a Columbia librarian wasting so much time to dig up papers on some vanished anthropologist for her? She'd even asked for updates when Sierra had met her at the library. Nydia must've met Wick at Columbia, or maybe gone there to seek him out.

And Sierra had been happily feeding her info on how everything was moving along. She cringed. She'd been so thrilled to find someone that looked like her on the otherwise unfriendly campus that she had played right into their hands. Nydia probably had Robbie at the library with her — she could easily hide him amidst those labyrinthine stacks. *Well, I'll straighten it all out one way or the other,* Sierra thought, rolling down the window and letting the cool night air swoosh against her face.

"Smoke bothering you?" Neville asked.

"Nah, just wanted some fresh air. Just . . . thinking."

"You know, if you wanna talk about it, I'm actually pretty good at keeping a secret."

"I wish I could tell you, Uncle Neville. I really do." She shook her head. Once someone you trusted turned out to be spying on you, it called *everyone* into question. "You ever been betrayed?"

Neville laughed. "Oh, plenty a times. And it never stops sucking."

"What do you do?"

"Officially?" He swung hard into the right lane to get around a slow-sauntering Jeep. "It ain't Sunday morning and we ain't in the country, fool!" He laughed and tugged on his smoke. "I mean, depends on a few things, but generally I cut the offending party out of my life and keep it movin'. Once all the damage has been repaired, that is." He screeched the car back into the fast lane and revved it forward.

"Yeah," Sierra said. "It's the damage control part I gotta figure out."

Neville grunted in commiseration.

"Can you drive any faster?"

"Well, damn, Sierra, thought you'd never ask."

The night guard, an ancient Irish cat with a wooden cane, was staring intently at one of those seven-day medicine holders. Sierra flashed the student ID Nydia had given her and the old guy barely glanced at it. "Workin' late?" he mumbled without looking up from his medicines.

"Something like that. Anybody here?"

"One or two lonely souls," the guard said. Sierra headed in. "And that lady who's always in the basement, of course."

"Nydia?"

"Uh-huh, that's the one. Little Spanish señorita like yourself."

"Anyone with her? Maybe a tall kid with locks?"

The old man squinted at Sierra. His left eye was foggy with cataracts. "You're mighty inquisitive, my dear."

"Forget it," Sierra said, hurrying along.

She had no plan. It was a stupid time to be thinking such things, rushing as she was down the endless flights of stairs toward a potentially ghost-wielding sorceress. But still, the thought remained: She had no plan. She had simply landed on an answer and run headlong into whatever mess awaited her. She'd have to do better in the future, if she survived. If Robbie was down there somewhere, surely, and if she could find him before Nydia found her, maybe they'd have a chance. Maybe. Then again, maybe Nydia wasn't even helping Wick.

Sierra reached the thick metal door that led to the archival basement and turned the handle ever so gently. The room was dark except for a dim light coming from somewhere deep in the stacks. She checked her pockets and scrunched up her face. She'd have to get in the habit of carrying around stuff to draw with if she was going to be any kind of shadowshaper. A fire extinguisher gathered dust in a little alcove right next to the door. Sierra unhinged it and heaved it onto her shoulder bazooka-style. It was ridiculous, but it felt good to at least have something heavy in her hands if things got hairy.

This is stupid, Sierra thought, making her way as quietly as possible down a corridor between two bookshelves. But all she could envision was Robbie being tortured to death at the hands of a throng haint. She shuddered and crept forward, trying to force the thought away.

Nydia stood at a table between two stacks. The Wick file was splayed out messily in front of her, and she hunched over it, her back to Sierra, flipping through pages and mumbling to herself. Sierra held her breath and slid silently into striking distance. She wrapped both hands around the neck of the fire extinguisher, bracing her body to swing. One hit and it would be over. Well, over for Nydia anyway. Sierra still wouldn't know where Robbie was, and Wick would still be out there somewhere. She paused.

Nydia spun around, her eyes wide. "Sierra!"

"I . . . I know everything . . ."

"What?"

Sierra held tight to the extinguisher, suddenly out of breath. "I know . . . what's going on."

Nydia raised an eyebrow. "Could you explain it to me, then?"

"Don't try and be coy with me, Nydia! I know you're a shadowshaper —"

"Me? I wish!"

Sierra shook her head. "No, stop! Stop talking. I know you've been helping Wick, spying for him —"

"Now, hold up." Nydia stepped toward her.

"Stop! Don't come any closer! Where's Robbie? Where are you and Wick keeping him?"

Nydia's eyes got wide. "What are you talking about? You think that I'm helping Wick? Sierra, no . . ."

"Of course you are. It all makes sense. You've been keeping track of my every move, letting him know where I'll be next."

"Sierra, listen." Nydia's voice was firm; her dark eyes didn't waver from Sierra's. "I haven't been tracking you. I've been tracking Wick."

Sierra lowered the fire extinguisher and then raised it again. Her head was spinning. "Stop lying."

"It's true." Nydia took another step closer.

"Stay back. I'll smash your head in." She wanted to break down and sob. Everything was happening way too fast. "You know about the Sorrows. You were surprised when I asked you about them, like . . . like I was onto you."

"Sierra, I study the spirit world, yes, but more than that, I study other anthropologists who study the spirit world. That's part of my research: how researchers get involved and change spirit-worker communities, both for better and worse."

Sierra put down the extinguisher. "You're like, what, an anthropologist super spy?"

Nydia smiled. "You could say that. I been watching Wick's moves for a while now. He really does mean well. Or, he did . . . but I didn't trust him. And when he fell off the map, I started looking deeper. That's when I found out about the Sorrows. Been researching them for the past couple months. It's . . ." She shook her head. "It's dire stuff."

"But . . ."

"Sierra, I want to help you. Trust me."

"You know how to find them, don't you?" Sierra said slowly. "The Sorrows. You said they were in some church uptown."

Nydia's eyes went wide. "Yes, but . . ."

"Take me."

"To the Sorrows? No, Sierra, that's not a good idea. They're horrible and immensely powerful and . . . they'll kill you. Kill us both."

"How else are we going to find Wick? Do you know where he is?"

Nydia frowned. "No, but —"

"Wick has my . . . He has someone I care about. He's after my whole family. He's . . ." Sierra fought back a lump in her throat. "He killed my friend Manny and made my granddad incoherent. He's almost wiped out the shadow-shapers. I have to find him. Tonight. The Sorrows gave him his power, but I'm pretty sure they aren't getting along so well anymore. If I can just —"

"Sierra, you can't reason with creatures as ancient and powerful as the Sorrows. You can't . . ."

"You said you wanted to help me. That you weren't working for Wick. If you mean it, Nydia, then this is what I need. If not, fine. I'll find the church on my own." She turned and headed through the stacks.

"Wait," Nydia said.

Sierra stopped.

"You're a shadowshaper, aren't you?"

She nodded. She was more than that, but the title of Lucera didn't feel real to Sierra yet; it was still some strange inheritance she couldn't fully grasp.

"You know shadowshaping won't work on the Sorrows? Your spirits won't even go near them probably, especially when they're on their home turf. All their power is centered in that shrine behind the church."

"Does this mean you'll help me?"

"It means I want you to know what you're getting into. You're still gonna go after them, even though your powers will be useless?"

"I don't have a choice, Nydia. The Sorrows will know where Wick is, how to find him — and Robbie. I've already seen people I love turned into horrible monsters. I'm not losing Robbie too."

Nydia raised an eyebrow again. "You've seen the Sorrows already, haven't you?"

Sierra smiled. "I'll tell you about it on the way."

They walked quickly through the corridors of books. "The church is at the top of Manhattan," Nydia said. "You know anyone that has a car and can drive fast?"

Sierra grinned. "Do I ever."

THIRTY-SIX

Neville's Cadillac Seville screeched to a halt outside an old iron fence on a deserted street.

Nydia exhaled loudly in the backseat. "Jesus."

Sierra caught her eye in the rearview. "You alright?"

"I will be." She patted Uncle Neville's shoulder with a shaking hand. "It's really nice to meet you, sir. You drive like a wild maniac, and I respect that."

"The pleasure is all mine," Neville said.

They were at the highest point of Manhattan, not far from the river, in a little corner tucked away behind the West Side Highway. Beyond the fence, a dirt trail led into the darkness. A heavy chain hugged the two elaborately crafted sides of the gate together.

"How we gonna get through that chain?" Sierra said.

Neville smirked. "Oh, I'll handle that."

"What if a guard comes?"

"Then I'll handle that too."

"Sierra," Nydia said. "I like your godfather. Let's do this."

Neville retrieved an ax with a long wooden handle from

the trunk, and Nydia and Sierra watched as he demolished the chain with five swift chops. The gate swung open with a high-pitched whine. "Ladies," Neville said, bowing slightly. "I would join you in there, but I have a feeling I'll be more use keeping things on the level out here. I'm no good with the kind of baddies y'all prolly abouta deal with."

"You . . . know?" Sierra stammered.

Neville winked. "Don't forget that your grandpa and I were good friends back in the day."

"You're not a shadowshaper, are you?"

"Nah. I had his back through some bad situations, though. I seen enough to know what's what when there's some woo-woo mess goin' down. I'll stick to the human side of being a badass, thank you very much."

"Wow," Sierra said.

"Oh, and here." He handed her the ax. "Take this."

"Uncle Neville, I really don't think . . ."

"I know, but take it anyway. You don't know what you gonna find in there, and *I'll* feel better if you're armed."

"Won't you —?"

"Don't you worry about Uncle Neville." He dapped Sierra, blew a kiss at Nydia, and then posted up by the gate.

Sierra looked at Nydia. "You ready?"

"Is your godfather married?"

"Nydia! Focus! We doin' this or what?"

"Yes! I'm here."

Sierra heaved the ax onto her shoulder and they started

up the path into the shadows. "What's your plan?" Nydia asked.

"Plan?"

"Sierra. You asked me to help you reach out to some of the most corrupt, powerful phantoms in the known universe. I brought you here, to their nasty lair, because I like you and I want you to nail Wick for what he's done to your family. You do have a plan, don't you?"

"Just show me where they are," Sierra said. "I'll do the rest." She hoped she sounded more confident than she felt.

Nydia shook her head. "Come on."

Up ahead, a building towered over them. Steeples stretched up to the moonlit night, and Sierra could make out the gnarly silhouettes of gargoyles jutting out to either side.

"The place was a convent way back when," Nydia said. "Then it was a mental hospital for a hot second in the seventies, then a crack house. Now it's abandoned. City doesn't know what to do with the property, I guess."

"Charming."

"Everything in my research points to this spot as the Sorrows' nesting ground and center of power."

They reached the top of the hill. Graffiti covered the elaborate wooden doorway of the old cathedral. The statues on either side had their faces scratched off and hands removed. A mountain of trash lay scattered along the steps.

"C'mon," Nydia said. "I think the churchyard is around back."

They followed a smaller dirt path around the side of the chapel, past the charred remains of a motorcycle.

"How do you even research something like that?" Sierra asked. "Where an ancient gang of spirits hangs out, I mean."

"A lot of it's oral histories, the ones most scholars ignore. Tying together urban lore, gossip around the way, and historical documents. A rumor about hauntings here, a scrap of info about some ancient cursed family there. That kinda thing."

"Sounds kinda awe —"

Sierra stopped in her tracks. Up ahead, the path led to a foot-high stone wall. Beyond it, drooping willow trees presided like mourning gods over a tiny churchyard. Golden light poured out of a circle of pine trees at the far end. "Whoa," she said.

Nydia blinked. "I didn't think . . . I . . . wow."

The golden haze illuminated the edges of the willows and a decapitated angel statue. It sent long, trembling shadows reaching toward Sierra and Nydia. A few moments passed.

"You ready?" Nydia whispered.

Sierra nodded.

"Let's do this, then."

"No," Sierra said. "I gotta . . . I gotta handle this on my own."

"Sierra . . ."

"I know. I know you think I'm crazy, I know it's suicide. I get it. But you gotta let me do this my way, Nydia. You brought me this far, and I appreciate it, believe me I do. But I don't even know you that well. I can't go getting you killed too."

Nydia shook her head. "I don't like it, Sierra. I know they always say that kinda crap in movies and it all works out okay, but this isn't that. You can't do this alone."

"I know," Sierra said. "And I'm not alone." She hugged Nydia, turned, and walked down the dirt path toward the cemetery.

The shadows rose up on either side of her. They pulsed with the same gentle light she'd seen in Coney Island as they glided with long, magnificent strides. She knew they wouldn't be with her all the way, but just their presence on the short walk to the churchyard made Sierra feel like she was protected.

Sierra walked through a rickety gate and into the church-yard. The shadows hesitated, then breached the low stone wall as one.

The trio of towering shrouds emerged from the pines. Sierra felt the heat of their golden glare on her face. In the grove behind them, three marble statues of women stood beneath the shadowy pines, their hands raised and touch-ing, their legs extended as if frozen in mid-dance to some long-lost music.

The shadows fell into a line on either side of Sierra. She took a breath, banished the tremble from her voice, and spoke: "I am Sierra Santiago, shadowshaper."

For a few seconds, all she heard was the warm night wind shushing through the willows. Then the three Sorrows swept forward around her. The shadows tensed but Sierra waved them back. The Sorrows spun in a slow circle, faces concealed beneath their drooping hoods, their glowing robes swaying slightly in the breeze.

She is the child from the brotherhood of shadows, ay? The whisper cut through her mind. It was sharp and gravelly.

Ay, but is she ready? said another.

Pssshhh, hissed the third, *this is no child, sistren, this is Lucera. She has transformed.*

At last!

Ay, but is she ready?

She will be soon.

"Enough!" Sierra yelled. "I've come for information, not to be glared at and spoken about like I'm not even here. Tell me where Jonathan Wick is."

The Sorrows stopped spinning and the three voices spoke as one: *He has been watching all along.*

Sierra rolled her eyes. "What does that mean?"

He has been watching all along.

"I don't have time for these riddles, y'all. Just tell me where he is, how I can destroy him."

Wick cannot be brought down. He is too powerful now.

"No!" Sierra said. "I don't believe you."

We are no longer concerned with Wick. He has failed us.

"Meanwhile, he'll destroy everything I love."

No concern of ours.

Sierra stomped her foot. "You made him what he is! You bear the responsibility."

It is you we are concerned with now.

"What? Why?"

One of the Sorrows stepped forward. *Our destinies are entwined, Lucera. Our futures and pasts. We will soon be one, as we have always been, and on that day, the Sisterhood of Sorrows will attain its ultimate power. It has been prophesied, child. We strengthened Wick so that he could infiltrate your shadow fellowship and take on the role of the Lucera.*

Or Lucero, in his case, one of the other Sorrows added.

He seemed worthy of such a task. But to complete it, he had to track down the current holder of that position, which he failed to do, as you know. We gave him a year. The year has run out. Instead of finding Lucera, Wick became drunk with the power of binding magic. His ego was so wounded when the shadowshapers didn't embrace him as their leader, his vision became clouded. He began destroying them in the quest to save their legacy. And still he failed.

Another Sorrow swept forward, this one closer. Sierra took a step back.

You, on the other hand, found Lucera, and we see she has passed on her power to you, child. You are Lucera now, Lucera is you. And Lucera and the Sorrows are destined to become one. Your grandmother was of an archaic generation, not so open-minded as you are, Sierra Santiago.

"It'll never happen," Sierra said.

We simply ask that you lis —

"No," Sierra said. "I'll never be one of you. If you won't help me, back off and I'll . . ."

The first shroud that had spoken lurched toward her. Sierra leapt back. *Who is this fool who thinks she can address the Sisterhood of Sorrows with such audacity?* The Sorrow's shrill voice cut like a rusty knife.

Back, Septima! another voice howled. *Do not touch her. The child is stained.*

"Stained? What are you — is that why you send others to do your dirty work for you? You won't touch us normal people?"

You are impure, the three voices whispered together. *Just like your grandmother. We thought if you were willing to hear us out, to purify yourself, you could one day be amongst us.*

Sierra shook her head. "Never."

And in exchange, we would give you the information you desire.

"You send this madman to destroy my family, my friends, and then you demand I join your stupid club or you won't tell me where Wick is?"

The Sorrows stood perfectly still, staring at her.

"Go to hell," Sierra said. "I'll find Wick myself." She turned and stomped out of the churchyard, shadows swarming in her wake.

"What happened?" Nydia asked.

"They said he's been watching all along," Sierra said. "That's all they'd tell me."

"So he's got a camera on you? He's got a spy, what?"

Sierra shook her head. "I don't know. But I'm done with this crap. Give me the ax."

"What? Sierra, you can't . . ."

Sierra took the ax from Nydia and marched back down the path into the churchyard. The shadows swooped along with her and fell into formation at the gate.

You have returned, Little Lucera! the Sorrows said.

Sierra stormed directly into their midst, watching with satisfaction as they swerved out of her way.

Where are you going, Little Lucera?

She made a beeline for the pine grove.

Little Lucera! the Sorrows howled. *Do not go in there!*

"No more riddles!" Sierra shouted. She swung the ax in a wide arc and smashed it against the first dancing-woman statue. It clanged against the marble with a satisfying crack, carving a chunk out of the figure's swirling robe.

Lucera! The Sorrows billowed around her. *Stop this!*

She's mad!

Do not corrupt the Queen Phantoms with your filth!

"Where is Wick?" She swung again, taking a sizable chunk of the next statue's hand.

Stop this!

"No" — Sierra raised the ax over her head — "more" —

she brought it down directly on the third statue's foot, shattering it — "riddles!"

The Tower! the Sorrows yelled as one. *The Tower above the lot of trash that your friends recline within. The greedy professor makes his domain in the Tower.*

Sierra lowered the ax. He really had been watching all along. Biding his time. Listening. She shuddered.

There he has brought the young shadowshaper, there he will raise his army of throng haints. For he is a man of observation, but his own creations fail to take. What's more, the use of corpses has proven problematic for him, as you have seen. The decaying human form cannot sustain the power of spirit for long. You are so fragile, children of blood and bone. The boy shadowshaper will provide the forms for the throng haint army with his painting.

Sierra turned and headed back out of the churchyard.

But you will be destroyed there, Little Lucera. One of the Sorrows floated after her as the other two tended to their damaged shrine. *You have been warned. The greedy professor will not be toppled. And his army will not be stopped. Your family will be destroyed. And even if you live, Sierra Santiago, ruler of the shadowshapers, what you have done here tonight will not be forgotten.*

Sierra swung around suddenly and reached for the Sorrow. It darted out of the way, hissing. "That's what I thought," Sierra said. "Now scatter. I've gotten all I need from you."

THIRTY-SEVEN

"This is it." Sierra shuddered as she gazed up at the Tower. It gave her chills, thinking that Wick had been up there all along, was probably up there now, watching her every move. Neville had dropped her and Nydia off and then blasted away to Sierra's house, promising to keep everyone safe inside. Somewhere far away, police sirens wailed into the night. A stray cat trotted away from a torn-open trash bag, but otherwise the street was empty.

The blue construction tarps on the Tower flapped angrily against its concrete shell. The windows on the ground level were boarded up, but a few random lights blinked on and off in its uppermost floors. Robbie had to be up there somewhere. He had to be.

"So we gonna . . ." Nydia started.

"Go up there and whup some —"

"Sierra . . ."

"Psssst!"

Sierra nearly jumped out of her skin with fright. "What the . . . ?"

"It's Bennie!" She stepped out of the shadows, followed by Juan and Tee.

"You guys!" Sierra almost yelled. "What are you doing here? You can't —"

"Sierra," Bennie said. "We got your text."

"But that was to warn you guys to stay away from the Tower, not to —"

"Don't be an ass. You wanna die alone? That's not how we roll."

"But I can't. I don't know what's gonna happen in there. I don't wanna get you involved."

"It's a little late for that," Tee said, smiling. "Anyway, we brought weapons." She held up a heavy garden shovel and passed Sierra a baseball bat. "Who's the hottie?"

"Who? Oh . . ." Sierra realized Nydia was still standing beside her. "This is Nydia Ochoa, everyone. She's a librarian at Columbia and she's been helping me out with all this. She's good people."

"Hey, guys." Nydia waved and forced a smile.

Juan snapped the broomstick he'd brought over his knee and handed half to Nydia. "Here you go, miss."

"Uh, thanks," Nydia said.

Tee shoulder-punched Juan. "Hands off, little man. She's mine."

"You got a girl," Juan hissed.

"Listen," Nydia said to the group. "I know the situation's

dire, but y'all sure you wanna go up in there now? Maybe we gather our strength, head in tomorrow?"

Tee, Bennie, and Juan turned to Sierra. She looked up at the Tower. If Wick really was putting throng haints into Robbie's paintings like the Sorrows said, he would surely send them after Sierra and her family first. There was no tomorrow to wait for.

She started walking toward the Tower.

"You don't even wanna wait a day?" Nydia called. "Maybe figure out your powers a little more?"

Sierra looked back. Tee, Bennie, and Juan were crossing the street toward her, each carrying something heavy and wearing their toughest frowns. Nydia looked around and then followed behind them. Sierra's hands wouldn't stop trembling and her mind kept dreaming up gruesome ways to die. But her friends were with her. She would not die alone, and she wouldn't live her life having abandoned the one boy she'd ever really cared about to the mercy of some madman.

Sierra turned back to the Tower, put her hand on the brand-new front door, and pushed it open.

It shouldn't be this easy, she thought, just before all the lights in the building flickered out.

"Good thing we brought flashlights," Juan said jauntily as they stumbled inside.

"I don't like this at all," Nydia muttered.

They took a few steps in, beams of light darting across the vast entrance space, and then just like that, the overheads flickered back to life.

"See?" Juan said. "Not so bad after all."

Sierra was not convinced. They stood in a huge concrete hall. Plastic shrouds hung from various scaffoldings. Exposed pipes crisscrossed the high ceilings, snaking in and out of some fleshy-looking gooey substance. The air reeked of paint and sawdust.

But there was something else. A heaviness hung all around them, a staticky, unpleasant feeling that seemed to coat the inside of Sierra's lungs every time she breathed in. No tall shadows awaited them. "You don't see any spirits?" she whispered to Juan.

He shook his head. "Just abandoned high-rise creepiness. No ghosts. Yet."

Nydia stepped up beside them. "You have a plan, Sierra?"

"I was thinking that we could spli —"

"We're not splitting up," Bennie whispered hoarsely.

The overheads fizzled out again. Someone said "Crap," and the flashlights clicked back on.

Sierra sighed. "If we're in smaller groups, I figured we could —"

"No!" Bennie said. "Come up with a better plan. If we get separated and then they attack one group, how's the other gonna know? And we don't even know what we're dealing with."

"Look," Juan said, "Bennie has a point, but . . ."

The lights flicked on again. Everyone moaned and put away the flashlights.

"You guys hear that noise?" Juan said.

Sierra slapped her brother's arm. "Juan, this is no time for your jokes."

He frowned. "I'm not kidding."

"I heard something," Tee said. "But you were talking so I couldn't really make it out."

"Like a muffled scream?" Nydia said.

"Ugh," Bennie groaned. "Stop it, you guys, that's too creepy."

Juan sighed. "Maybe."

"C'mon," Sierra said, starting toward the far wall. "I think there's a stairway over there."

They crept toward the open metal stairs, stopping only once when Juan accidentally kicked a paint scraper across the floor. He shrugged off their four glaring faces.

The heaviness in the air seemed to increase as they got closer to the stairs. Sierra felt as though it was suffocating her, a tension eating away at her very cells. She rubbed her eyes, tried to take a deep breath but coughed instead, and then started toward the second floor. Her feet made soft clangs on each stair, and soon the answering clangs of her friends' footfalls rose behind her.

"They're close," Juan said when they were halfway up.

Sierra tightened her grip on the metal bat and went up

the last few steps to the second floor. Most of the windows didn't have glass, allowing a cool night breeze to swish across the room. The hanging plastic drapes swayed and dragged against the dirty floor, sending up gravelly whispers. Juan followed close behind her.

The first corpuscule stood perfectly still, partly concealed by a drape, its gaze fixed straight ahead. Sierra caught her breath, raised the bat up, and waited. The corpuscule didn't move. She tried to make out its face, see if she could recognize it as one of the shadowshapers from the photo, but it was too dark. Sierra heard her friends reach the landing and freeze as they noticed it. A flicker of motion caught her eye and she swung around to see another corpuscule stand up behind a shroud a few feet away. Beside it, another one rose.

Juan trembled next to her. She could feel the rage and terror build inside him as clearly as if it were her own. He let out a scream and ran forward, swinging his broomstick just as the three corpuscules burst toward them. Tee stood beside Sierra for a moment, panting, and then followed Juan. Sierra tightened her grip on the bat and stepped toward one of the charging corpses. She wound up and swung, catching the thing under its arm. The corpuscule grabbed the bat and yanked it hard, pulling Sierra off balance. She screamed, gripping the handle harder even as she stumbled, vaguely aware that keeping the weapon was her only hope for staying alive. She wrenched the bat out of the thing's grip, planted a foot behind her, and swung hard as it barreled toward her again.

Something solid cracked and reverberated down the metal bat shaft and through her arms. For a terrible second, Sierra had no idea what was happening. She heard her friends scream, the sounds of scuffling around her. Dust and gray particles exploded in what seemed like slow motion toward the ceiling, and something slapped against her face. She stepped back and saw the corpuscule slump to his knees and then collapse into a heap. His face was crushed in, and a huge area of dried flesh was missing entirely from just above his left eye.

Sierra wiped dry dead-guy head off her face. She steadied herself and turned toward her friends just in time to see another corpuscule running toward her. It was Bellamy Grey, or had once been — one of the newly smudged shadowshapers in the picture. It closed on her too quickly for her to get a good swing, so she threw her body into its charge.

The corpuscule's icky cold fists rained down on her back as they both plummeted to the ground. All was blistering chaos for a second; Sierra felt a painful blow smack across her face and almost blacked out. Tee was screaming something in her ear. The corpuscule writhed beneath her, swung its torso up hard and threw her off, then was on top of her, its deathly hands grabbing her wrists, holding her down as his weight crushed the air out of her lungs. A flush of panic swept up Sierra's airway and took over her thoughts. This was it. They had tried and failed. She struggled, but each breath brought more of that heaviness inside her, pulled her down toward some dizzy oblivion. It was over.

And then it wasn't. Hands snaked around the corpuscule —
brown hands. Tee's hands. Sierra gasped for air. The thing
tried to shrug Tee off it, but she wouldn't budge. Then more
hands appeared: Bennie's and Nydia's, Sierra thought. Her
wrists suddenly free, she shoved her thumbs into the corpuscule's eyes and pushed. There was a spirit in there — some
poor enslaved thing that Wick had summoned for the sole
purpose of doing Sierra harm. It wasn't the human being
whose dead face stared emptily back at her. It was something
else. She pushed harder and felt the dried-up, dull flesh give
beneath her thumbs, the eyes squish into nothingness.

Then it was gone. Sierra sat up, gasping for air. A few
feet from her, the corpuscule staggered backward, flailing
its long arms. Nydia stepped forward, swung her shovel
hard, and caught it smack in the chest with a dull thud. The
thing toppled backward, sliding over the side of the stairwell
and landing a few seconds later with a terrible, wet crunch.
Nydia peered gingerly down to the first floor and then made
a "done-deal" sweep of her hands to the others.

Sierra stood, brushing the ickiness off her, and walked
unevenly toward Tee and Bennie. "Where's Juan?"

Bennie nodded toward one of the plastic shrouds. Sierra
stumbled toward it, trying to ignore the sickening thuds that
were coming from the other side. Juan stood over a crumpled corpuscule. He was panting; sweat poured down him.
A nasty black-and-blue swelled along his right cheek.

"Juan."

He shut his eyes, and tears streamed from them.

"What is it, man?"

"I knew him," Juan whispered. "His name was Arturo. He was . . . I met him when I was a kid."

Sierra put her hand on Juan's trembling shoulder. "It's not him anymore, Juan. It was something else. And it's done."

He lowered the bat and turned his tearstained face to Sierra. "I destroyed him."

"No. You destroyed the body. His spirit's long gone. You know that. Come on, Juan." She put her arm around his shoulders. "We gotta keep moving."

Juan nodded and allowed Sierra to usher him back toward the others.

"Everyone pretty much alright?" Nydia asked when Sierra and Juan rejoined the group.

"Cuts and bruises," Tee said. "Nothing broken."

Bennie nodded. "Same." But her eyes were wide and watery.

"It's not too late to turn back," Nydia said. "It's not gonna get any easier, I suspect."

Bennie shook her head. "No turning back. You okay, Sierra?"

"Sore as hell, but yeah."

"I'm fine," Juan put in before anyone could ask him.

"Think there's more of 'em?" Bennie asked.

"I don't doubt it," Nydia said.

But it wasn't the corpuscules Sierra was worried about.

THIRTY-EIGHT

They made their way upward in silence. Once Juan stopped them, sent an uneasy glare across the empty floor, and then grudgingly motioned to keep moving. Sierra felt like her heart had snuck up to her brain so it could blast that pounding pulse directly into her eardrums. Every sliding shadow, each creak and crack, sent her mind spinning off into a thousand horrible visions. She struggled to stay focused and push forward, but the culminating weight of everything that had happened that week wouldn't leave her alone.

Sierra felt a distant flurry of motion erupt somewhere nearby. The air suddenly felt thick around her. It was a gathering: the ferocious swell of a wave before it breaks.

"There's something . . ." she said as they crept up the stairs. ". . . Something . . . happening." Everyone froze. "I don't know . . . what." Her face was scrunched in concentration. She turned her head slowly from side to side, her eyes closed. "You feel it, guys?"

Juan nodded. "I can't describe it, though. Like nothing I've ever sensed before."

"Something coming?" Bennie asked.

"Yes. But . . . not for us," Sierra said. "Just coming. Many, many things."

"Hundreds," Juan added. "Thousands, maybe."

"Is whatever's coming dusty and white?" Tee said from the top of the stairs. "Cuz something just moved up here, and that's all I could make out."

Sierra rushed up the rest of the steps and peered out onto the third floor. "Where?"

"It slid down that wall," Tee said, nodding to the far end of the room.

The construction had come a little further along on this floor; half-finished plaster dividers rose up between the metal beams, and electrical wiring snaked alongside the ceiling pipes. But nothing, as far as Sierra could see, was moving. "You sure?"

Bennie was beside them now, squinting into the dimness. "I don't see nothing."

"I'm telling you guys," Tee said. "It was about the size of a person. It slid down the far wall and was gone. A dusty cloud of white."

Chalk. Could it be that Robbie had escaped somehow and sent a spirit to help them? The thought gave Sierra a little surge of hope, and she stepped out onto the floor.

Bennie reached for her. "Sierra . . ."

Whatever she was going to say, the words stopped short in her mouth. A white dusty figure slithered across the floor toward them. It was blurry — the chalk was heavier in some parts and almost nonexistent in others — but Sierra thought she could make out a human form to it.

Just before it reached them, the shape vanished completely. And then all Sierra saw was dull whiteness — a billowing cloud that resolved into a screaming face. *Robbie's* screaming face. His mouth opened wide; his eyes were two empty sockets, surrounded by swirling chalk. For a terrible moment, the phantom hung in the air, a reverse shadow, long, dusty fingers reaching out toward Sierra.

And then it pounced.

Sierra stumbled backward, swatting blindly at the air. She felt like someone had splashed boiling water across her face, like a thousand tiny knives were stabbing into her body. People around her yelled. Then hands were on her, all over her; she prayed they were friendly hands because she still couldn't open her eyes or even think straight through the pain. Someone swatted at her, then more people. They brushed frantically at her face, her clothes. She felt them lower her to the ground, and she realized she was screaming. She was screaming as hard as she could.

The hands kept brushing against her body, and gradually the vicious stabbing feeling gave way to a harsh, full-body sting. Well, it wasn't getting worse, anyway, and that was something. She squinted her eyes open. Tee, Nydia, Bennie, and Juan were staring down at her with their faces creased with terror.

"What . . . happened?" Her face throbbed like she'd just gotten the worst sunburn of her life.

"That thing . . ." Bennie said, glancing around nervously.

"It was Robbie . . ." Sierra gasped, the horrible memory of his ghostly face jumping back at her. "It was . . . ugh."

"What do you mean?" Nydia said. She reached down and helped Sierra stand.

"I mean the chalk phantom . . . It . . . It had Robbie's face. He was . . . It was screaming. Where'd it go?"

"We brushed the chalk dust off you, and it just dispersed into the air," Juan said. "You okay?"

Sierra scowled. "Kinda." She looked at Juan. "Does that mean . . . he's . . . ?"

He shook his head. "Not necessarily. But it's not good."

"Guys," Tee said. "There's more coming."

Everyone spun around. Four — no, *five* chalk-dust phantoms slid down the far wall and onto the floor. They all looked just like the first one: Robbie's face stretched into that silent scream.

Nydia turned toward the stairwell. "Run!"

Sierra threw her back against a wooden crate and slid to the ground. She'd made it to the fourth floor, the chalk-dust phantoms close on her trail. She didn't know if it was from fear or exhaustion, but she could barely breathe. Something metallic clinked a few feet to her left, and she jumped.

A minute of silence passed, during which Sierra struggled to slow her breathing, ease her heaving chest. Suddenly, she heard a desperate scramble of feet; someone screamed — was it Bennie? Tee? And then nothing. Her breath came heavy again, like invisible hands were squeezing her lungs closed from the inside. *Calm yourself, damn it!* She closed her eyes, saw only flickering chalk-dust phantoms, and opened them again. *You're useless when you're frantic.*

If only she could catch her breath for a second and concentrate on her shadowshaper magic. It was there somewhere, churning inside her, a weapon she didn't even fully understand. Sierra shuddered. Anyway, she hadn't seen a single shadow spirit since they'd entered the Tower, and what good were her 'shaping skills with nothing to 'shape? She hated that everyone had been separated. That for all she knew, her friends were already dead, or worse. That it was all her fault. She didn't have the metal bat anymore, and even if she did, what good would it do against a floating pile of dust?

Something clattered to the ground on the other side of the room. If she yelled out, those ghouls would know exactly where she was. If she stayed still, they'd find her anyway. And surely they were coming.

Ever so carefully, Sierra wrapped her fingers around a tarp that was slung over the crate beside her and pulled it to herself. She would run. There was no other choice. Make for the next floor up and hide again. Keep going till she found Robbie or . . .

She would count down to zero and then go. The thick tarp wasn't much, but at least it would give her something to block the chalk-dust phantoms with if they caught her.

Four. She would beeline for the stairwell.

Three. She was a good runner. She could make it.

Two. She wanted her breath to slow down, but it only got faster and faster.

One . . .

She put one hand on the ground, clutched the tarp against her chest, and shot sprinter-style across the floor. She didn't have to turn around to know the phantoms were there; a sudden flurry of movement erupted in the room all around her.

"Sierra, go! They're coming!" It was Bennie. Sierra almost burst into tears knowing that her best friend was still alive. Of course, her shout meant that Bennie had given up her hiding place to distract the phantoms. Sierra strengthened her resolve, willed her legs to stop feeling so gooey, and rushed toward the stairs.

Then something — a sixth sense? the shadowshaper magic kicking in? — *something* told her to turn around. A chalk-dust phantom was almost on her, its long dusty arms out. Sierra swung the tarp at it as hard as she could just as the thing dove at her. The tarp slowed as if it was wrapping around some vague shape for just a moment, and then it pushed through, scattering the dust into oblivion.

Sierra stood in total disbelief. Was that simple? "Bennie!" she yelled, snapping back into emergency mode.

"Use a tarp! Anything that'll scatter the particles!" She gazed out into the dim room, hoping to catch sight of her friend, but nothing moved. Had the phantoms gotten her?

Chalk-dust phantoms flitted along the floor toward her. Four . . . five . . . six of them. She wound the tarp behind her head, trying to calculate how many she could take out with one swipe. Her legs had stopped trembling. She had, at least, figured out some way to fight them. And fight she would.

"Sierra, go find Robbie!" Juan shouted from somewhere across the room. Two of the phantoms spun off toward his voice. "We'll get these chalk bastards!"

"Hey!" Bennie yelled at the phantoms, stepping out into the center of the room with a plastic sheet wound up like a whip. "Come on, suckas; I'm right here!" Two more phantoms reversed course to take her challenge.

Sierra was speechless for a second, then the two remaining phantoms sprung up toward her. She swung, scattering one of them into nothingness and clipping the other.

Bennie swung at her pair, disintegrating both with one slash. "Sierra, go!" she yelled.

The damaged chalk phantom had collapsed to the ground in a muddled heap and was crawling forward like an injured dog. Sierra stepped backward toward the stairwell. Three more phantoms slid down the walls and onto the floor. She had to trust that Juan and Bennie could handle them. She turned and sprinted up the steps.

THIRTY-NINE

It was there, waiting for her. She felt it as soon as she stepped onto the fifth floor, and the suddenness of it almost knocked her over. The throng haint's foulness seeped into her mouth like the aftertaste of sour milk.

No. Sierra shook her head, steadied her knees. She wouldn't be overwhelmed by fear alone. Not by that acrid taste, not by the dread of facing the thing that had pursued her through Flatbush and down the shore at Coney Island. She would not succumb. She took a few wobbly steps forward, then firmed up her stride.

On the far wall of the fifth floor, a metal staircase led up to the roof. The place was empty except for some crates tucked in the corners and a floor-to-ceiling section of wall stretching ten feet along the center of the room. She heard a faint shuffling noise and some scratches. Something was on the other side of that wall.

Could be anything, she thought as she crept toward it. Could be Robbie. Could be the throng haint. Or more of the chalk phantoms. Or something worse — whatever tidal wave of spirits she'd felt coming. Sierra was too exhausted and emotional to bother with all the terrible possibilities. She reached the wall and peered around to the other side of it.

Robbie stood there, a paintbrush in his trembling hand, his eyes open wide. Then they got wider. "Sierra?"

The paintbrush fell to the floor. He crossed the room with a long stride and wrapped around her, hugged her tighter than she'd ever been hugged. Sierra tried to catch her breath. "Robbie," she said. She held him at arm's length and inspected his face. His nose was broken. Dried blood had caked around one nostril and a fine layer of white chalk covered his face and clothes. He looked exhausted and terrified but otherwise okay.

She pulled him to her, found his lips, and devoured them — a messy kiss, tasting of chalk, but it felt so good! He was alive! She kissed him over and over, realized there were tears coming down her face and wiped them away, kissed him again.

"You're not dead," she whispered.

He shook his head.

"And you saved my life. Juan's life, back on the boardwalk."

A noncommittal shrug.

"Your tats, Robbie." She lifted his arm and saw only faded ghosts of the glorious art that had once been there. "No!"

"It's okay." He smiled weakly. "They'll come back. Just not yet."

"What happened to you?"

He shook again. "I can't . . . It's horrible, Sierra. You gotta get outta here before Wick comes back."

"I'm taking you with me."

"No!"

"Whatdyou mean . . . ?"

"If I'm gone, Sierra, he'll kill all of us. He'll kill you for sure. He's been talking about it all night. Believe me! He's the one that made me do all of this." Robbie gestured to the walls.

Sierra's mouth fell open. She hadn't even noticed the wall in her excitement at finding Robbie. Tall, hideous creatures lurked in the still-wet paint behind him. Each painted demon had gangly arms with razor-sharp nails drooping down from hunched shoulders. Their faces were frozen into malicious grins and screams.

Sierra felt a chill just looking at them. "He wanted new vessels for the throng haints because the human corpses are decaying."

Robbie nodded.

"What happened, man?"

"I woke up covered head to toe in chalk." He paused, gulped back a sob. "Wick was standing in that corner, talking to himself. 'It's not enough,' he kept saying. 'It's just not enough.' I would've fought him, but I wanted to get a sense of what was going on before I tried to get away. When he noticed I was awake, he lifted me up and threw me into the wall. He did it to make a print of my chalk-covered face — something he could 'shape a spirit into and send against you. I blacked out after the third or fourth time he threw me. Woke up with the worst headache ever, bleeding, and he was still there, muttering to himself."

"Oh, Robbie . . ." Sierra reached out to him, but he stepped back.

"No, let me just . . . explain. He brought me these paints and told me what to make. Said he'd kill you and me and both our families if I didn't do what he said. And I knew he knew how to get at you. He knew your name, your address, everything. Sierra, he knows *everything*!" Robbie had worked himself up into a frenzy, pacing back and forth beneath his angry demon paintings. "I was gonna try to 'shape a spirit into one of these but there were none around."

Sierra tried to steady her voice. "Robbie, he's going to kill us all anyway. Don't you see? We're in his way. First, he just wanted to fill the gap Lucera left behind, but now he's going after shadowshapers. All of us. Soon as he gets what he wants out of you, he'll kill you too."

"Sierra, we can't . . ."

Sierra's voice went cold. "Where is he?"

"He went to the roof," Robbie said. "He said he's . . . ugh . . . he's building the throng haints."

"Come on." They walked to the stairwell in the corner of the room and crept up it. The door at the top was ajar, a sliver of night sky visible on the other side. Sierra peeked through.

Wick stood at the far end of the roof, his arms raised toward the sky. He was in a T-shirt and jeans, like any random dude. Behind him, Manny's poor gray body stood, the throng haint within it heaving ragged breaths that burned through Sierra's mind.

"It's time," Wick called out. "Come to me, spirits! Tonight we save the shadowshapers and begin anew."

The air thickened, like they were in a big crowd. "You feel it?" Sierra whispered.

Robbie nodded. "It's been coming and going all night. I'd feel it, then it'd be gone. Now it's back, but even louder than ever. If you can call it loud."

The feeling seemed to be gathering toward a climax of some kind, a rush of movement around them so fierce it was almost deafening.

"What is it?"

"Spirits," Robbie said. "Lots of them."

"Why?"

"I don't . . ."

"They're here." Sierra gazed at the night sky above the Tower.

Hundreds and hundreds of souls filled the air. They stormed across the rooftop in long, shadowy strides, slender arms dangling at their sides. Some glided up through the floor, puffy dark clouds churning with faces and stories from their lives. Others flitted across the sky like autumn leaves.

"I've never . . ." Sierra started.

Robbie shook his head.

"So many!"

He nodded.

". . . Beautiful! . . ."

Another nod.

Wick was spinning in a slow circle, arms outstretched. "This is more than I requested," he said. "I see some of you have come to bear witness. Very well." Shadows were accumulating on his arms as he spun. They reached out desperately, trying to wrench themselves away from him, but it was no use.

Binding magic, Sierra thought. The power the Sorrows had given Wick allowed him to hold spirits even against their will.

Soon two hulking masses of spirit stood on either side of Wick. The anthropologist closed his eyes, muttering under his breath. He clenched his fists as the spirit masses congealed and then took shape. The newly formed throng haints stretched long, spiny arms to either side and roared. Sierra watched in horror as mouths opened along their shadowy flesh, gnashing and churning in silent protest of their sudden enslavement.

Wick spun again, more shadows gathering along his

arms. Around them, the air grew thicker with the billowing outrage of the spirits. It felt like a thunderstorm about to break. "Come, my children," Wick said when two more throng haints stood heaving beside him. "Let us place you in your brand-new vessels."

They turned toward the door, Wick, Manny, and the four still-shadowy throng haints. Sierra and Robbie crept back downstairs and dashed to hide behind the crates at the far edge of the room.

FORTY

A fierce murmur swam through the remaining crowd of spirits as they flooded onto the fifth floor ahead of Wick and his throng haints. Sierra felt them bristling like a pack of feral dogs. Wick strode across the room, swatting away shadows as they dove around him. *"Come to the crossroads, to the crossroads come,"* he muttered. *"Where the powers converge and become one."* He reached Robbie's first painted demon, placed one hand against it, and turned to one of the new throng haints. "It is time."

A throng haint stepped up, momentarily engulfing Wick, and then disappeared. Robbie's demon writhed to life, snarled, and hurtled out of the wall. It became three-dimensional, a towering monster glistening with fresh paint, long arms stretched out in front of it as it raced back and forth.

"You know what to do," Wick said.

The demon haint bellowed and then rushed down the stairs and out of sight.

"They're going for our people," Robbie whispered.

The throng haint in Manny's body stepped up to the wall. Sierra almost screamed as the hulking shadow emerged from Manny's open mouth. His corpse collapsed in a heap and the haint vanished into another of Robbie's demon paintings, which burst to life. It ducked quickly into the dark recesses of the room and disappeared.

Sierra felt strangely calm, as if her fierce warrior of a grandma was right there beside her. "Robbie," she said quietly. He looked up. "Lucera has passed on the legacy." It felt good to say it, felt true. She spoke slowly, feeling out each word as it came. "I'm the new Lucera." Robbie nodded. His face changed from shocked to slightly smitten. "We can stop this. We have to. You have chalk?"

"Always." He produced a stick from his jacket, and she took it from him. "But a chalk spirit could never stand up to one of those demon haints, Sierra."

"Hopefully it won't have to for very long. I just need a distraction so we can make it to that window." Sierra nodded to the wall across from them. She'd been thinking it through as the spirits swarmed in: Their mural on the outside of the Tower — the dragon and the elegant, guitar-playing skeleton — reached all the way to the fifth floor. It wasn't fully done, but hopefully close enough to work. If Robbie could make it to that window and have a few seconds of safety to touch the mural, he could ignite the whole thing with spirit. It was a long shot, but at least they'd have a chance and some backup.

Sierra used the chalk to scribble two women with machetes and long capes. She stood over one, raised her left arm, and touched her right hand to the picture. Nothing happened. The spirits were still all around them, glaring toward Wick and his burgeoning army. "C'mon," Sierra whispered. A tremble of fear began gathering in her stomach. "C'mon." She took a deep breath, tried to picture a spirit moving through her, exhaled, and slapped her hand onto the chalk drawing.

She felt it instantly — the sudden rush of coolness flooding through her veins. For a second she thought she might pass out, but then it was gone as quickly as it'd come, and the chalk warrior shivered to life and took off across the floor.

"You did it!" Robbie hissed.

Sierra smiled. She was about to 'shape the other warrior when one of the towering throng haints came slouching toward them.

Sierra steadied herself. That familiar holy terror tore through her blood vessels and wrapped a vise grip around her heart. She refused to scream, although her whole body begged to release the sudden burst of fear.

Her first chalk warrior charged the throng haint and shattered against it. She needed a stronger form for her shadows.

She remembered Wick chanting the poem, *her* poem: "*Where the powers converge and become one . . .*" *Become one. Become one.* Mama Carmen had passed along the poem to help her understand the legacy. *Become one.* The spirits formed a whirlpool of shadows around her. They pulsed with the rhythm of her breath. She could taste their rage at Wick's abominations, distinguish each soul's flickering memories as they buzzed through the air. *Become one.*

Sierra was Lucera, a fierce spiritual warrior like her abuela. She was stepping into her destiny. The spirits' intentions unified with hers. They were righteous, these spirits, and ferocious. They were not about to see their world destroyed at the hands of some old fool like Wick. No. They, Sierra and the spirits, would not be manipulated, dogged, oppressed. Not after so many years of struggle.

Sierra didn't know which thoughts were hers and which were the spirits'. She knew death was all around, breathing down her neck like some ancient god, like the giant painted throng haint now rushing toward her. She raised her left hand. If there was no vessel for her to transmit spirit into, she would be the vessel.

The demon thundered toward her, only a few feet away. She took a deep breath, closed her eyes, and placed her right hand to her forehead.

Everything flashed and light flushed out the world, as if the sun had exploded. Sierra's limbs were barely moving; ancient rivers gushed through her body, an ocean raged inside her heart. She might have been floating. Certainly, her feet were not on solid ground. And this feeling of lightness . . . Perhaps she didn't weigh anything at all.

Gradually, things began to resolve around her: There was the large empty room, the demon-painted wall, and Robbie standing nearby, looking shocked. The long-armed haint that had been rushing her was now struggling to get back onto its feet, its long mouth hanging open in surprise. What had happened? Where was Wick? Where were all the spirits? The air around her was empty where hundreds of shadowy souls had frenzied just seconds earlier.

The painted demon rose and lunged toward her again. She swung one arm over her head and brought it down across the haint's face. She felt the dull resistance of its physical presence, felt her hand cleave easily through it. Watched the thing gasp in surprise, stumble backward, crumble.

She had to remind herself to breathe. *Become one.* One wasn't a person: It was a state. One with the spirits. Their purpose, energy, power, ferocity had all unified with her body. She was no longer the conduit; she was the form, the vessel. She, they, had become one.

"WICK!" Sierra's voice boomed across the building, echoing back and forth amidst the empty light fixtures and dusty piping. Her voice carried the voices of a hundred thousand souls in it; a whole history of resistance and rage moved with her. It felt terrific. She stepped over the crumpled body of the demon she'd just murked. Wick had to be nearby, the little worm. And she would deal with him. She would end this right now.

There was only one demon painting left on the wall.

That meant four were roaming free, some in search of Sierra's family and friends. She growled, an unfathomable rage welling up inside her. What she needed was a little battalion of her own. A few spirits that could handle those demons while she . . . Of course! Her plan came swimming back to her. She turned to the boy standing by her side. "Robbie."

He looked at her with wide, worried eyes. "Sierra?"

She reached nonchalantly toward his bruised face and placed her hand on it, allowing tiny flecks of light to seep into his cells and follow along his neural pathways. The black and blue became brown as she watched.

"I'm going to send spirits into the mural and then go after Wick," Sierra said. "Go with them to my house. Make sure my family is safe. Please."

He nodded.

"And Robbie? Be careful. Some of those painted throng haints might still be in the building."

He had a strange expression on his face, something between a smile and grimace. He'd be alright. She smiled at him, vaguely aware that her whole body was glowing with a supernatural flare. "Go," she said. He smiled back and turned toward the stairwell. "I'll deal with Wick."

FORTY-ONE

The night air felt fresh against Sierra's face. She reached a glowing arm through the window and slapped the wall at the top of the dragon's head. "C'mon, Manny," she whispered to the sky. Surely his spirit was one of the many that had come.

She held her hand there, allowing some of the spirits to flow through her into the paintings, making sure they had enough time to fully engage. The swirling tingle of energy was an incredible feeling, like all the twinkling lights of the city were bursting through her bloodstream. Slowly, the painting came to life: The dragon stretched its long neck as if waking from a thousand-year sleep, blinked a few times in the glare of the streetlight, and then looked directly at Sierra. For a moment, they held each other's gaze, and then it smiled slightly. In that smile, Sierra saw Manny. His spirit had entered the painting and was taking control.

The guitar-playing skeleton woman stood up beside the dragon. The churning city of her musical notes flurried into the air.

Go, Sierra whispered in her spirit voice. *Find the haints. Scatter them, destroy them. Save my family.*

The paintings slid off the wall, now full, three-dimensional spirits in the sky, and disappeared into the night.

Sierra turned and looked back into the room. A few shadows still flitted back and forth throughout the building. She shut her eyes and became instantly aware of the many spirits working for her, as their vision was hers. It was like looking at monitors in one of those big security rooms: There was the third floor stairwell. There Bennie crouched behind a crate, panting. There were Juan and Tee, backs flat against a pillar. Where was Nydia? A few crates away from Bennie, grasping her arm in pain.

Robbie rushed down the stairwell to the first floor. He hadn't met any resistance yet, and Sierra was glad. She had a feeling she was about to have her hands full.

A tinge of panic sent her attention reeling back to the fifth floor just in time to see one of Robbie's painted giants swing down on her from the rafters. The thing was tremendous, a gangly sprawl of clawed arms and legs, and just the sudden intensity of its presence threw Sierra backward. The demon landed in a crouch and sprang at her, painted claws reaching out.

Sierra almost floated back to her feet. She didn't remember getting up — she was just up, and furious that she'd been startled. She swung a shimmering left hand, catching the haint across the face, and watched the foul thing sprawl backward.

WICK!

Her spirit voice had an even greater reach than her human one. It thundered out across the Brooklyn skyline, making Manhattan pause and wonder what was going on over there.

Come out!

The painted demon squirmed at her feet like a giant water bug. Sierra could feel that Wick was close, but it irritated her to no end that she could find everyone else in the building except him. Spirits raged and swirled inside her, hungry to find this arrogant human who'd enslaved so many of their own.

Something fluttered from a dark corner of the room — another shadow about to burst to life, surely. Sierra scowled, stepped heavily on the demon at her feet, and strutted toward the movement.

I'm coming for you, Wick.

A panicked strobe simmered across Sierra's mind. She swung her attention out across the building tops, along narrow alleyways, and finally toward that familiar corner at the edge of her block. One of the painted throng haints stood perfectly still in the middle of the street, glaring with empty eyes toward her house.

Hurry, Robbie! Please . . .

She slipped back into her own consciousness just in time to see the flickering shadow scatter toward her. Another one was coming at her from behind; she could feel the monstrous vibrations of its attack. They were strong, these two. Wick must've been saving his most powerful demons for last. They would crush her between them, tear her to pieces, and leave her body scattered amidst the dusty crates, a macabre blurb in tomorrow's obituaries.

No. They would not get what they wanted. Sierra side-stepped, and the demon behind her tumbled past. It was larger than she'd counted on, and one of its claws slashed across her face. Blood trickled down her cheek, and a wave of nausea sizzled up and down her body. Poison. The thing's very touch was a sickness of the soul.

Woozy, Sierra stepped back a few paces as the other throng haint charged her. She caught a quick glimpse of Wick by the far wall, his eyes wide and desperate. Too many things were happening at once. She lashed out with her right hand, focusing all of the raging spirits inside her, and caught the demon haint full across the face as it rose toward her. The force of their collision sent both Sierra and the haint backward. She couldn't even strike it without some of its foulness seeping into her, draining her life force. Spirits flurried around inside her to rejuvenate whatever damage had been done as she rose and took an uneasy step forward.

With Wick handled, the painted demons would be lifeless again. Simple. She took another step, firmer, and then broke into a run, gathering her swirling spirits as she went.

The last haint rose directly from the floor, a sudden tower of fury glaring down at her, heaving with sharp uneven breaths.

Sierra.

It was that same eerie cacophony of voices she'd heard in Flatbush and on the beach at Coney Island, the same foul stench. Behind the haint, Wick cowered, glaring out at Sierra.

"Don't you see we want the same thing, Sierra?" he called.

"You killed Manny," Sierra said, glaring back past the haint's hulking form. "You destroyed my abuelo's mind. Scattered the shadowshapers."

Wick shook his head. "Your abuelo was responsible for the destruction of the shadowshapers. I'm trying to save them. You don't understand any of this, Sierra. This is not your world."

"It is my world!" Sierra's voice reverberated down alleyways and out toward the sea. Each of the myriad swirling spirits inside her spoke the words too. *"And you tried to take it from me. Tried to tear my own heritage away."*

Wick raised his eyebrows. "I see your old grandmother passed on her magic."

Around her, the spirit music began to swell.

Loooooooooooooooooooooooooooooooooooooooo . . .

The spirits were calling her — a harmonious battle cry. She felt them gathering their strength inside her, felt each passing second crystallize into a map of strategic striking points wrapping around Wick's body.

Saaaaaayraaaaaaaaaaaaaaaaaaaaaaaaaahhhhhhhhhh . . .

They had always been calling her. She'd been too scared

to realize it at first, and then too confused. Now she knew. It wasn't her abuela the spirits were summoning. It was her, Sierra, the new Lucera, heir to the legacy of shadowshapers.

At a signal from Wick, the haint tensed and planted one clawed foot onto the ground to steady itself for a lunge. For Sierra, time slowed. The spiritual power inside of her burned so intensely, she felt that if she simply burst forward, she could plow through the haint and obliterate Wick. Scatter him into some molecular puree across the wall.

But that didn't seem right. This was time for precision.

The throng haint swung its long, spiny arm toward her.

Sierra pitched forward into its body, hands first.

The thing let out a bellow of surprise, but quickly regained its composure and brought claws down on her back with devastating speed. She felt them — its blows thunderous jolts along her spine — but not enough to slow her down. She kept pushing, her hands enmeshed in the haint's horrible rubbery flesh, the stench of death and fresh paint suffocating her. Every cell of her body begged to let go, but the battle-hungry spirits inside of her were not about to quit. Neither was she.

Mama Carmen's poem surfaced in Sierra's mind. *"See my enemies fall,"* she whispered. The throng haint bellowed again, this time from pain. Mouths opened and closed all across its painted form. Sierra felt its solidity beginning to give way between her fingers, felt the twisted sorcery that held it together loosen. A stream of some foul liquid trickled down from the thing's mouth. When its blows weakened, Sierra knew that it wouldn't be long. She dug her feet in and pressed forward. Wick still stood just behind his haint, staring in horror as his creation came apart before his very eyes.

LOOOOOOOOOOOOOOOOOOOOO . . .

She was the shimmering culmination of all her ancestors' strife, joyfulness, and struggle. She was a radiant child of spirit. She was a hundred different souls vibrating within a single living body. *"My spirit voice calls . . ."* she whispered.

SAAAAAAYYYYYYRRR . . .

"And the energy surges . . ." Sierra took a deep breath, steadied herself, and then heaved forward one final time, releasing a tiny, furious fraction of that pent-up spiritual rage. *"Like a thousand suns!"*

AAAAAAAAAAHHHHHHHHHHHHH!!!!!!

And the throng haint gave way around her, splattered back across Wick and the far wall in a thick coat of nastiness.

FORTY-TWO

Sierra stumbled forward, startled by the sudden emptiness. Several trembling shadows scattered off into the night. She spat at them and turned to Wick. He crouched against the wall, covered head to toe in thick, murky haint ichor.

"It started as fascination," he stammered. "It was an act of l-love. To spread the knowledge. Knowledge of the tradition. It's what your grandfather wanted to . . . to spre —"

"Don't talk about my grandfather," Sierra growled.

"Sierra." He raised a shivering hand. "I just want to — to — to explain . . ."

"I don't want your explanations." Sierra closed her eyes for a second and immediately heard her mother screaming again. She slid her spirit vision along the streets till she found hers, watched in horror as María Santiago and Uncle Neville came tearing out of the brownstone and ran down the dark sidewalk. Two throng haints lurched out the door a second later, galloping after them at full speed.

Then a great wall of swirling colors flooded forward from the far end of the block. Robbie was a tiny dreadlocked general beneath the Technicolor onslaught of painted warriors, the old guitar-playing skeleton and the Manny dragon rearing above him. María and Neville fled toward them, the demon haints only a few feet behind.

With a terrific smashing, the two forces collided, and María and Neville disappeared in the chaos.

Sierra whirled on Wick, her every muscle aching to crush his windpipe.

"Sierra," he whispered.

She stalked over to him, slid her hands around his neck. It would be so easy. Just a flicker of her suddenly ferocious fingers and it'd be all over. She squinted at him writhing in her hands, acutely aware of the huge battle raging on her block, her mami caught up in the midst of it.

But no. Death was too simple an ending for Dr. Jonathan Wick. It left him too much room for some nefarious rebirth in the afterlife. Sierra studied his trembling lips and tear-stained eyes. She could do better than death, she decided. She was a surgeon, not a butcher. She concentrated for a half second, and then simply allowed all the spirits churning inside her to surge forward into Wick.

They left memories behind as they passed from her hands. A dizzying collage of smells, moments, emotions, longings sped through Sierra's entire body. She was on a horse in the rain forest, galloping toward freedom. She was alone in a cell, coming to terms for the four hundredth time with her imminent death and the deaths she'd dealt. She was

in the full rapture of love. She was ashamed. Her brain simmered with bursts of lilac, cigar smoke, sweat, the cringe of
a missed opportunity, pangs of hunger. Most of all, though,
she felt alive. The dead were so alive! They carried their
whole lives with them in those tall, walking shadows,
brought each second, each thrill and tragedy with them
wherever they went.

She looked down at Wick. He screamed as the spirits
swarmed through him, burrowing into the most intimate
reaches of his soul. Sierra sharpened her mind and allowed
her vision to slip alongside the spirits as they thundered
through the old anthropologist's inner workings. *Take his
powers,* Sierra told them, but they were already on it. Little
flashes of light blinked out as the spirits sped through his
blood vessels and entrails, crisscrossing synapses and cell
membranes. *All his powers.* Sierra could feel the purge,
feel the tremendous vacuum as every last echo of Wick's
spiritual power was obliterated like a ramshackle hut in a
monsoon.

The vacuum changed him on the outside as well. His
skin became ragged and dry, sagged into pathetic folds on
top of itself. His mouth hung open, drool trickling out; his
teeth turned black and crumbled in seconds. She let go of
his neck and stood back. The spirits were leaving him now,
shadows flickering off into the thick warehouse air.

Wick slumped to his knees, shriveled and broken.
"You've . . . murdered me . . ."

Sierra rolled her eyes, then closed them to check on her mami. Her block was awash in color. Sierra's dragon mixed with several of the skeletons and mermaids from Club Kalfour. Robbie's demons were now paint puddles on the sidewalk, the spirits of the throng haints scattered. María Santiago stood panting beside Robbie and Neville.

Sierra let out a sigh and opened her eyes. She took a last look at the splattered walls, then stepped over Wick's whimpering body and walked down the stairs. Juan, Bennie, Tee, and Nydia were rising wearily from their hiding places, dusting themselves off. The five friends exchanged hugs, tears, stories, gasps, and laughter, and then walked together to the ground floor.

Sierra could hear the spirits still humming their sacred harmonies, calling out her brand-new name. They strode in slow circles around her, breathing in and out like the summer breeze. She smiled for what felt like the first time in a long while, and then she and her friends all walked out together into the dark blue Brooklyn morning.

EPILOGUE

"How I look?" Sierra asked.

"Fit to become one with," Robbie said.

"Whoa! Easy there, playa." She felt like her smile was about to explode off her face. She wore a flowing white strapless dress, and her matching white shawl flapped around her like wings in the ocean wind. Robbie took her in with a mix of hunger, awe, and curiosity, as though he might either pounce and try to make out with her, or drop down on the sand and kiss her bare feet. Wasn't a bad look at all for him, as a matter of fact.

"Sorry," Robbie said. "I just . . . you look really beautiful."

"Ah, there, that wasn't so hard, was it? A straightforward compliment! Thank you."

Robbie didn't look so bad himself. He'd pulled his locks back into a slick ponytail and wore linen slacks under a white guayabera.

"Your ancestor tats are coming back!" Sierra said, running her fingers along his arm.

Robbie smiled. "They always do." He put his hand over hers and then wrapped her arm around his elbow, and together they promenaded down toward a secluded area of Coney Island beach by the edge of the water. "How's Lázaro?" Robbie asked.

Sierra shook her head. "I haven't been back up there yet. I don't know if I can face him. I don't even know what to . . . say? I will, though. I will." She took a long breath. "But whatever: Today is for celebrating. C'mon."

María stood on the shore wearing a lovely white dress of her own. When she saw Sierra and Robbie coming down the dune, she offered the saddest, most genuine smile Sierra had ever seen on her mom. Juan was there too, and Tee, Bennie, Jerome, Izzy, and Nydia, all dressed to the nines. Jerome and Izzy had heard the story of the battle from Tee, and called to make up afterward. They all stood in a half circle, facing the ocean.

"Go 'head, Sierra," María said. "You asked us here."

The shadows rose up in the dimming light and began dancing their soft circles around the arc of the living.

"I brought you all here today," Sierra said, "to honor the memory of Mama Carmen Siboney Corona, my abuela, may she rest in peace. I didn't know my grandma that well, really. But she still showed me a lot about life, taught me a lot about what it means to be who I am. And for that, I honor her."

There was a pause. The spirits' steps grew wider and their hum stretched across the open sky, filled Sierra's soul with a melancholy contentment. They were mourning Lucera too. Mourning one and welcoming another. Everyone seemed lost in their thoughts and memories for a few moments.

"We're also here to honor Manuel Gomez," Sierra said, "aka the Domino King."

The bodies had been recovered, and the past few days had seen a swirl of funerals and tributes to Manny and the other shadowshapers. María wrapped her warm hand around Sierra's. Tears rolled down her face, but she still had on that sad sweet smile.

"I'm here today," Bennie said, "to honor the memory of Vincent Charles Jackson, my brother. May he rest in peace."

"Today," Robbie said, "I come to honor the life and spirit of Papa Mauricio Acevedo, my mentor and friend."

They went around the half circle, each calling out the name of one or several loved ones who had passed. The spirits swirled faster around them, flitted this way and that through the darkening sky. Sierra watched them. She was beginning to see subtle differences in how each spirit moved — the clenching of shadowy fists on an upward flush into the sky, the curve of a spine from a life of hard labor. Their stories, the same stories that had flashed through Sierra just a few nights before, still lived with them, made up the fabric of who they were.

When all the names had been called out, Sierra looked into each of the faces around her. Bennie smiled through her tears. Juan had his hair slicked down and was wearing one of their dad's white uniform shirts; his smile was serene for maybe the first time ever. Tee just grinned like all this was the most natural thing in the world. Nydia's eyes were wide, like a little kid on the first day of school, and Jerome and Izzy gaped in amazement. María and Robbie stood smiling on either side of Sierra.

Each of them nodded at her and joined hands. Above them, the spirits began pulsing gently as Sierra took a deep breath and closed her eyes. She could feel each of her loved ones, their passions and fears. They registered as flashes of color in her mind's eye. She exhaled and sent a ray of power out from her center, felt it blitz along beneath her skin and then enter her mom on one side, Robbie on the other. Their colors brightened. Bennie and Nydia were next, and then the brightness worked its way to Juan, Tee, Jerome, and Izzy.

"It's done," Sierra said. "My shadowshaping friends, it begins anew."

She felt her mom squeeze her hand. They smiled at each other and then looked up to where the spirits danced wild circles across the darkening sky.

ACKNOWLEDGMENTS

I am hugely grateful to Cheryl Klein for lifting this book out of the slush pile, believing in it, and bringing it closer to its true heart with every single edit. Thanks also to the whole team at Arthur A. Levine for making *Shadowshaper* the book it is. Many thanks to my agent Eddie Schneider and the whole team at JABberwocky for all their fantastic work. Nathan Bransford was patient and brilliant as he helped me through many early drafts; his kindness and creativity still echo in the pages. Thanks to all the brilliant folks who read *Shadowshaper* and gave their thoughts, doubts, and encouragement, including but not limited to: Ashley Ford, Anika Noni Rose, Justine Larbalestier, Dr. Lukasz Kowalic, Sue Baiman, Troy L. Wiggins, Marcela Landres, and Emma Alabaster. To Bart Leib and Kay Holt at Crossed Genres and my *Long Hidden* co-editor Rose Fox.

Thanks to my amazing family, Dora, Marc, Malka, Lou, and Calyx. Thanks to Iya Lisa and Iya Ramona and Iyalocha Tima and my whole Ile Omi Toki family for their support; also thanks to Oba Nelson Rodriguez, Baba Craig, Baba Malik, and all the wonderful folks of Ile Ase. To the many teachers who inspired me, encouraged me, and sharpened my skills along this path, especially Connie Henry, Inez Middleton, Charles Aversa, Ron Gwiazda, Lori Taylor, Mary Page, Tom Evans, Brian Walker, Orlando Leyba, Warren Carberg, Gloria Legvold, Michael Lesy, Lara Nielsen, Vivek

Bhandari, Yusef Lateef, Roberto García, Alistair McCartney, Jervey Tervalon, and Mat Johnson. Huge shout-out to the whole VONA/ Voices community. Stefan Malliet is the Internet wizard who made my website awesome, many thanks to him. I'm grateful to Nisi Shawl and Andrea Hairston and the whole Carl Brandon Society for their support. And thanks to Aurora Anaya-Cerda and the team at La Casa Azul Bookstore in East Harlem.

I am deeply grateful to two amazing writers who found room under their wings for me: Sheree Renée Thomas, who believed in my voice from the very beginning, and Tananarive Due, for her guiding wisdom throughout.

To Jud, Tina, and Sam for many strolls and good meals along the way. To Sorahya Moore, the best mentee and friend a writer could ask for. To Akie for long talks with cigars and making great music. To Nina for always demanding I stop writing and play with her just when I'm getting into the swing of things. To Lenel Caze, Carlos Duchesne, Rachelle Broomer, Rudy Brathwaite, Walter Hochbrueckner, Derrick Simpkins, and all the EMTs, medics, supervisors, nurses, doctors, and staff at the ERs and ambulance stations at Brooklyn Hospital, Beth Israel, Montefiore, and Mount Sinai, as well as the good folks at FDNY EMS battalions 57 and 39.

To the Pattie Hut & Grill for the best jerk chicken in Brooklyn and A&A Bake & Doubles Shop for the best doubles in Brooklyn.

To all the hilarious, brave, outrageous, incredible folks on Twitter who've been there to challenge me, cheer for me, and keep me on point and laughing during those hours when I felt stuck and didn't know how to move forward.

To Nastassian, my heart and soul, woman of my life, dream come true. Thank you for being you.

I give thanks to all those who came before us and lit the way. I give thanks to all my ancestors; Yemonja, Mother of Waters; gbogbo Orisa; and Olodumare.

Daniel José Older's first young adult novel, *Shadowshaper*, received four starred reviews, won the International Latino Book Award, was nominated for the Kirkus Prize and the Andre Norton Award for Young Adult Science Fiction and Fantasy, and was also recognized as a *New York Times* Notable Book and an NPR Best Book of the Year. It went on to become a *New York Times* best-seller. Daniel is also the author of the Bone Street Rumba adult urban fantasy series and the short story collection *Salsa Nocturna*. His essays on race, power, and publishing have been published online and in the collections *The Fire This Time* and *Here We Are: Feminism for the Real World,* and his short stories have appeared in many science fiction and fantasy magazines and anthologies. He also writes music and plays bass in the soul-jazz band Ghost Star.

Daniel lives in the Bedford-Stuyvesant neighborhood of Brooklyn, New York, where the Shadowshaper Cypher is set. You can find his thoughts on writing, read dispatches from his decade-long career as a New York City paramedic, and hear his music at his website, danieljoseolder.net, and follow him on social media at @djolder.

READ ON

FOR A SNEAK PEEK

OF SIERRA'S NEXT ADVENTURE

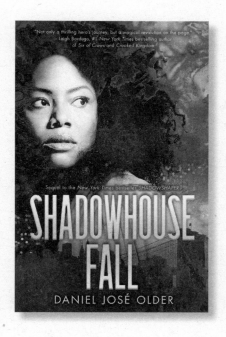

"A magical revolution on the page." — Leigh Bardugo, #1 *New York Times* bestselling author of *Six of Crows* and *Crooked Kingdom*

"Older leaves us openmouthed and speechless, asking 'What just happened to me?!'" — Jacqueline Woodson, *New York Times* bestselling author of *Another Brooklyn* and *Brown Girl Dreaming*

★ "Lit." — *Kirkus Reviews*, starred review

★ "Dynamic, smart." — *Booklist*, starred review

★ "Exciting.... Older has upped the ante with this second installment." — *School Library Journal*, starred review

ONE

Sierra Santiago closed her eyes and the whole spinning world opened up around her. A brisk wind whispered songs of the coming winter as it shushed through browning leaves then whisked along the moonlit field, throwing Sierra's mass of curls into disarray. Up above, the first round of overnight flights leaving JFK cut trails across the cloudless sky. Traffic whirred along just outside the park walls, and beyond that the shuttle train sighed and screeched to a halt; doors slid open; weary passengers collected their personal belongings as instructed, adjusted their earbuds, and headed off into the night.

But that was the simple stuff. Sierra had learned to expand her senses out further than any normal human. It wasn't easy, but when she quieted her mind and the spirits were close, she could hear the city's clicks and groans halfway across Brooklyn. Tonight wasn't about meditation or the ongoing urban symphony, though. Where were her spirits?

As if in response, a vision sizzled into view in her mind's eye: There in the forest, not too far from her, a figure crouched. She could make out the silhouette leaning against a fallen tree, see the person's fast-beating heart telegraph frantic pulses out into the chilly night. The person scratched something onto the tree and looked around for nearby spirits.

I see you, Sierra thought, tensing her face into a smug smile. *Whoever you are. Now who else is out there?* She let the image go and immediately another appeared: In the field she sat on the edge of, a figure lay facedown in the grass, breathing heavily. After a few seconds, the person hunched up on their elbows and peered into the darkness. *Okay.* Sierra nodded. *Got it. What else?*

The next vision appeared so suddenly it almost knocked her over. Dark trees whipped past; someone was running. Panting and running. Sierra felt her own heart thunder in her ears. The other views she'd seen had been through the visions of her spirits: a cadre of shadows she'd come to think of as her own Secret Service detail. But this was different — it was someone alive. Or some*thing* . . . Branches whisked out of its way as it bounded across the forest. *Which forest? Was it . . . was it close?* Sierra tried to scan for clues, but everything was moving too fast.

Spirits, Sierra beckoned. *Find this . . . thing.* She didn't remember having stood up, but she was on her feet. A wave of dizziness rushed over her as the half-dozen views of Prospect Park swimming through her mind veered suddenly skyward and then turned toward the shadowy fields and forests below.

All but one.

Whatever the running thing was kept storming through the forest, panting. Its whole body was tensed with intent. It was . . . it was hunting. Sierra felt its hunger deep within herself; saliva flooded her own mouth. Flesh would be torn, a panicked heart would race and then falter, finally fail in this monster's jaws. The thing lunged and Sierra's eyes popped open as a hand landed on her shoulder.

"Gotchya!"

Sierra screamed and spun around, elbows first. She hit something soft and jumped back.

"Ow! What the hell, Sierra?" Big Jerome stood there rubbing his chest and pouting.

"I . . . Jerome . . ." Sierra scanned the field behind him, the forest beyond. Nothing. "I don't know . . . what happened."

"I do. You were so surprised I actually won a practice round, you damn near cracked my rib."

"No . . ." Sierra rubbed her eyes. A branch snapped in the woods she had been facing. She spun around and probed the darkness for movement.

"Sierra?" Sierra's mom, María Santiago, called. "¿Qué pasó, m'ija?" She walked up next to Jerome. "I was hiding and then I saw this guy barrel past and actually reach you, and I knew something had to be going on."

"Whoa," Jerome said. "Mrs. Santiago with the snark. If you hadn't tangled your chalk spirits with my twig monsters at the last training run, neither of us would need extra practice."

"Mind your manners, jóven," María snapped. "What's a twig monster supposed to do anyway? Set itself on fire and dive-bomb the bad guys? Come on, man. Anyway, you didn't 'shape anything this round to win, you just ran through the field like a lost moose! That doesn't even —"

"Shh," Sierra said, her eyes still on the forest.

María scowled. "Sierra, don't you —"

"*Shh!*" Sierra hissed. "Something's out there."

If María asked a bunch of annoying parenty-type questions instead of being quiet, Sierra was going to scream. A year ago, that's what her mom would've done, but since embracing the family legacy and becoming a shadowshaper four months back, María had let go of some of her extra-eyeroll-worthy mom habits. She sighed, but said no more.

Sierra exhaled and squinted into the forest. Her spirits had swooped back down into the park and were springing along through the underbrush. The charging, starving whatever-it-was was gone. At least, she couldn't see through its eyes any more. Maybe it was right there at the edge of the darkness, watching her.

Sierra narrowed her eyes and steeled herself. She had done enough running away over the summer, when she first learned about the magical art of shadowshaping and her family's legacy. It had only been a few months, but she wasn't that scared little girl anymore. She wasn't even just a shadowshaper — her dead abuela had passed on the mantle and made Sierra into the next Lucera, the beating heart of the shadowshaping world. She was still figuring out what all her powers were, but one thing she had promised herself was no more being that freaked-out, screaming girl she saw in horror movies. No more running away. She took a step toward the dark forest.

"Uh, Sierra," Jerome said. "What're you doing?"

"There's something in the trees."

"I get that. Why are you going *toward* it?"

Shadows rose up around Sierra, tall, long-legged spirits that would leap into her drawings and lash out if needed. Their gentle hum rose in the night air and filled Sierra with that familiar mix of ferocity and calm — a loving hurricane within. She pulled two pieces of chalk from her hoodie pocket and put one in each hand. "Stay where you are, J. I got this."

"But —" Jerome started. María must have calmed him with a hand on the shoulder, or probably a gentle slap. She knew better than to try and stop her daughter in one of Sierra's gung-ho moments.

Sierra reached her arms out to either side and strutted into the shadows. She scraped the chalk along the trees around her as she walked, then tapped the marks once with her fingertips. Even with the spirits heightening her vision as they slid along in smooth, sparkling strides, it seemed like a blanket of darkness had been thrown over the whole world. The chalk scratches sped along the tree trunks, flashes of color, and then disappeared in the gloom up ahead. They weren't the best weapons to have — nowhere near as strong as a painted mural, for example — but they'd be able to keep an enemy busy till she could work out something better.

Hopefully.

And then, very suddenly, Sierra stopped. She wasn't alone. The certainty of someone else there, a presence, tickled along her shoulders and the back of her neck.

"Don't be afraid," a girl's voice said as Sierra spun around.

"Mina?" Mina Satorius was a grade above Sierra at Octavia Butler High, but she looked fourteen. She had big eyes and her strawberry blond hair was ponytailed, with bangs at the front and a spindly curl framing her face on either side. She stood in the middle of a clearing, wearing a plaid shirt over a tank top and a sweater tied around her waist. Despite what she'd just said, Mina herself looked terrified — eyebrows creased with worry, bottom lip trembling slightly, arms wrapped around her slender frame.

"What are you doing out here?" Sierra asked. Her towering shadows emerged in a circle around Mina; their gentle glow pulsed in time with Sierra's own heartbeat. Shimmering chalk marks appeared on the trees, poised to flush forward and attack.

"I'm . . . I . . ." The girl looked like she might collapse into a puddle any second. Sierra resisted the urge to walk up and hug her. Something had been out here hunting, something ferocious. It was hard to imagine Mina could have anything to do with that panting monster whose eyes Sierra had seen through, but . . .

"Spit it out, Mina. We're not safe here."

"I know," Mina said. "That's what — that's what I'm here to say. A warning."

The shadows around Mina rustled, seemed to whisper to each other. Mina glanced up, her eyes widening even more. She had the spirit vision, Sierra realized, just not very advanced. At least, that's how she made it seem.

"You have a warning for me, so you hide out in the woods and wait for me to come to you? You couldn't send a text or something? This is creepy."

"No, I know, I — I was gonna come out and talk to you but then I felt it nearby and . . ."

"Felt what, girl? Come on, now."

"The . . ." She shook her head. "Here." With a trembling hand, she held up what looked like an old playing card.

Sierra didn't move. "What's that?"

"It's from the Deck of Worlds. Take it."

Sierra shook her head. "My mama told me not to take freaky magic cards from strange white girls I meet in the woods."

"Sierra, I'm . . . I'm not here to hurt you. I know you've had problems with the Sorrows before, but —"

"You're with the Sorrows?" Sierra narrowed her eyes. All the shadows tensed and took a step forward. "Get out of here. Leave. Don't talk to me in the hallway. Don't talk to my friends. And definitely don't let me catch you skulking around these woods while I'm working with my shadowshapers."

"It's not like that, Sierra, listen —"

"I listened. I heard what you said. Get out of my sight before I let these shadows loose on you."

Mina shook her head and took a step backward. "You don't understand," she whispered, placing the card in the soft forest soil at her feet. "But when you do, come find me. I'm not . . . I'm not your enemy, Sierra. Take the card. Don't leave it there. You need to . . . you need to take it." She turned around and ran.

Sierra took a step toward the card.

"Sierra?" María called from behind her. "¿Estás bien, m'ija?"

"Sí, Mami," Sierra said. "Ya voy."

She crouched down to get a better look at the card. An archaic, faded drawing was scrawled on the front. It showed a white wolf with glowing blue eyes, its jaws open and lips pulled back into a snarl. Gleaming castle towers spiraled toward a stormy sky in the background. *El SABUESO de la LUZ,* was scrawled across the top in elegant,